TRUTH OR DARE

Non PRATT

WALKER
BOOKS

Non Pratt's real name is Leonie, but please don't call her that unless she's done something really bad. She grew up in Teesside and now lives in London. After graduating from Cambridge University, Non decided to work in children's publishing. Since then she has worked as a non-fiction editor at Usborne and a fiction publisher at Catnip. She now writes full-time. Her first novel, *Trouble*, was shortlisted for the YA Book Prize and longlisted for the Carnegie Medal. Her second novel, *Remix*, was described as "smart, funny and very real".

Follow Non on Twitter (@NonPratt).

www.nonpratt.com

Other books by Non Pratt:

Trouble

Remix

Unboxed

AUTHOR'S NOTE

A writer's one job is to be good at imagining what it would be like to live many different lives. Regardless of the research I've done talking and listening to other people with different experiences, at the end of the day, I'm still just making stuff up and hoping you want to listen.

But perhaps you would also like to listen to the people with those different experiences instead? Perhaps you'd like to read *The Good Immigrant*, edited by Nikesh Shukla, featuring 21 black, Asian and minority ethnic writers whose experiences of living in Britain are closer to Sef's than mine.

Or maybe you would like some insight into what it would be like to live with a neurodisability, in which case I'd suggest reading Jean-Dominique Bauby's *The Diving Bell and the Butterfly*. (There's a film, but the book brings you closer to Bauby's experience.)

Any book written by one person can only really represent one way of looking at things and my way of looking at things may not match up with yours. This is why we need more writers, with more voices and different experiences – so that every reader finds a writer who can truly speak for them.

ACKNOWLEDGEMENTS

The characters in this book are fictional, but the problems they face are not. These are some of the charities that provide support for people with brain injuries:

The Royal Hospital for Neurodisability – www.rhn.org.uk
Headway – www.headway.org.uk
Child Brain Injury Trust – www.childbraininjurytrust.org.uk

As Sef says at one point, "Isn't the point of having money to make life better, even if that life isn't yours?"

Thank you to Susan Patterson at the RHN and Tamsin Ahmed at Headway, and especial thanks to Speech and Language Therapist Gerry Roxburgh at the Frenchay Brain Injury Centre for all your help on getting the facts straight.

Thanks also to Humaira Ashraf Din, my editorial consultant on this project, who gave me fantastic feedback and is only responsible for making the book better, and to Sasha Jawed, for answering some preliminary questions.

Consultation doesn't stop a writer from making mistakes, or deciding to bend procedures a smidge to suit the story. Any inaccuracies in the book arise from me.

My deepest gratitude goes to Denise Johnstone-Burt and (even though she wasn't able to see it to the end this one time) Annalie Grainger. Apologies/thanks to the ever-patient Daisy Jellicoe, who I think I nearly broke, and Maria

Soler Cantón for a knockout cover. Everyone at Walker Books, I love you, from Publicity, Marketing, Sales and Rights through to Design, Editorial and the oft-neglected Production department.

Amazing Agent Jane Finigan, my champion.

George Lester and Lauren James, two of the most adorable humans I know, thank you for being excellent first readers.

The internets, this book captures only a fraction of my feelings about you – you are both the worst *and* the best. Shout out to everyone who responded to my call for reports of dares you did as youths: Soizic Le Courtois; Daniel Shipley; Paul Black; Rachael E Bellis; Richenda Thompson; John Bardsley; Sally Teare; Ceinwen Brunt; Emma Reynolds. Even if your dares didn't make it into the book, you inspired the ones that did. People of twitter, you are ever-helpful, this time round thanks to @Charli_TAW for suggesting which YouTubers to follow, @storytellersinc for suggesting Sef and Amir watch *Taken*, @saramegan for some in-depth historical video game answers and @ShinraAlpha for Rich's injuries.

The UKYA community continues to be my favourite place in the world, thanks to bloggers, librarians, booksellers and bookfans. It is also the place I've found the best friends – Lucy Ivison, Lisa Williamson and Robin Stevens have been particularly awesome this time round.

My family. If there's anything that makes you appreciate your own, it's learning what can happen to others'. Thank you for putting up with me crying all over you.

*For Denise J-B, who challenged me
to write something different*

First published 2017 by Walker Books Ltd
87 Vauxhall Walk, London SE11 5HJ

2 4 6 8 10 9 7 5 3 1

Text © 2017 Leonie Parish
Cover design by Walker Books Ltd

The moral rights of the author have been asserted

This book has been typeset in Fairfield and Avenir

Printed and bound in Great Britain by Clays Ltd, St Ives plc

British Library Cataloguing in Publication Data:
a catalogue record for this book is available from the British Library

ISBN 978-1-4063-6693-8

www.walker.co.uk

PART ONE: CLAIRE CASEY

All I ever wanted was to be noticed.
Now all I want is to disappear.

SEPTEMBER

CHAPTER 1

It's freezing in the school hall and Rich's shirt is so tight you can see his nipples. Disturbing as this is, I can't seem to look anywhere else – it's like they've hypnotized me.

"Is this assembly ever going to end?" Seren slumps sideways onto my shoulder as Mr Chung, the head, stands up from his chair at the back of the stage to walk towards the lectern.

"Apparently not," I murmur in reply.

Rich leans across to whisper, "If it's this or Maths…"

On stage, Mr Chung clears his throat before addressing us.

"Some of you will already know what happened over the summer when Kamran Malik fell into the Lay river."

We've all heard about it one way or another, but that doesn't make it any less awful and there's a collective burst of gasps and horrified murmurs. There's also an indiscreet "Fall or jump?" from one of the sixth-formers behind us. West Bridge has an unofficial and entirely stupid tradition of people tombstoning off the viaduct after their exams. There's rumours that Sef Malik – Kam's younger (gorgeous) brother – did it at the start of summer, but it's not something I'd ever imagine Kam doing.

"Kamran – or Kam as most of us knew him – was taken

straight to hospital with a suspected brain injury. Having been in a coma for over two weeks, he regained consciousness yesterday." Someone does an uncertain sort of cheer, but you can see from Mr Chung's face that this is not the right time. "Once Kam has recovered sufficiently, he will move to a local rehabilitation unit. The injuries he has sustained as a result of his fall mean he will have to relearn a lot of the skills we all take for granted. Such lessons take a long time and require medical support. His family, too, will require support."

Like everyone else, I'm glancing round the hall looking for the Malik brothers – or at least the one I would recognize. His friends are here, towards the end of the row of Year 12s – tall, quiet Finn Gardner and the infamous Matthew Lund – but no Sef.

"Yousef and Amir will be coming in next week and we ask that you treat them with the respect befitting of West Bridge students. Those who count yourself friends, be watchful and patient, and those of you who are nothing more than a face in the corridor, make sure that face is friendly. No staring, no whispers, no rumours.

"As one of last year's head boys, I know Kam is well liked." Our murmur of agreement is even louder than our distress. "And I know you all wish him the very best. If you would like to send Kam a more personal message of support, you have until next Friday to sign the card outside my office, where there's an envelope for donations to the Recreare Hospital for Neurodisability."

I sit up in my seat at hearing the name of the place where I'm volunteering as part of my Bronze Duke of Edinburgh.

I've got training there next Friday.

Mr Chung nods once and row by row, we're guided out of the hall, the teachers furiously shushing the rising tide of voices.

"God, that's *awful*," Rich says, like he can't quite process it.

"And he was going to Cambridge…" Seren shuts up at the sharp look Rich gives her, but it's too late. They're off.

"Would it have been better if he was heading to Hull or art college or –" Rich slaps a sarcastic hand to his face – "worse still, *he wasn't going to university*?"

"Oh, shut up, Denver Richards – that's not what I'm saying at all!"

"Then what are you saying?"

"I don't even know, all right? I suppose I mean that it can happen to anyone. That studying hard and being head boy and all those things that make you good don't protect you from … *this*."

I leave them to it, lost in my own head, trying to work out the implications of Kam moving to the Recreare the same time that I'll be there. It's not like we knew each other – the only time we spoke was when I thanked him for stopping the Year 8 hockey team from pushing ahead of me into the lunch queue – but still…

Behind me, a familiar hyena laugh rises out of the voices in the corridor and my blood chills. I managed to dodge the Cave Boys during registration, but the press of bodies by the stairs has slowed me down and there's nowhere for me to go.

This will be the first time I've seen them since it happened.

It was one of the hottest days of the year and me and Rich and Seren had squashed onto a single blanket in a three-gradient paint chart: me at one end, the luminous white of someone who has lived in a cave their whole life, and Seren, with her blessed-by-a-Turkish-father brown, at the other. Rich sat between us with his top off, exposing an almost-tanned chest.

"Six," I said.

"It doesn't count if it's the same one twice," Seren said.

We'd been counting how many people checked Rich out on their way past.

"I'm feeling objectified by the female gaze," Rich grumbled.

"That one was male." I didn't need to see her to know that would make Seren smile.

"If you're so worried about objectification, put your top on," she said.

"Victim blamer."

"I'll be honest, Rich – my heart's not in this one. I'm on your side. Wear what you want. It's a scrawny naked torso, not an invitation."

Rich was too busy taking affront to notice Chloe King and Gemma Brogan until they were close enough to cast shadows across our blanket. The pair of them were drenched, Gemma's skin goose-pimpled and glittering, Chloe's white dress turned translucent over a two-piece that could have been stylish underwear or sporty swimwear.

"The Cave Boys have conquered the fountain and we came to ask if you'd help us take it back?" Chloe might have been the one asking, but I didn't miss the way Gemma cast a glance over Rich and I silently added her to his tally.

Rich and I were happy to sign up. Seren was not. Leaving her to guard our stuff, we joined the others.

It was carnage – everyone within splashing distance of the fountain was soaked. The spray and the screaming made it impossible to know what was going on until Vijay Dinn caught me round the middle – and because I'd always had a soft spot for Vijay, I let myself enjoy the attention, scream-laughing as I tried to wriggle free, my skin slippery against his.

When I broke free to spin round, ready to retaliate, the horrified delight that blossomed across his face caught me off guard. Tracking his gaze down, I saw that the string of my halterneck bikini had come undone, releasing my bare boobs for the whole park to see…

They draw level with me on the stairs and James Blaithe – the biggest and most brutish of the three troglodytes – stares without shame at my chest before miming taking a photo. His slight underbite gives a predatory edge to his grin and runtish little Isaac sniggers into his fist as I draw further into my school jumper.

We all know that there's no need for James to even joke about taking a picture. Not when he filmed the whole thing on his phone before posting it onto an anonymous gossip site with the tag: *#MilkTits*.

My whole existence boiled down to a Ctrl+Z moment that can never be undone – a moment that has been shared over a thousand times in twenty-two days.

After lunch Madame Cotterill asks James to hand out the worksheets in French and I pretend not to notice him lumbering between the desks towards where I sit with Seren. But he stops just short of my desk, holding the paper so that I have to reach for it.

"One for Milk Tits…"

A hand lashes out to snatch the sheets from him.

"Her name is *Claire*!" Seren hisses fiercely. I whisper at her to leave it, but afterwards I can tell by the way she's stony about the past participle that she's annoyed with me.

"You should report it," she bursts out at the end of the lesson, firing a glance down the corridor to where James and Isaac are making fart noises with their armpits as if competing to see who is the biggest cliché. "It's sexual harassment. He can't get away with it."

She doesn't understand that he already has. They can take the link down, but they can't wipe people's memories. Any time I've caught someone's eye today, I've wondered whether they've watched the video or commented…
Udder alert! Check out her mammaries! Bit NIPPY, was it??? ((@))((@)) They follow you wherever you go…

We're still arguing about it when we reach the lockers, where Rich has been waiting.

"… can you just leave it? I'm not going to."

"What's Claire not going to do?" he asks.

"Report James about the video," I say at the same time as Seren says, "The right thing."

Rich gives me a sympathetic look.

14

"If Claire's said that's not what she wants—"

"You mean, it's not what *you* want?" Seren rounds on him, her smooth black bob swishing like it's been CGI-ed into existence by someone who used shampoo ads for reference.

"Hey!" Rich raises his hands in surrender.

"Now you're captain of the football team, it's important to keep James onside, right?"

"What's football got to do with it? I'm listening to what my best friend wants instead of assuming I'm the only person capable of deciding what's right."

"This isn't about *deciding*!" Seren's staring at us both, brows lowered. "If you don't report him for this, then he'll do it again."

"He's going to keep calling me Milk Tits whatever I do…"

"It's not just *you* – next time it might be someone else. James Blaithe is a giant toddler, and if someone doesn't set the boundaries, then he'll carry on like there aren't any."

I wish Seren wouldn't get so angry with me – and I wish she could understand that ratting on James will make things worse. I'd rather be the joke than have everyone think I can't take one.

"I get where you're coming from. I just don't want that someone to be me."

"I'll do it, then—"

"Seren. Please." Her will is the kind that mine usually bends to, but not on this. "The only people in this school who haven't seen my boobs are the teachers. I'd like to keep it that way."

Seren flares her nostrils the way she always does when she's holding something back.

"Fine." She yanks her locker open and swaps her French books for English ones, marching off down the corridor, too annoyed to walk at a normal pace.

As we follow her, Rich slings an arm round my shoulders and gives me a squeeze.

"Just to be clear, *I've* not seen your boobs."

"Not even the live show?" I stare at the floor as we walk.

"Looking the other way, wasn't I?"

And I half turn to give him a flimsy smile. "Hashtag not all men, Rich?"

"Hashtag not this one."

CHAPTER 2

"Has anyone here met someone with a neurological condition before?" The man leading the training session sweeps a look round the conference room. His name is William and he's rocking a *fierce* monobrow. Of the five volunteers, I'm the youngest by at least a decade and I feel conspicuous in the hideous maroon of my school uniform.

"It's a different way of being from what you're used to," William continues. "The brain dictates so many of the things you take for granted in other people – how polite they are, the control they have over their emotions, their ability to process what you're saying to them…" He pauses to give us another searching look before adding, "It can affect someone's appearance. Many of our residents have had operations that leave a hole in their skull, or have a condition that's misshapen their head in some way. Many have no control over their facial muscles. It takes a certain character to withstand the confusion of the unfamiliar and see through to the person for whom such confusion is their life."

After that scary start, William talks us through things we're not expected to do (medical stuff, unwelcome physical contact – consent is an issue for a lot of the residents) and more positive things like how to use different communication aids and what we should do if someone falls asleep during our session (let them).

Coming at the end of my first full week of school, I'm not capable of much more than doodling tapirs in the margin of my notepad. Once the session is over, it takes me a while to pack away my things because of how overstuffed my bag is.

"Everything OK, Claire?" William's come over for some reason.

"Seems to be." I give him a bit of a confused stare. Should it not?

"I didn't want to single you out because of your age, but –" he thought he would anyway – "I wanted to see whether you had any further questions about dealing with someone who has neurodisability?"

This feels like a trick question.

"I – er – I planned on treating whoever I'm with like they're a person." Because that's exactly what they are.

"Actually, that's what I wanted to talk to you about. I understand you might know one of our patients – Kamran Malik?"

I nod. "He was at my school. We had an assembly about what happened."

William does something weird with his rubbery mouth. It might be a smile. "Excellent. Well, his family have indicated they'd be interested in having a volunteer visit him and I thought perhaps I'd talk to them about that volunteer being you?"

"I'd really like that," I say. It's what I've been hoping for since that assembly.

I head back to reception, past frosted-glass signs to the aquatherapy pool and the physio suite – there's even one directing me to a private cinema. On the ground floor, I pass a woman using a walking frame. She's helped by three other people as she makes slow but determined progress towards the double doors that lead out onto wide, flat lawns.

This place isn't what I'd expect of a hospital and, while I'd prefer never to have to, I could imagine worse places to stay.

Outside, I take a seat on the low wall around the car park and get my phone out. Dad was supposed to be picking me up at half past, but I can't see his car anywhere. When he answers, there's the familiar fuzz of him Bluetoothing it in the car and a brief "There in ten!" before he hangs up.

Which would be fine if my father measured minutes the same way as the rest of us. I find the Recreare's Wi-Fi, unable to resist the toxic lure of #MilkTits. Knowing I shouldn't isn't enough to stop me, and a broken, pathetic part of me is almost disappointed when there are no new comments to feel bad about.

There's a bang over by reception. The double doors have swung wide open and a boy about my age walks out.

The one I was looking for in that first assembly.

Sef Malik is tall – gangly – his glasses are hipster cool (if you like that sort of thing), his hair is brushed back in a soft quiff and he's the sort of stylish that just about pulls off a denim jacket and skinny jogger combo. His skin is brown, hair black, and I like the curve of his jaw and the slight hook of his nose.

I like *him*.

So I look away. If school has taught me anything, it's that hot boys should be seen and not heard, spoken to or even fleetingly acknowledged. And… *Oh God, what if he's seen the video?*

I desperately tap away from what I've been watching as Sef's footsteps draw too close.

Then they stop.

"Hey."

When I look up, he's standing in front of me, the faded print on his grey T-shirt showing where his jacket pulls apart as he drums his fingers lightly on the roof of the car next to him.

I try a cautious "Hi?"

"You go to West Bridge then?" Sef nods at my uniform.

"Er, yeah." And because it's socially acceptable for me to recognize everyone in the year above, I add, "So do you."

Sef's fingers drum a little harder, a smile emerging fast and bright. "Do I now?"

"I saw you in *West Side Story*. You were great as Tony." Which makes the whole thing sound more legitimate and less stalkerish. Our race-bent adaptation made the local papers with the headline WEST BRIDGE SIDE STORY.

"Thanks!" His proud glow warms me through. "Are you going to tell me my name too?"

"Your name is Sef."

"Yousef, technically." He pronounces it differently to the way Mr Chung did last week, swallowing the second syllable so that it sounds more like "suff". "But you can only call me that if I'm in trouble."

My palms prickle at the look that accompanies those words. Sef is someone I imagine gets into a lot more trouble than me.

"And are you going to tell me *your* name?" he asks.

"Claire Casey."

Sef walks between the cars to sit next to me on my wall, close enough that if I'm not careful, I might brush his arm with mine.

"So, Claire Casey, what are you doing sitting on a wall outside the Recreare?" He smells like pencil shavings and ginger biscuits.

"Volunteering as a reader."

"A what?"

"They have a scheme where you can come in and read to the residents and I've just had my training."

"For reading?"

"It's very complicated." I nod knowledgeably and he smiles again. It's pleasing. "They've said I might read to your brother, actually."

Sef's joy dims, smile slipping, and his attention turns away from me to the car park, to the sky, to a worn patch on the cuff of his jacket, where he starts pulling at a thread.

"Yeah, well, you'll have to wait a while. Kam's not moving here till next week and the post-traumatic amnesia means it's going to take a while for him to settle in." He flicks a glance up that doesn't quite meet my eye. "Sorry. I must sound like a textbook."

"Not really," I say, wishing I knew what post-traumatic amnesia actually was. "But if you're not here visiting Kam...?"

"Drove Mum up to drop some of his stuff off," he explains. "Get the room ready."

I get the impression that this boy, shiny and confident as he seems, would rather talk about anything else in the world than what's happening with his brother, so I reach for a desperate, "You drove?"

It's like magic. The second the subject changes, he perks up.

"I did indeed." Sef gives the Honda next to him an affectionate kick and casts me a glance that's approaching smug. "Impressed?"

I notice the L-plate. "I'll reserve my admiration for when you pass."

"Why wait when I can take you for a spin now?" Sef's up and off the wall, the keys slipped from his pocket before I can blink. "You coming?"

His grin is irresistibly wicked.

"For a ride in a strange car driven by someone yet to pass their test? No thanks."

"Her name is Mrs Bennet."

"You named your car Mrs Bennet?"

"My brother did. It was that or Bent." He nods at the letters on the number plate by way of explanation. "So now you're acquainted with her..."

"There's still the small matter of you not having a full licence."

Sef shrugs like laws are for other people. "Go on, live a little. I dare you."

But there's the sound of an engine by the entrance and a familiar black Audi pulls through the gates.

"That's my dad," I say, wishing it wasn't. "Gotta go."

The bricks catch at the back of my tights as I slide off the wall and by the time I've picked my bag off the floor, Sef is ahead of me, stepping out to open the passenger door of Dad's car.

"See you around, Claire Casey," he says in a voice that's low and pleasant and has a strange effect on my heart rate.

As Dad turns the car round, I look over to where Sef is leaning on the boot of his car, arms crossed, watching. When he sees me, he lifts one hand up in a casual farewell.

We're pulling out of the gates as Dad says, "That's an interesting shade of puce you've turned there, Little Bear."

CHAPTER 3

Three weeks back at school and the bickering between Seren and Rich has escalated. Yesterday's vicious faux feminism debate started during afternoon break and carried on over messaging, with insults flashing from my bedside table long after I'd turned out the light and put my phone on to charge.

It's been no better this morning. I've had Seren in one ear and Rich in the other.

"Rich is such an entitled toadling."

"... she's so arrogant..."

"He never lets me finish – has to interrupt whatever point I'm making."

"... insufferable..."

"You can't seriously think it's feminist to have a half-clad woman with no head as your screensaver."

"... winds me right up."

I can't face it over lunch too and head, via the vending machine, for the relative peace of the Media Suite. Miss Stevens is too busy talking to a sixth-former to take much notice of my violation of the no food or drink rule, and my heart does a double bounce when I recognize the back of Sef's head. He's not someone I'd expect to see in here.

Ducking down behind a console, I take out the Fanta,

Wotsits and Toffee Crisp that would have my mum sprinting for a NutriBullet and, with nothing better to read, I flip through the notes I made on viral marketing campaigns and admire the bullet point that consists solely of the word *HASHTAG* written in short savage strokes. Obviously I didn't think there was much more to learn about the power of a catchy hashtag…

"… talk to Claire."

The sound of my name has me knocking my Wotsits across the table and I look up, sheepish. Miss Stevens and Sef look down at me, one with a resigned arch of the eyebrows, the other suppressing a smile.

"I'll pretend I didn't see that," Miss Stevens says. Then, to Sef, "If you want advice about starting a channel, Claire's an expert on all things YouTube."

"Oh, me and Claire go way back," Sef says, prompting a glance from Miss Stevens that would set Seren off on a rant about heteronormative assumptions.

"Well, as I said, Claire's an expert. I'll leave you to it." Miss Stevens nods at my crisps – "Don't make any mess!" – and turns back to her desk.

In one smooth and startling move, Sef sits down next to me and swipes a Wotsit from the table top.

"Er, that's my lunch you're eating," I tell him.

"Nutritious." He eyes the Toffee Crisp and Fanta. "And orange."

I nod, not really knowing what to say to that.

"So what qualifies you as an expert?" he says, as he reaches for another Wotsit, from the packet this time.

"A fierce YouTube habit, I guess. What did you want to know about starting a channel?" I'm surprised he's not already into this, being a Drama type.

Sef tuts, his leg bouncing a restless rhythm beneath the table. He's wearing skinny jeans today. Dark purple.

"Actually it was equipment I was after, not advice." His leg is still going, but he doesn't appear to want to say anything more.

"Equipment for what?"

"Something I didn't want to tell Miss Stevens about."

"Or me?" I venture.

"We don't know each other." His tone is so dismissive Sef may as well have backhanded me right in the face.

"Right. OK," I say, my voice tight, wishing Miss Stevens had never brought him over here.

Sef's leg has stopped moving, his gaze on me, eyes like needles. "Look –"

"You don't have to tell me—"

"– it's for Kam." Sef pauses, weighing up how much more to say. "I want to set up a channel where people can donate to watch me do dares."

"OK."

"I'm serious."

"OK." Maybe if I keep saying this Sef will stop looking at me like I'm trying to argue with him?

"I'm sorry." He runs a hand down his face like he's tired of talking, but then he mutters something that sounds like, "Guess *you* should know." Then a little louder, "He has six months."

"To live?!"

Sef gives me a patronizing stare and I regret deviating from "OK".

"To get better," he says.

"I'm sorry, I don't understand."

"There's no reason you would, but you asked, so…" Sef splays his hands like that's all the explanation I'm going to get.

What I gathered from training is that most brain injuries last a lifetime, one way or another, and from everything I've been told about Kam, his is a pretty big one. Like, change-the-rest-of-your-life massive. I don't know what Sef means by getting better, but I can't imagine much of it happening in under six months.

"So … you want to raise money for his care?" I try.

"If we want him to stay on at the Rec." Sef glances up over the frame of his glasses. "Which we do."

"How much money?"

"Sixty thousand pounds."

My mouth falls open and the words tumble out in a horrified whisper: "That's *loads*."

"Tell me about it," Sef says with a bitter twist to his mouth, as he stares down at the cartoon tapir Seren drew in my notebook.

"I know you weren't serious about asking for help…" I feel stupid for what I'm about to say. "But if you wanted any…?"

"And what is it you're offering, Claire Casey?" There's a sceptical slant to his eyebrows. "You going to read to me, too?"

That stings.

"I'm offering ideas and time." I pause before playing my trump card. "Equipment."

CHAPTER 4

Do you think Rich has a problem with me? Seren writes in the margin of my French sheet.

Did something happen at lunch? I write back.

Didn't see him. Seren isn't someone who uses emojis on her phone or little faces in her notes and you have to actually look at her face to be sure what she's feeling. She's not happy.

For all she acts like a crusading robot with a heart of tempered steel, my best friend isn't quite as immune to insecurity as she pretends.

Do you want me to ask Rich?

Yes please.

Rich and I have Art together next and after examining possible angles of subterfuge, I come out with, "So, what's going on with you and Seren?"

There. That should do it.

Only Rich ignores me. He painstakingly adds a fraction of red to the blue he's already got in his palette.

"Rich? Did you hear me?"

"We all heard you…" mutters Oliver Martinez from the other side of the table.

Rich adds a touch more red before saying, "I'm just ignoring you."

"Well, don't." I reach over and brush a thick yellow line across his knuckles. "Or I'll annoy you into talking to me."

He tuts and wipes off my brushwork, but he doesn't blow up the way he would if I were Seren.

"Fine. I'll talk. Cease your torture. But not now, OK?" He makes his eyes go extra wide as if that's supposed to mean something.

"OK." I make my eyes go wide too.

"We've got a match tonight. Would you wait for me?"

I had planned on going home to think about Sef and his channel...

"Sure," I say and Rich breaks out into the purest smile I've seen since term started.

"It'll be the first time you see me play as captain."

It turns out that Gemma Brogan's at the match too, so while I sit on my coat and half-do some of my homework, she cheers and makes disparaging remarks about how useless her brother is in defence.

"They should try a diamond formation in midfield," Gemma says afterwards as we wait by the changing block.

Since I did not pay enough attention to the match to know what this means, I go with a vague "Mm".

"Denver's better with someone who can feed him a short ball."

Denver. I always find it funny when people use Rich's real name. He hates it. Such a waste of a cool name.

"Well, he couldn't exactly have been worse, could he?" I say. "Strikers are supposed to score."

Gemma feeds me a short ball of a look and I shrug. There's a swell of noise and a few of the players emerge from the changing room in a miasma of Lynx infused with the scent of mud and wet leather.

Without even knowing whether James Blaithe is among them, I've crossed my arms, the stitches straining in the sleeves of my jumper as I pull it tighter around me.

"Lads! We've a fan club." James swaggers over and even Gemma, one of the more boy-confident girls in my form, shrinks away from him.

"Go away, James. We're not here for you."

"Speak for yourself, Brogues. Milk Tits and I are on intimate terms."

"No, we're not," I say, several decibels too quiet to be defiant.

"That's what you think." And he bites his lip as he reaches down, pretending to jack off as he steps past. The rest of them – boys who aren't even in my year – pat James on the back and laugh as my skin tries to crawl from my body and slither down the nearest drain.

"I hate him," Gemma says, leaning into me a little, offering comfort in solidarity.

I nod along, thinking that what I really hate is how James makes me hate myself.

At home, with no one more threatening than Rich around, I finally relax, pyjama bottoms on over my tights as I sit cross-legged on my bed with a tin of wasabi peas. My house isn't the best for snacks and Rich has already fallen into a pit of

First World despair at discovering the fizzy stuff in the door of the fridge is elderflower nonsense and not lemonade.

"We should have got Mrs Brogan to drop us off at the corner shop," I say as he picks out the sweet potato crisps from the bag of root vegetable crisps.

"I fancy her," he says.

"Who? Gemma's *mum*?"

He gives me a look.

"Gemma?"

Rich frowns, tilting his head to the side. "Gemma's all right, I guess."

All right? Gemma's one of the most attractive girls in our year with a ridiculously stylish haircut and the sort of figure that makes me think (fleetingly) about taking up sport.

"Who, then?"

I'm rootling around in my pea tin, vaguely thinking about confessing to Rich that I've been talking to Sef Malik, when he replies, "Seren." And then, "Stop looking at me like that."

Apparently my mouth has fallen open.

"You fancy *Seren*?" I sound like it's impossible to believe, but it's not. Seren looks like an angrier, plumper version of a young Catherine Zeta-Jones and even the Cave Boys have been known to give her thoughtful looks.

It's just that Rich's crush – anyone's – is doomed to failure.

Girls, boys, whatever, Seren just isn't interested. She's asexual and pretty political about it – Seren's campaigning is the reason West Bridge has such comprehensive LGBTQ+ lessons in PSHE.

"You can't fancy Seren," I tell him helpfully.

"And yet, I do."

"Have you tried, just … not?"

"Because it's that easy."

I love how Rich thinks he's the first of us to experience an unrequited crush, when they make up ninety-five per cent of my love life.

"You'll have to get over it," I say, because that really is his only option.

"What do you think I've been trying to do?"

What I think he's been doing is punishing Seren for the way he feels about her, but I'm not sure my pop psychology would go down too well. Instead, I put my peas to one side and shuffle over to give Rich a consoling hug.

"Ignore it until it goes away." I pat his back. "And in the meantime, try being nice to her."

"Rich is really starting to grow into himself," Mum says later over the miniscule M&S meal for two that meant having him stay for tea wasn't an option.

"I guess." Rich has always been passable, but his skin's looking better these days and his hair's grown nicely – along with his chesticles – but he's still just Rich. I can feel Mum's speculation regardless. "No, Mum. Don't even think it. I would rather eat my own vomit than go there."

"Claire!"

"Don't give me those sorts of looks then." I poke at a rubbery mushroom. "Where's Dad?"

"Busy with other things."

"Having an affair with the vicar?"

"Assuming you're using 'the vicar' as a euphemism for 'his spreadsheets', then yes."

There's no high ground for the taking when it comes to work. Since Mum's company moved offices, she's been coming home late too. The pair of them have been arguing about her looking for a new job, forgetting that it doesn't matter if I'm three rooms away on a different floor – I can still hear them if they shout.

Once tea's cleared, Mum goes to take a conference call while I head upstairs to research things Sef could do for his channel. The next I see of her is when she puts her head round my door on her way to bed, warning me not to stay online too late. I don't see Dad at all, but I hear him creeping past my door, trying to hide how late home he is the same way I'm hiding the light of my laptop under the duvet.

CHAPTER 5

Saturday night and I find it hard to sleep, my mind flipping between what I'm doing tomorrow morning, when I visit Kam for the first time, and what I'll be doing in the afternoon, when I meet Sef. Nervous as I am about spending time with Sef, imagining multiple scenarios that end up with him laughing at me, it's his brother I'm more concerned about, trainer William's words haunting my thoughts.

It takes a certain character to withstand the confusion of the unfamiliar and see through to the person for whom such confusion is their life.

What if I don't have that character? What if I do something completely dreadful and insensitive? What if I find out I'm not the person I want to be?

It's William who meets me in reception, signing me in and pointing out where the cafe is as we pass, leading me through the building and up some stairs where there's a sign for the BUELLER WING. I have to press a buzzer to enter and he hands me over to the charge nurse, Adele Goethe.

"You're Claire, are you?" She has an Australian accent and a firm handshake. "Let's go find your friend, Kam."

"I – er…" I have to hurry to keep up. "He's not exactly my friend, we went to the same school, but he's three years older than me and we didn't…"

Nurse Goethe looks confused. "But you're friends with his family?"

"His brother." Maybe. I'm not sure what we are yet, but my answer seems to suffice.

Kam's room is empty when we get there and Nurse Goethe leaves me in the doorway while she goes to find him.

There's a window opposite, a globe and some Lego on the windowsill and framed posters on the wall: nerd-boy classics *Planet of the Apes* (the original) and *The Big Lebowski* either side of *Moon*, one of my top films of all time. Edging inside to see what's on the nearest wall, I find an enormous photo collage, with a few special snaps in individual frames arranged on the chest of drawers underneath.

The first picture is of Kam's parents with a younger boy that must be Amir. Looking at him now, I recognize him as being in the same year as Rich's sister, although he looks a lot happier in this picture than I've ever seen him at school. They're posing along the Thames with the Houses of Parliament in the background and Mr Malik looks like he wishes the photographer would get on with it. I can see where Sef gets his glasses and his height from, if not his looks. His mum is shorter, wider, rounder, with a girlishly pretty smile.

Next to this there's one of the three brothers. Amir is a child, arms crossed, smile broad as he takes pride in posing with his brothers and Sef's stooping slightly like he's not yet used to being tall. Between them stands Kam. Short and broad and strong, confidence rolling off him, hands resting on the picnic table behind him, ankles crossed as he cocks his head at the camera.

It's an attitude echoed in the last picture, set inside one of those cardboard frames that comes with a school-endorsed photo. Kam and his friends – two boys I recognize, without knowing their names – arms round each other for the formal photo taken at the Leavers' Cruise along the Lay.

The sight brings a lump to my throat that I can't seem to swallow.

"Claire?" The voice at the door makes me jump and I flush pink with guilt as Nurse Goethe looks in. She frowns, then steps back to let someone in.

To *push* someone in.

Kam's wheelchair is tall, supporting his spine, a cushioned brace stopping his head from lolling too far over and a footplate keeping his legs in a comfortable position. There's a tray across the front of the chair, where one of his hands rests, the other crooked up towards his chest, fingers curled inwards. His hair's shaved shorter than in the photo with his friends, an observation followed by a rush of comprehension when I see the dressing strapped to his skull.

William's words of warning about how a brain injury can affect someone's appearance have not prepared me for the change in Kam's face.

There's a doughiness to his cheeks, as if the muscles beneath have softened, giving his whole expression a lack of purpose. His eyes – a more distinctive bronze than Sef's – have none of the same spark and when I try to meet his gaze, Kam's attention slides off me to rove around the room.

There's so little of the Kam I knew in the one I'm here to see that it is impossible not to feel wholly and uncontrollably horrified.

"Claire, this is Kam," Nurse Goethe says. "Kam, this is Claire."

I swallow, determined not to cry. Not everything in this world is about me, and Kam does not want my pity.

"Hi, Kam," I say.

An hour is a long time to read out loud. It's also a long time for Kam to have to concentrate on anything and he falls asleep several times during our session – although given the book I was reading, I can't blame him.

"That went well," Nurse Goethe says on the way out.

I say nothing, still processing just how severe Kam's condition is. When I'd started reading, he'd been fretful, forcing out low, strained moans as I talked and each time he woke up, he seemed startled to see me still there. Apparently he won't recognize me next week, either – new memories are hard for Kam to make.

Sensing my mood, Nurse Goethe slows to a halt. "How do you feel about it?"

"I thought Kam would be using communication aids?"

Nurse Goethe looks at me with a gentle sort of pity. "He will eventually, but Kam has complex cognitive issues and he's only been with us for a couple of weeks. Progress will be slow across many different aspects of his life, including his communication skills."

"Would he be able to choose what book to read next

week?" I ask, thinking of how dull the book was that I'd picked off the shelf outside his door and wanting to give Kam some control over the session too.

"Perhaps not next week," Nurse Goethe says, "but in time you'll be able to present him with options and see if he wishes to choose."

"Are you sure that went well?"

Nurse Goethe sighs. "I thought this was what you wanted—"

"I do." My vehemence surprises her. "But I don't want to assume that's what Kam wants, just because it's what *I* want."

"Then trust someone who's been working with him, who knows his moods." She softens once more. "If you spend time with him regularly, as you plan to, you'll come to understand Kam better – and he will come to know you. It just takes time."

CHAPTER 6

Sef said to meet him at the arts cinema at the end of Halstead Street, where all the edgier people from school buy one-of-a-kind second-hand clothes. Walking past windows dressed with vintage evening gowns under grandad cardies and racks of Georgian-era military jackets, I glance at my unremarkable checked-shirt-over-vest-over-long-sleeved-tee combo. Even my shoes are generic.

The cinema itself is up two flights of steps, the walls lined with posters for the sort of films I can never persuade my friends to watch. At the top, I take a moment to regain my breath and my dignity before opening the doors to a foyer of flaking gold columns and a once-plush maroon carpet.

Sef is sitting with his back to me at one of the tall tables by the window. The collar's turned up on his black polo shirt and the afternoon sun cuts a slice of gold across his shoulders, highlighting the word STAFF.

I like him too much for this to be a good idea, but last night's feverish conviction that Sef is only humouring me doesn't seem quite so important now that I've actually met Kam. It doesn't matter whether I'm about to make a monumental idiot out of myself – I still want to try.

* * *

Sef is charming and I blossom under the attention, smiling as he talks and laughing at his jokes. Flipping through my notes, he scans the things I've jotted down, asking questions like he's genuinely interested in the answers.

"Who's Moz?" He points to where I've written a list of single-camera vloggers.

"His channel's called MozzyMozzaMeepMorp—"

"That's a ridiculously long name." Sef twinkles with amusement.

"He's good at what he does…" I fizzle out with a shrug, losing confidence as rapidly as I'd found it. No one I talk to has ever watched his stuff, but Moz has hundreds of thousands of viewers and I find his videos addictive.

On the next page I've boiled my plan down to three bullet points. It doesn't look like much.

Sef plays truth or dare to the camera (picks own)

Invite viewers to donate and then copy the video, linking their post back to channel

Grow audience and invite people to post challenges in the comments

"How much am I asking them to donate?"

"A couple of pounds." He glances up, disappointed, and I add, "People won't donate if you ask for too much. That's all people had to donate for the Ice Bucket Challenge and that made *millions*."

It's an optimistic comparison, but the principle still stands.

My phone goes before I can say any more and I step away to answer it, getting it in the neck because Mum forgot I said I'd be out all day and she wants me to help in the garden. Such is my vibrant teenage life.

Sef's been flipping further through my notes to the page where I brainstormed brand identity, but when I finish my call and see what he's looking at, I want to reach over and flip the book shut.

"Ignore that," I say, trying to pull my notes back across the table. "I was just messing about."

I'd been thinking about how Sef could make his channel stand out and latched onto the idea of him having an alter ego, like a superhero, and started sketching a few designs – only I got a bit carried away with the superhero thing and added a sidekick.

Me.

"It's good!" Sef keeps a firm hold of the notebook and levels me with a look. "We should do this."

"Are you serious?" I say, because it's very hard to tell whether Sef means anything he says.

"Why not?" The energy that's been humming through him all through our meeting has increased frequency.

"It's just … you're an actor and stuff. Don't you want to be the star?"

He waves the suggestion away. "I'm better with someone to spark off –" my lungs contract in a hiccup of excitement at the way he looks at me – "and me and you, I reckon there's a spark."

"Is there?" I manage as my ears reach the temperature required to melt right off my head.

"You don't think so?" Sef tips his head to one side and

gives me a rakish grin. "And you say in your notes that we need a good brand…"

"It doesn't say anywhere that *I'm* a part of that brand!"

"But you could be," he says. I can almost believe he means it.

"Can I think about it?"

"No. You're very good at thinking." Sef taps the notes I've made, then runs a finger down the page to where the two be-masked figures strike superhero poses with Truth Girl and Dare Boy written on their T-shirts. "This is about your gut, Truth Girl…"

Hearing him call me that feels strange.

"I was only messing about!"

"Messing about with me would be better, though." My senses are so overloaded by Sef that it's hard to know what I really feel – whether he can really be trusted.

My instinct is to say no. I haven't got it in me to face another #MilkTits situation. Every other second I'm in school, I'm fighting against an anxious narcissism, convinced everyone's looking at me, whispering about me, laughing at me…

Yet maybe what Sef's offering is a way to build myself up? With the channel, I could dictate what I will and won't do in front of a camera, I would be the one editing the result. I'd be hidden by a mask … no one would have to know it was me.

Since James posted that video, I've been struggling with making eye contact with the boys at school, but I can't seem to keep my gaze off Sef for more than a few seconds at a time and when I look up he's looking at me like he knows exactly what I'm thinking.

I have a feeling it's very difficult to say no to Sef Malik.

CHAPTER 7

In the next week, Sef sorts out the biggest of our problems by suggesting we film in his Uncle Danish's static caravan while he's away working on a building contract in Oman. I get the impression Sef wishes his uncle wasn't gone for so long, but at least we'll have a private studio with electricity and running water from now until the end of February.

That's the date by which the Recreare needs guarantee of funds to pay for another six months of Kam's care. Long-term – "Level 2" – care at the Rec is limited, and expensive. Whenever I press Sef on how unfair this is, asking what will happen if there's no money, he gets testy, as if by questioning the system I'm questioning whether Kam needs the care and I soon leave off asking. It's not like griping about it is going to change anything.

There's a lot to be done before Saturday, when we've agreed to start filming. My phone's on overdrive, messages firing back and forth with Sef about T-shirt designs and eye masks and channel names and social-media accounts and how we'll structure filming to maximize editing efficiency and what we're actually going to film.

We've been discussing that one since last night and I'm on the bus, my screen angled away from Rich, when yet another message comes through from Sef.

Right, so, nothing illegal, nothing dangerous and no nudity... You do understand the concept of a dare, don't you, Claire???

I do. I also understand the concept of *getting people to copy us*.

People are a lot less bothered by these things than you think they are, Sef replies and I resist the urge to type back a slightly snarky **Only people like you!,** distracting myself by reading what Rich has written about tidal drifts as he does Geography homework on his lap. If he knew what I was up to, Rich would tease me about spending so much time with a boy from the year above and Seren would pick everything apart with a brutal kind of logic that takes no account of the need for hope. For now, I'm keeping them out of it.

I return to Sef.

1) We can't make any videos if we're arrested. 2) We can't make any videos if we're dead. 3) Even if the dangerous things we do don't kill us, how would we feel if they killed someone else because they'd copied us?

I send it then add, **Case closed.**

Rich and I have Computing first thing. While I thought my coding on point, it seems my grasp of error handling is so far off point that Mr Lester is unable to locate it. Still, he spends so long looking that by the time he's done with me, everyone in my class has left and the sixth-formers who are in next push past me as I leave. When I get out into the corridor, I find there's one who's yet to make it into the classroom.

Sef's leaning nonchalantly against the wall, faffing with his phone.

"Fancy seeing you here," he says with a lazy sort of grin that does unprecedented things to my insides.

"You mean in the school that we both go to?"

"I'm trying to be cool and secretive," he says as my phone bings and I glance down to see that he's just sent me a message, which I regret reading while standing in front of him.

Fine. But no one ever died from legal nudity.

But they might die from talking about it.

"You got my message then?" he says, watching my reaction.

"Yeah. Look." I *really* do not want to bring this up, but I can't see how else to shut down any further nudity discussions. "Haven't you seen the video?"

Sef's eyebrows do a cute little quirk, a comma-shaped hollow appearing above the frame of his glasses. "What video?"

One of his friends – Matthew Lund with the blue eyes and bad shirts – sticks his head out of the classroom.

"If you're skipping, mate, maybe do it where Lester can't see you?"

When his pretty baby blues slide my way, I tip my head forward to hide behind my hair. Matthew Lund has *definitely* seen the #MilkTits video.

"Two secs, Matty." And Sef waits to be sure he's gone before saying again, "What video?"

"The Milk Tits video." I keep my head down. "The one

that literally everyone in this school has seen of me having a wardrobe malfunction of the bikini-top variety."

Perhaps if I stare hard enough at that smear of chewing gum on the floor, it will turn into a vortex that will suck me into another dimension?

"Claire –" Sef's shoes shuffle into my vision – "I don't know what video you're talking about."

"You really don't?" I look up to scan his face for the lie, but all I find is an implacable honesty that makes me want to fling my arms around him and thank him for not being like all the others.

"I'll co-sign your no nudity clause," he says, taking a step towards the door before he turns round to add, "YouTube screens for anything gratuitous anyway."

And he actually winks.

"I'm going to have to do something," Rich says on the bus home.

I'm tired and Rich's shoulder is my pillow. "Do something about what?" I murmur into his jumper. We had PE last lesson and he smells like other boys' deodorant.

"My *feelings*. For Seren."

Rich's ego must be the size of Mount Everest, the difficulty he's having getting over himself, and I'm bored of how long it's taking. Bored of playing referee. Bored of lying to Seren about why our friend is acting like a humourless goat turd. Bored of having the same conversation running across three separate chats – one for all three of us, one just for Seren and one just for Rich – Seren moaning and Rich mooning and me getting RSI.

"Please stop talking to me about it," I say.

"Unhelpful."

"I've told you. Be nice to her. Get over it. In that order."

"And…?"

"And I'll stop worrying that my two best friends might kill each other in a debate over what the difference is between Brie and Camembert."

"That's not what I meant." Rich shrugs me off his shoulder so he can look at me. "Do you really think I shouldn't say anything? It's not like I'm some random…"

He's wearing me down and, buried deep below layers and layers of more honourable parts of my character, there's a seed of hurt that Rich has chosen Seren. It's like hating netball, but still not wanting to be the last person picked for the team.

"It won't change anything," I say, when I should really just say "No". Again.

"Maybe not," he says, picking at the skin around his nails. "But it'll mean I don't have to keep hiding it from her."

"I love you to bits, Rich," I say, laying my head back down and shutting my eyes. "But my advice is don't say anything unless you really can't not."

Since he had last period free, Sef's been setting everything up at the caravan for tomorrow morning and when I check my phone after Media Studies, I find a picture of where he's hung the bedsheet backdrop and questions about equipment – can I bring a couple of extension leads and maybe a desk lamp if I have one? I'm about to reply when he sends through a series of ridiculous selfies of him lying on what appears to be a leopard-print bedspread.

Sef rubbing his face against the material … tilting his chin to look down over his glasses … a finger hooked over his teeth as if biting it…

Excitement writhes around in my belly at the sight of them.

Think maybe I should take up a career modelling?

No. I amble slowly after Gemma and Chloe as they round the corner, heading for our lockers.

Wow. Harsh much.

Models have to look serious.

I can look serious.

Shortly followed by a picture of him in a pose you'd find on the back of a book, the author with their chin resting on their fist, deep in creative thought.

I take it all back. You're clearly the next Gandy.

Gandhi? I guess all us brown people look the same to you…

Usually I'd agonize over the right response to a joke like that, but everything with Sef – even uncomfortable jokes about race – seems so much easier than with anyone else.

David Gandy. The model??? Think Gandhi was famous for something more than his physique.

Are you saying you only like me for my body?

Who said I liked you at all?

Stop flirting with me, Claire. It's unprofessional.

My smile is snatched from my face as someone grabs me from behind.

I say me – I mean my boobs.

"Guess who!" James Blaithe's voice is loud and hot in my left ear.

"Get off me!" There's a desperation in the way the words squeal out of me as I squirm away, but James laughs as if this is a joke I'm enjoying as much as him. Before he lets go, he gives my breasts a gentle little double-squeeze, like it's a private treat just for us.

Disgusted and humiliated and desperately sad, I watch as James walks off down the corridor, high-fiving someone from the football team as he passes.

CHAPTER 8

My bag is packed with everything except the desk lamp, since I'm not sure I can convince my parents I need one for the Film Club I've fabricated to explain my Saturday morning absences.

Hopefully, once Sef passes his driving test in two weeks' time, I won't have to worry about logistics as he'll pick me up from the layby at the end of my road, but for now, Mum drops me in town on her way to Pilates. From there, I catch a bus up to the caravan. It takes a while and I would have missed the stop if it weren't for Sef waiting to meet me.

Despite the rain pattering applause in the trees, he's wearing nothing more substantial than his denim jacket and I wonder why it is that boys look so much better wet.

"Truth Girl."

"Dare Boy." This feels strange.

Taking my bag, Sef heads towards a sign for Sunny Slopes Caravan Park. Slopes that are more slippery than sunny as we pass rows of static caravans. Some have flowers outside marking homes more permanent than temporary, the washing hanging inside for today. It's only once we're inside that I realize our caravan falls into the same category. I'd thought it was somewhere Sef's Uncle Danish spent his holidays, not his life, but there's no doubting that this is someone's home – pictures up on the wall, mismatched mugs on the shelves, the carpet and furnishings displaying a softness that speaks of regular, affectionate use.

Thanks to Sef's prep the day before, it doesn't take long to set up, the camera balanced on one of the chairs and strips of tin foil stretched over some of Uncle Danish's bigger cookery books to act as reflectors.

"Here." Sef pulls a pair of black eye masks out of his pocket.

"Let's do a screen-test." I wave him forward, more comfortable behind the camera than in front.

The same cannot be said for Sef, who bounds into the spotlight. His brown skin and bright T-shirt stand out against the white backdrop.

Hitting record, I tell Sef to say something.

"Like what?"

"Something long enough to get a sense of what the microphone picks up when we're on camera."

Sef clears his throat, staring out of the window a moment before he turns to look at the lens.

"Thou, Nature, art my goddess; to thy law my services are bound…"

At first I watch him through the camera, but then I sit back to watch for real, Sef slipping out of his own skin to wear the words he speaks, his expression shifting to accentuate the feeling behind them, voice rolling and rich.

It's a little bit magic.

"What?" Whoever Sef was pretending to be is shrugged off in a matter of seconds.

"What was that?"

"Shakespeare, bruv." He laughs. "Edmund the bastard's soliloquy from *King Lear*. We all have to study one for Drama."

"Is that what you want to do? Act?"

"Maybe." He shrugs. "I'd like to try. World needs all the brown faces on telly it can get."

"Yeah. You're right. Of course." I'm not used to people talking so frankly about stuff like this. Even Seren seems more comfortable talking about gender than she does race and the unwelcome thought that this might be because her best friends are white scurries across my conscience.

"But I'm not sure I will," Sef carries on. "There's no money in acting, no stability."

"You sound like my parents – about making films, not starring in them." I think of how hard I had to fight to convince them to let me take Media Studies as one of my options – how dismissive they've been of my vague dream of making films or TV shows, or safety videos about what to do in the event of a fire.

"You're about to star in one now." Sef hops off his stool.

"So long as you know I can't act as well as you..."

"Anyone who thinks they're bad at acting doesn't realize they're doing it every single day." He holds his fist up for me to bump, and yet again, I wonder whether or not he's being serious.

"All you can see is my mask!" I say as we watch the clip of me telling the camera my name and mumbling out a bit about what I had for breakfast. "How come you look so much better?"

Sef holds his arm next to mine, every cell of his skin the same rich ochre as the freckles that pepper my wrist. "Slightly different complexions, Snow White."

He tilts his head back as if studying me and I try not to get too twitchy under his scrutiny.

"Don't suppose you brought any make-up with you?"

Ten minutes later and we're giggling uncontrollably as we duel with a blusher brush and a kabuki brush, each of us trying to swipe powder on the other's nose. It's getting a little dangerous and a lot silly.

"That's cheating!" I protest when Sef snatches my brush with his free hand.

"You've met me, right?" He flashes me a careless grin. "Rules aren't really my thing."

Picking up some black kohl, Sef bites his lip and raises his eyebrows as he waggles the pencil at me.

"What are your feelings on boys wearing eyeliner?"

"Hot," I say, not specifically meaning boys wearing eyeliner so much as Sef looking at me like that. I can feel myself blotching at this slip-up when his phone vibrates, making us both jump as the name "Laila" flashes up.

For a moment, we both stare at the phone buzzing between us, until Sef looks up at me and says, "Gotta get this."

He picks up, edging away towards the bedroom, but not before I catch him saying, "Hey, babe…"

Well *obviously*. Why wouldn't he?

I have the length of that phone call in which to get over the fact that the boy I've been trying my hardest to flirt with all morning and – yes, all week – has a *girlfriend*. No matter how hard I try and rationalize this, no one calls their cousin or co-worker or boring old friend "babe" do they? It's a word you use for people you think are actual babes.

People who aren't me.

The sickness rising within me isn't so different from the wave that washed ashore when I found out about the #MilkTits video going live – the shame that comes from feeling exposed.

I glance to where Sef is still talking in the other room. If I change how I am around him when he comes out, he'll know that I fancy him – that I was only acting like that because I thought I might be in with a chance…

The tide rises higher.

Of course not.

Sef's easy manner is just that.

"You all right there?" Sef re-enters the room, sliding his phone screen-down on the breakfast bar.

For a moment, when he meets my eyes, there's a hint that he's asking me for real, like maybe he knows I've had a mini emotional crisis in the last sixty or so seconds.

"Sure. Just thinking about what to film first…"

I pick my eye mask up and put it on. Claire Casey might fancy the pants off Sef Malik, but I came here today as Truth Girl.

"You good to go?" I ask him.

CHAPTER 9

The only light in my room is coming from my laptop where there's a thumbnail image of me and Sef. We look cute. Or at least, I do, my face contoured into shape, iridescent-purple eyeliner popping beneath my black mask, my hair coiled up into two buns atop my head, like a pair of pale orange panda ears.

Sef looks *hot* – sharp – the way he's lined his eyes, hair combed flat and slicked into a side parting like an edgier Clark Kent.

I hit play for what might be the thousandth millionth – and hopefully last – time.

"Hi!" My voice sounds so much higher than in my own head.

"Hi!" Whereas Sef appears to have dropped his an octave.

"I'm Truth Girl and he's…"

"Dare Boy."

I spliced in a static shot of the pair of us doing stupid poses overlaid with the words *INTERNET SUPERHEROES!*

"And we challenge you to copy us –" Sef punctuates all of this with his hands – *"doing dares and telling truths and…"*

"… generally being complete idiots," I finish. Then, so stilted it's hard to believe I was actually trying to act natural,

I say, *"So far, so like any other challenge channel – am I right, Dare Boy?"*

God. I actually put a finger to my mouth as if I've googled "questioning pose" and copied the first image I found.

"No! You are wrong – this isn't about the challenges, this is about the cause." Sef's much more comfortable than I am in front of a camera. And probably wasn't excruciatingly self-conscious about how much he fancied the person next to him. *"We're asking you to help us raise money for a friend of ours who has suffered a massive brain injury and needs our help."*

"Every time someone copies one of our videos, we ask that you donate two pounds to the Doing Dares, Saving Lives fund –" as I talk, Sef is pointing to where the link will be at the bottom of the screen – *"link back to our channel and use the hashtag to spread the word."*

#DoingDaresSavingLives appears as an overlay.

Onscreen I hold out homemade Truth or Dare? cards to the camera like a tarot reader.

"One of us picks a card… If it's a dare, no matter how silly, how embarrassing—"

"How downright dangerous!" Sef interrupts and I had to cut out the nervous little glance I gave him for that.

"… the person challenged must accept."

"If it's a truth card, we both confess."

We finish with us throwing the cards up into the air, doubling over in hysterics.

As trailer videos go, it could be worse.

It also took over an hour to film and three to edit.

Tomorrow night we're scheduled to post two videos: one DARE, one TRUTH – and then the same on Wednesday. If all four take as long as this to edit, my hands will have curled into claws before the week is out.

I open up my phone to let Sef know it's loading privately onto the channel so he can check it over before posting. After a pause, I scroll through and re-read the conversation I had with him earlier.

Hey Sef, was just wondering – how secret are our identities?

???

Are we telling people what we're up to? Does your girlfriend know? Your family? Am I OK talking about this with my friends?

It's not exactly subtle and if I blurted this out in person I'd be mortified, but messaging has always been easier than talking face to face.

Sef answered my question in a series of short replies.

Hm. Wasn't planning on telling anyone, is that OK?

Can't face the idea of people knowing and it not working.

False hope and that.

Something I can identify with.

When I tap on my Instagram app, it opens straight onto Laila Jalil's account. There's only one Laila in our school so it wasn't exactly hard to find her.

Half her feed is made up of heavily filtered photos layered with fragmented poetry, the rest recording the minutiae of her life – home-cooked food and close-up selfies of artfully flicked eyeliner and fancy plaited hairdos. Pictures taken on nights out with her friends. And her boyfriend.

He's only there once, months before we teamed up, before his brother fell from the bridge, his arms around Laila, their faces pressed together, lips twisted as if trying to kiss as the pair of them look right into the lens.

Celebrating the end of the exams with my favourite boy.

I read the comments below, also for what might be the thousandth millionth – and hopefully last – time.

FINALLY.

You guys are officially the cutest.

More like that until there's one from someone called @HisMalisty:

I'm your favourite boy, am I?

To which Laila has replied:

Don't fish for compliments, @HisMalisty. It's undignified.

But she's added a row of hearts in brackets.

I resist the urge to click through to @HisMalisty's account. I feel stupid enough having looked at Laila's.

CHAPTER 10

Hallie has infected me with the plague. Can you make sure people collect notes for me? Maybe drop them round after school???

Ever since her sister started preschool, Seren's been getting ill, but she stresses about missing lessons and this is the first time this term she's actually been off. It's possible she's not exaggerating about the plague.

But I've my own problems to deal with – the video for *TRUTH: When was the last time you picked your nose?* was supposed to go up last night, but I spent so long on the dare video that it's still not ready.

"Rich…" I sidle up to him during registration and hold out my phone for him to read Seren's message.

"No worries. I'll get a lift with Charlie after practice – he lives over Seren's way."

I'd forgotten he had football. "You don't have to—"

"Shush now." He pats my head. "Anything for my favourite girls."

The mug of tea I made when I got home has gone cold by the time I finish editing the video and I leave the file transferring to Sef for approval, padding downstairs to make myself another drink, wondering how many videos it takes to get good at editing…

Deciding I deserve a treat, I pop a hot chocolate capsule into Dad's posh coffee machine and pick my phone up from where I'd left it by the kettle.

There are *thirteen* notifications – all from Seren.

OH MY GOD CLAIRE!

Rich came round with my homework.

It was horrid. SO. VERY. AWFUL.

He was all twitchy and he smelled like a scratch-and-sniff David Beckham advert and then he asked me if I liked him.

Of course I like him, he's my best friend, but then he said he didn't mean it like that.

(*One* of my best friends. You're the other one.)

Why aren't you replying???

Where are you???

He said he has "feelings" for me and that he needed to get things out in the open.

HE TOLD ME HE LOVES ME!

"What?" I hiss in horror at my phone.

So I told him that I loved him too, but he didn't let me finish and then he tried to kiss me. (WHY? WHY WOULD HE DO THAT? I'VE GOT SNOT LEAKING FROM MY EYEBALLS! DID HE WANT ME TO ASPHYXIATE?)

And then we had a fight and… I can't do it like this.

Can I come over?

The last one is only a couple of minutes old and I tap back a message apologizing for going AWOL and saying *of course* she can come over. As I'm sending it, a message arrives from Rich.

So, I cleared the air with Seren – atomic-bomb style. I don't think we're friends any more.

Half an hour later and Seren is on my doorstep. There are dark bags beneath her eyes, two feverish flares of pink on her cheeks and she reeks of Olbas oil and sweat. It's intoxicating – not in a good way – and I wonder if Rich was high on the fumes when he thought it was a good idea to *kiss* her.

Up in my bedroom, windows open, I hand Seren a box of tissues and in between sips of the hot orange I made her, she tells me what happened. A longer version of what she said in her messages, essentially, but with more nose-blowing and shouting.

"Are you OK?" I say when she's done.

"No."

I wait, but Seren can be very literal sometimes and won't say anything more than you ask.

"How do you feel?" I try.

"Nauseated."

"I meant about Rich."

"Like I said: nauseated." She gives me a weak little smile as she breathes out and collapses into her own lap. I reach over and stroke her back. "Why, Claire … *why* would he tell me all this? He *knows* – you both do. It's not like that for me. I'm ace and I'm aro and … I don't … ugh!" She pings back upright to blow her nose.

Until Seren told us she was asexual, I didn't know you could come out as anything other than gay or bi and I'm not always up on the terms she uses. I spend a lot less time on Tumblr than Seren does.

"What does aro mean again?"

"Aromantic. No interest in romance. As in, zero interest in having a relationship beyond the platonic variety and certainly not wanting to be accosted on my own doorstep."

"OK, but, wouldn't you rather Rich was honest with you?" I try, wanting to defend him.

"No," she says, her voice quiet. "Honesty isn't everything. His crush or love or whatever it is he thinks he feels, that's *his* problem – all he's done is offload it onto me."

I could weep for her, because that is exactly what I should have said to him. Only I didn't.

"I'm sorry," I say.

"You don't have to be. It's not your fault, is it?" She smiles, but it falters when she sees the way I'm looking at her.

"I'm *really* sorry, Seren—"

She's shifted round out of reach. "You *knew* about this?"

"I—"

"How long? Have you been talking about it behind my back? Did you tell him he should do this?"

"No!" I'm hurt by this. "I told him it wouldn't change anyth—"

"But it has!" she snaps, not listening. "It's changed *everything*."

"It doesn't have to, though, does it?" I say, trying to talk her down. "You could just take it as a compliment and—"

Seren rises up out of her chair, a little wobbly, before

she starts walking towards the door. "I'm not doing this. Not with you."

"What do you mean, *not with me*? I'm your other best friend."

She whips round and I'm shocked to see that she's crying. "Exactly! Almost anyone else and maybe, yes, I could take it as a compliment, but you and Rich – you're supposed to get it, you're supposed to get *me*!"

"Why are you shouting at me?" I'm wheedling and I hate it.

"Because I thought you were on my side, but you're acting just like everyone else, like asexuality isn't real, that it's something I'll grow out of when I meet the right man or woman or whatever."

"When have I said that?" I yelp. "And what's all this about sides? What battle do you think you're fighting?"

"I think I'm fighting *this one*!" She's so upset that she's shouting now. "I don't want to do sex stuff with Rich any more than you want to do it with a giant squid."

"No one's saying you have to do any sex stuff!" My voice rises to a squeak.

"But they *are* – don't you get it? Society thinks women are only good for sex and babies and I don't want either."

Why does Seren always have to do this? Turn something as small as an unrequited crush into some giant conspiracy.

"This isn't about *society*," I say. "It's about Rich—"

"And Rich isn't like that," she finishes for me, but with a lot more sarcasm. "You know he's had sex with the last two girls he kissed at a party, don't you?" I didn't, and I wonder where she got that information from. "You really think if I agreed to go out with him, he wouldn't want the same from me? And when he did, what would you say to him? Give it a go, she might say yes?"

The parallel she's drawing strikes me silent with horror.

"That's how people like me get 'cured' in some places." Seren puts the tissues she was going to take with her down on the bed. "I'll go now."

"Seren, please—" I find my voice.

"I said I'm going." She doesn't look back when she says, "Please don't call me."

CHAPTER 11

Despite being nothing short of a walking, oozing corpse, Seren is back at school on Tuesday, too proud to give in to the temptation of hiding from her problems the way I would have done.

She doesn't sit with me in registration – not on Tuesday, Wednesday, Thursday or Friday – and it's strictly business in lessons. If I get any of our native language out of her during French, it's as clipped and civil as if she's reciting it from the textbook, and in English, where we're allowed to move tables, Seren's taken to sitting with Oliver Martinez – the human Switzerland. She and Rich pass each other with the calculated disinterest of two rival cats and I'm fielding questions from half our class as to why they've fallen out.

As I sum up to Gemma Brogan while we're waiting together for Media Studies, "Rich did something stupid and Seren won't forgive him."

I don't add that I'm not forgiven either.

Rich has been predictably infuriating about the whole thing.

"Have you even tried to sort this out?" I ask him during Art.

"Like she'd listen."

It's hard resisting the urge to tip dirty paint water over

his head. "So what if she doesn't? You should still try."

"You weren't there, Claire." Rich glares at his attempt at a self-portrait. "Seren made it very clear she won't be listening to anything I have to say ever again."

On Friday, I cave. If Rich isn't going to try, I am.

Hey. So I know you're mad with me and I'm so so so sorry. Please can we talk about it? I hate leaving it like this.

When she replies almost immediately, my heart soars so high it practically flies out of my mouth…

I'm sorry you hate this, but I'm not in a talking place right now.

Her message fires an arrow from my phone to my heart, catching it mid-flight so that it flops feebly onto the floor.

I'm sorry. Please don't hate me.

Her reply isn't so much a long-distance arrow to the heart as a volley of them fired at close-range.

I don't hate you, Claire. I just don't want to talk to you. Please stop trying to make me.

Seren's message casts a cloud over my weekend and filming with Sef on Saturday feels a bit flat. He ploughs so much energy into trying to cheer me up, that by the time we're riding back into town on the bus, I feel exhausted. Also disappointed – it would have made me feel better if he'd simply asked me what was wrong and given me a chance to talk about it.

"Wish me luck," he says, after we get off.

"What for?"

Sef mimes driving. "Got my test on Wednesday."

When I wish him luck, I mean it. It'll be much easier once he can pick me up from my house.

The brightest spot of the weekend emerges on Sunday when I visit Kam and learn that he's been working with his speech and language therapist on basic communication skills. Although it *feels* like we might be getting on OK – Kam's loud when I arrive and quiet once I'm reading – it can be hard to read his expression. The way Kam's muscles hold his mouth open could be mistaken for a smile whether that's what he intends or not and it's not always easy to catch his eye when you're looking down at the words in a book.

Our attempts at Kam choosing what I read to him don't quite work out, but he seems to enjoy having a chance to try. When I talk to the charge nurse after our session, she writes down his therapist's email and encourages me to ask for advice ahead of our next session.

"Kam's been working hard on this." The nurse on duty is younger than Nurse Goethe. "It won't be long, I'm sure."

The accident robbed Kam of his voice, but that doesn't mean he hasn't anything to say and I look forward to finding out what that is.

Over the next week, the channel progresses, even if things with Seren don't. Dare Boy and Truth Girl's banter is breezy and flirtatious and our challenges cute enough to get a few thumbs-up from the people who watch us – an audience that is almost certainly down to Sef's social-media offensive, posting across our accounts as one or other of us, signing off on comments as "DB" or "TG" – although if you read enough of them, you can guess who is behind them without the sign-off. Truth Girl is encouraging and unfailingly optimistic – she is also, like me, an emoji enthusiast, whereas Dare Boy is flirty, funny and has a sketchy approach to capitalization and exclamation marks.

Two different characters, both played by the same person.

Someone I get the impression is keeping me at arm's length. The way he is on camera, the playful messages, it's exactly the same as it was when I met him in the car park. The easy and open manner that tricked me into thinking we were closer than we are. Whenever I push for anything more substantial, Sef pushes right back. He never talks about his friends, or Laila. He never says much about his family.

The weekend after Sef passed his test, driving home I told him I was looking forward to seeing Kam, but when I asked him how he felt about Kam's progress communicating, he shut down in much the same way he did in the car park.

"You'll see for yourself tomorrow. Kam's life, what he can do and that, isn't always the same day to day. You know that."

And that was it.

I guess Sef prefers to focus on things he can control, like making money – if only that was what we were actually doing.

If I'd written down our strategy and handed it in to Miss Stevens, it would have come back with top marks. But the real world isn't a Media Studies assignment, and for all our efforts, the channel isn't working.

My phone buzzes long after I should have been asleep, but Sef's messaging doesn't seem to follow any particular schedule.

Videos are going up. Nice work this week.

Thanks. But I replied while he was still typing.

We need to mix it up. Film stuff outside the caravan.

Despite the fact that I was just thinking the same thing, his suggestion ties a knot in my digestive tract.

What if someone unmasks us?

Lex Luther's more bothered about Superman, tbh.

I'm serious, Sef. We can't film round here.

Fancy spending Friday filming in London?

It's the day before half-term and we've got an inset day. Sneaking off to London would mean lying to my parents – and Rich. It would also mean spending nearly an hour on a train with Sef. No filming to focus our conversation, no mobile signal to hide behind. I wonder if the thought of actually talking to each other worries him as much as it does me.

Friday it is. I type. And for better or worse, I press send.

CHAPTER 12

When we round the corner to face the gauntlet of street performers leading towards Covent Garden Market, I grind to a halt.

I don't think I can do this.

Everything else we've done – from eating earwax to the blindfold spice test – has been fun, but this? This is scary.

"Can we grab a coffee or something?" I say, meaning *Can I lock myself in the toilets and never come out?*

"It'll only get busier, more people to watch you…" Sef thinks he's teasing me, but his words prickle like sweat beneath the surface of my skin.

For all Truth Girl's T-shirt, make-up and hairstyle transforms me on the outside, on the inside, I'm still Claire Casey, the girl whose boobs popped out of her bikini.

My hands have turned clammy, vision weird and swoopy and I'm no longer in a busy city street, but back in the park. The murmur of surrounding shoppers has turned to laughter, cries of "Oh my God!" and "Nip slip!" and I'm transported back to that split second between knowing that everyone was looking at me and understanding *why*…

"I can't do this!" I say, my arms instinctively wrapped round my chest. "I'm not – I can't…"

Turning away, I hurry down the nearest, narrowest

alleyway in an effort to escape the crowds, the dares, the humiliation and when I feel a hand on my back, I flinch away in surprise.

"Claire! Stop!" And then, "Please."

I stop, keeping my eyes down, not wanting to look at him.

"What's going on?"

I'm not sure whether to be pleased he's forgotten what I said about the #MilkTits video or sad that he's forgotten *me*.

I fix my gaze on a cigarette stub trodden into the cobbles. "I can't do this. Not in front of an audience."

"But all the stuff we've filmed—" he starts.

"… has been in the safety of the caravan."

"And recorded for the whole world to watch." Sef holds up the camera, drawing my attention away from the ground.

"We have thirty-one subs, Sef."

Sef reaches out and turns me to face him, fixing me with a frown. Sharp kohl lines trace the shape of his eyes, lashes fanning out to frame his gaze. "We don't have enough subscribers. We don't have enough donations." His voice is low and firm. "But you made me think we could do this and we can. *You* can."

"I can't."

Sef lets out a huff of frustration. "We came to London because we need to be seen to be taking more risks. So why are you here if you aren't even prepared to try?"

I think of that moment in the cinema, when I saw Sef before he saw me, when I was ready to risk him laughing at me and I remember what kept me going.

I'm doing this because I want to help Kam.

No one sees us coming as I walk towards a silver man sitting on an invisible chair. There's a semi-circle of disbelieving tourists studying him, a couple of kids daring each other to stand close enough for a photo. The statue man's gaze is fixed on some point in the middle distance, the crowd too distracted to pay any attention to a masked teenage girl or the boy filming her.

Breaking rank, I drop some coins in the box and lean in, half expecting the man to clout me with one of his silver hands. But he stays as still as … well, a statue – and I stick my tongue out, wide and flat and lick him all the way from chin to forehead.

There's a revolted groan from the audience and a flat tang of chemicals on my tongue and I'm off, not waiting to test the man's commitment to his art as I dash away down the street, dodging in and out of the crowds, legs pounding like pistons, adrenalin fizzing through me in a rush of relief.

I did it.

"At least human statues don't unload all over you." Sef's grumpy because it's taken him half an hour to catch a pigeon in Trafalgar Square, his arms flapping as frantically as wings until a pigeon flew blindly at his face and he caught it mid-air – the exact moment it emptied its bowels.

"We should order spare T-shirts."

"Or we could just wash the ones we've got." Sef dabs

ineffectually at the pigeon poo with a napkin as we queue to order some food.

"Like you wash your own clothes," I say, with a grin. "Bet your mum does it."

Sef pauses for a moment, not quite looking at me. "Not any more she doesn't – Mum's got more important things to worry about than laundry."

It's unusual for Sef to even mention something like this and I feel a fool for making the joke. It's too easy to forget how different Sef's life is from mine.

There's a nudge on my shoulder. "Had to google how to use the washing machine first time I tried, though."

After lunch we pay a visit to the National Portrait Gallery. Twenty minutes later we're escorted off the premises. Doing the dares is addictive and I'm giddy on broken rules, my mood bubbling over, making me as silly as Sef, falling into him as I giggle along the pavement until we find somewhere I can pretend to busk.

Half an hour of singing the theme tune to *The Fresh Prince of Bel-Air* on repeat sobers me up – having to perform in one place, where it's obvious people can see me, is hard and I'm relieved once it's over. Funny as it sounded on the card, I'm not sure anyone's going to want to watch the full thing and already my mind is whirring away, trying to think about how I can edit it into something more appealing, more funny, more shareable.

"We've got time for one more," I say, looking at my watch and glancing up at Sef. "Why don't you do a car walk?"

Sef picks the road and fear pinches at my throat – these

cars are *expensive,* but Sef is insistent. I set up with my back to the sun so Sef will come running along the roofs of the cars towards the light. Lifting my arm, I see him wave back in reply at the far end of the street before I bring mine down in a swoop to start filming.

Halfway along the row, there's a shout from one of the flats and Sef spins round on the roof of a shiny black Mercedes to look at the man hanging out of a second-storey window.

"What the hell are you doing?!" the man bellows and I zoom in on Sef's face as he turns back to camera, genuinely scared.

"Run!" I yell at him, but instead of jumping off the car and onto the pavement, Sef bounds across the last few cars in the row. A door slams further down the street, voices shouting at us as Sef leaps from the roof of the last car.

"Go, go, go!"

In a scrabble of arms and legs, the pair of us pelt off round the corner, almost colliding with a mum and buggy. Our momentum carries us through a break in the traffic on the main road, my heart in my mouth as I dash out in front of a slow-moving taxi. My lungs burn, limbs turning to jelly when Sef slows abruptly and pulls me into a crowded pub. No one notices as we both pile into the first toilet, pressing ourselves into the tiny little cubicle.

Neither of us speaks, hearts and breath slowing as we stand, tensed, listening for someone thundering in after us.

"I think we lost them," I whisper after a few minutes.

"Best to be safe." Sef pulls off his T-shirt so that I'm

confronted by his bare chest before he turns round, balling his top up with his eye mask and stuffing it in his rucksack. I try not to stare at the curve of muscle on his shoulders, the soft sweep of his spine, but it's hard when the only other place to look is the toilet bowl.

I'm relieved when he tugs down his hoodie and I can stop pretending that I'm cool with being this close to a half-naked boy.

"Reckon I'll just zip my coat up," I say.

"Shame." And he winks at me, the git.

CHAPTER 13

Saturday morning, I drive down to Devon with Mum to stay with Grandad and "Call me Nan if you want" Sylvia. Mum takes work with her, which means I get away with the same – no one needs to know I'm going through the London footage rather than actual schoolwork. In truth, I'm falling behind in that department without Seren around to guilt me into working harder.

It's been annoying, though, missing a session with Kam.

My contact with Sef, Rich – even Seren's silence – can coast along on my phone, but my friendship with Kam relies on time spent together. He's only recently started to recognize me and I'm worried about the effect of having a two-week gap.

We get back late the next Saturday and when I ask Dad if he'll drive me to the Rec in the morning, he seems surprised.

"Thought you'd want a lie-in?" His attention slides to the clock on the cooker while I appreciate the luxury of a coffee-machine hot chocolate before bed.

"I want to see Kam more," I say.

Kam's room at the Rec is *not* sympathetic to my lack of sleep. It's warmer here than at home and I'm stifling unwelcome yawns every other sentence until one finally breaks free.

Kam huffs out a phlegmy breath of a laugh and I catch his eye. He looks thinner and more tired than when I last saw him, but he's still much more expressive than when I first met him.

"OK, you got me, this book is boring," I say. "You can choose a different one."

I've taken to bringing a bag of books from home with me every time I come. We never finish any of the ones we start, but so long as that doesn't matter to Kam, it doesn't matter to me.

"Would you like this one…" I frown at the cover of what looks like it might be a detective thing and hold it up in my left hand. "… or this?"

The one in my right has a more exciting cover with a silhouette of someone looking up at a colourful sky packed with stars.

Kam holds his gaze steady on the second option for as long as he can.

"The spacey one." I hold it forwards. Then I swap the two around and wait for him to choose the same cover again, which he does. You have to do this in case the person you're asking looked in a certain direction by accident – like so many other things, Kam's eyesight has been affected by his injury.

But when I reach into the bag to put the rejected book back, I find another that makes me smile.

"Are you sure you wouldn't prefer this?" I bring it out and show him the cover of a super trashy, super ancient romance book.

Kam laughs.

"Is the shirtless pirate putting you off?"

He laughs some more, his head moving a little in what might be a nod.

"No shirtless pirates, got it…" I say with a grin and when he looks at me, there are crinkles around his eyes like there are in the photo with his friends.

Rich messages me after lunch while I'm posting the London videos on the channel. They're unlisted for now – Sef can choose what order they go live.

You back?

Yes.

Do you want to come out tonight?

I frown at my phone. Rich knows full well that I prefer to stay *in*. "Out" implies strangers. That I might have to talk to. You can't filter them in the real world the way you can online. In a bar or a house party or wherever it is Rich wants to go the conversations are private, you can't just sidle up, listen in and then repeat someone's joke back to them while crying with laughter or they'll think you are weird.

Not really.

Pleeeeeeeeeeeeeeeeeeeeeeeeeeeeeeeeeeeeeease.

Why? Where?

Gemma's friend's band is playing at some gig. She asked if I wanted to go.

Well? Do you?

Yes.

Then what do you need me for?

Company. I've missed you.

However annoying he is, I've missed Rich too.

The music that claws at my ears as we walk down the corridor gets swallowed up by soft bodies and the swell of half-shouted conversations in the main bar. I can't see Gemma, but I'm distracted by a boy wearing a ski hat with a unicorn horn emerging from it, shouting, "I'm a NARWHAL!" and attacking his friend, who has FUCK THE WORLD DEAD written on his T-shirt.

"Do you want a drink?" Rich asks. He's already managed to smudge the stamp on the back of his hand that marks him out as underage.

"No, thanks," I say and he gives me a look like he thinks I'm not trying. "Fine. You can buy me a Fanta, but I'm coming with you. I don't want to stand around on my own."

We queue in other people's personal space by the bar until Rich hands me a warm can of Fanta that I sip through a straw.

"What?" I say, noticing him frown.

"Are you wearing make-up?"

I'd applied a little of the knowledge I've gained from dressing up for the channel to tonight's look. Possibly a little too much.

"Yes. I am."

"Weird." On seeing my stare, Rich adds. "Good weird."

I think of sucking up a mouthful of Fanta and using the straw to spray it in his face.

We find Gemma with some of her friends from outside

of school and there's a brief round of introductions that mean nothing to any of us. Eventually, after half an hour pretending I'm part of the conversation, there's a squeal of guitars from the next room. The live music is so loud that conversation is (thankfully) impossible. In front of me Gemma keeps standing up on tiptoes and holding her mouth close to Rich's ear to shout something to him. Each time, she rests her hands lightly on his back, as if to balance herself. Between songs, Rich leans in to say something to her and when he's finished talking, he doesn't move back to where he was, but stands with Gemma, arms touching, his finger tracing patterns on the skin of her wrist once the next song starts up.

Bored, I open up my phone and message Sef.

Which video did you go with?

Check the channel yourself!

Can't. Am at a gig.

A GIG? Who even are you?

A dark horse … who does not want to be at this gig.

There's the Claire I know and love.

What you up to?

Work. Yawn. You could come and distract me?

If only. Maybe next time.

I glance over to where Rich is brushing Gemma's hair away from her ear.

I send another message. One tapped out a little more savagely than any I've sent to Sef.

Good to know that ruining your friendship with Seren hasn't put you off making the moves on Gemma.

I watch as Rich feels his phone go, before turning round to give me a wounded look. Rolling my eyes, I turn away to go and treat myself to another lukewarm Fanta, leaving him to it.

NOVEMBER

CHAPTER 14

Kissing on Sunday, kebab shop on Monday, awkward "So, would you, um, are we like … do you want to be my girlfriend?" conversation on Tuesday and Denver Richards and Gemma Brogan are a bona fide, blue-tick couple.

Ruin a friendship and reap a relationship – that's Rich for you. I'd like nothing more than to talk to Seren about it but she blanks me during Thursday's registration and when she gets up to walk to Maths, it's with Vijay and Isaac, not me. I watch as James Blaithe bounds up to join them, stung that Seren can forgive my worst enemy, but not her best friend.

In French, later, Madame Cotterill gets us all to research different medical maladies, then invites us up to the doctor's desk. James, who thinks that saying English words in a French accent is enough to get by, says he has "an 'orrible cold", which he demonstrates by sneezing all over the place and annoying the teacher.

Next to me, Seren flicks through the textbook, writing down phrases I barely recognize as French.

"What's wrong with you?" I ask.

She looks up sharply, then sees that I'm talking about the work.

"Malaria. I've just been on holiday to the Côte d'Ivoire and didn't take my tablets properly."

"I have a broken leg," I say, even though she didn't ask.

Seren looks a bit irritated with me and I know it's because she thinks I've gone for the easy option. All I've got written on my notepad is *"Mon jambe est cassé".*

"Je me suis cassée la jambe," she corrects. "And think of how you did it."

There's a tap on my shoulder and someone hands me a note. Gemma wants to know if I'm going to be watching the West Bridge game tonight.

Wasn't planning on it, I reply, passing the note back. When I twist to face the front, Seren's returned to her textbook and, without looking up, she says, "You two seem to be getting friendly now Gemma's going out with Rich."

I could point out that I've always been friendly with Gemma, but I'm willing to sacrifice the truth in favour of conversation.

"Pretty weird, huh?"

Seren's pen pauses halfway through the word *"oublié".* "You mean, pretty weird that one month ago Rich's supposed love for me was so overwhelming that he *had* to tell me and now he's chuffing along with someone else?"

Before I can tell her that *yes*, that's exactly what I meant, she's called up to the front. All the time she's up there with her malaria, I try and work out what I can do to make this right, when I should be more concerned about my broken leg. Madame Cotterill isn't impressed that I respond to her question about how it happened by adopting the James Blaithe™ approach and replying, *"Je ne sais pas!"* accompanied by a Gallic shrug.

The bell goes as I return to my desk and I pack up deliberately slowly, trapping Seren while everyone else files out.

"I know what you mean about Rich," I say. "About it being weird that Gemma's just slotted into his life—"

"And yours."

There's hurt in the way she says it.

"Seren—"

Seren tips her chin back as if to indicate there's someone behind me. "Good to know I'm so easy to replace."

When I turn and see Gemma waiting for me, Seren squeezes past without another word.

"What's up with her?" Gemma asks, watching Seren's curtain of hair swishing with every step as she strides off down the corridor.

"Ask your boyfriend…" I mutter darkly. I'm willing to take responsibility for being an idiot about what happened between him and Seren, but if my best friend won't talk to me, she can't be angry with me for talking to someone else.

Have you seen this?

I click on the link Sef's sent. Onscreen two girls run around a park chasing pigeons on a speeded-up film. It's almost exactly what I did when editing *DARE: Catch the Pigeon!* – right down to the Benny Hill background music – only I'd pause the sound every so often so the viewer could hear Sef cursing the pigeons he was trying to catch. Their video has loads of views and comments, but no credit.

Did they donate?

Sef's in charge of monitoring the donations page, but the last time I looked, there was more money in the change pot on our kitchen table than in Kam's fund.

What do you think?

And then:

This isn't working, Claire.

I know, I say, not wanting to.

Today is the twelfth of November and Kam only has four more months before his level of care changes. I think of the progress he's made since I've known him – and how much more there is yet to be made. An additional six months of the kind of care that the Rec can provide could make a huge difference to how fast that progress is made.

Another message comes in from Sef:

You want to meet up?

Now? It's gone nine on a school night.

You free?

Hurrying downstairs, I poke my head in the sitting room to find Mum with a glass of wine and her laptop. Dad's in the study. "Can I pop round to Rich's? He only lives two roads over."

She glances at the bottom corner of her screen.

"Bit late, isn't it?"

"Girlfriend trouble," I lie. Rich and Gemma are probably at Rich's house right now getting into a very different kind of trouble from the one I'm implying.

"Home no later than eleven. Just this once."

* * *

Sef picks me up from our usual layby. I'm muffled up in one of Dad's scarves and the heat of the car knocks the breath out of me so that I struggle to unwind myself as fast as possible. When I finally escape, Sef's watching me, lips curled up in amusement.

"You quite finished there?"

"It's cold out," I say defensively.

"Where shall we go?" he asks.

"Somewhere that means I'll be back by eleven." I notice the look he's giving me. "Some of us aren't allowed out on a school night."

Sef just laughs at me and pulls out in the direction of town. We go, surprisingly, to the arts cinema. The foyer is empty but for the girl working there, quietly wiping down the tables by the window. She's the same one who was here before, with stylishly scruffy hair and a tattoo of a needle and thread stitching something along her collarbone.

"Last showing went in thirty-five minutes ago," she says with a sardonic slant to her eyebrows.

"Just here for a drink, Mia."

She gives us a shrewd look and finds something to do over on the other side of the foyer.

"I've been thinking," Sef says, and I guess by the intensity of his fidgeting that he's reluctant to actually tell me his thoughts.

"About the channel?"

"Yeah…" He starts plucking at the ring pull on his can of Coke. "So. Here's the thing. We do the dares and ask people to pay to copy us. But that's all the wrong way round.

People need to pay first, then see the dares."

"Why would they pay, though?" That's kind of the point of YouTube – it's free.

"We give them an incentive…" He's refusing to look at me.

"What kind of an incentive?"

"Offer up dares worth paying for."

"Sef…" So far the most exciting dare I've done is licking a slug – and a human statue. Apparently Fate wants me to lick things.

"The amount we've raised averages out at fifty-four pence per video. The money you're planning on spending on a GoPro is more than we're ever likely to make if we carry on like this."

This is the closest he's ever come to acknowledging the privilege deficit between us and I'm hurt by the resentment that laces his voice.

"I don't mind *you* doing dares…" I start, wanting to change the subject. I only mentioned the GoPro idea to Sef the other week because we'd been talking about how cool it would be to have a head-cam. My parents spend money on me because it's cheaper than time and I figured I could ask for a new camera as a birthday and Christmas present rolled into one.

"People want to see *both* of us doing them – we're a team." Sef takes his phone out, already open on one of our videos as if prepared to convince me. "*OMG – you guys are adorbs. Freshest vid I've seen this week. Truth Girl's such a little cutie. Anyone else totally shipping these two?*"

He glances up, barely registering how uncomfortable this is making me. *"Love your channel – have you thought about opening up to challenges in the comments?"*

The idea makes me nervous.

"So you're saying they have to pay to challenge us?" Because that won't work either.

"No, but we should do this anyway, take up challenges from our viewers. You always said audience involvement was the key to getting people to come back – and what better reason to come back than to check to see if we've done their dare?"

"How does that—"

"Two different things: accept challenges as part of our regular posts and make it just about growing the audience. No donations. To make money, we offer up something big – a series of proper dares set up so that we have to reach a target amount of donations before we perform." The words come out hurried and desperate, his hands talking as fast as his mouth.

"What do you mean by 'proper' dares?"

Sef shrugs and I can feel his knee bouncing next to mine. "Things people want to see other people do that they wouldn't do themselves."

Things *I* would never want to do…

"Please, Claire." Sef leans across the table and puts a hand on my arm, eyes wide and vulnerable, and there's a tremor in his voice when he says, "I can't do this without you."

CHAPTER 15

I agree to the plan. How can I not? But Sef's wrong if he thinks people will donate just for the sake of whatever qualifies as a "proper" dare. They need a reason to care – and that reason has to come from Sef. We need to separate the truth from the Dare Boy.

After a wasted hour of trying to sleep, I get my laptop out and hunt for a video I once saw of some guy on a train. (It takes a while.) The video is of him looking at the camera, not talking or anything, just staring a bit, sometimes reacting to the stuff happening around him, but the audio is him talking about what's going on inside his head.

It's powerful, hearing someone's voice disconnected from their face, pulling you in, so that hearing their thoughts feels as close, as *real*, as hearing your own.

I send Sef the link, knowing he'll still be awake. I don't think he ever sleeps.

I want to film a trailer like this for the channel.

???

Just you, looking at the camera, while we hear a VO of you talking about Kam. Our viewers need to know why this matters.

His reply is a long time coming.

OK

x

I've never so much as put an "x" at the end of a message, but there's no other reply that would feel right.

At the caravan the mood is subdued as we set things up for the trailer – a single stool for Sef to sit on while we play the audio file out loud and film his reaction.

"You ready?" I ask.

Sef adjusts his eye mask and gives a tight nod for me to press play on the audio file saved on his phone. It'll be the first time I hear it and I'm not sure *I'm* ready...

"You know me as Dare Boy." Sef points silently to himself. *"But that's not all I am. And this channel might look like two teenagers doing stupid stuff for the camera, but again, that's not all it's about.*

"Someone close to us –" there's a subtle shift in his focus to where I stand next to the camera and I feel the pressure of tears burning behind my eyes – *"had an accident. He survived. But he can't come on here and tell you a truth because he can't talk. He can't come on here and do a dare because he can't move.*

"We're doing these things because he can't and we invite you to donate because a life like his is expensive and not everyone has that kind of money." There's a pause on the audio and I see Sef's eyes are glazed with tears that he quickly wipes away. *"Isn't the point of having money to make life better, even if that life isn't yours?"*

When the audio stops playing, I leave it a second before I go in and give him a hug where he sits, so that for once I'm the tall one. Sef's chin rests on my shoulder as I hold him. It must have been hard for him to show that much of himself on camera, to talk about Kam in a way he rarely does, even to me. When Sef lets go, he sniffs and thanks me and asks for a biscuit break.

We sit huddled on the step outside, my mug of tea steaming in the winter air. The air in the caravan is heavy with unspoken fears, hope the only thing stopping us suffocating, but out here it's cold and bright. A couple of tiny kids are swinging sticks at the skeletons of brambles along the bottom of the field. I laugh when one of them yelps, followed by a "Martin! You're not meant to hit *me*…"

But when I glance over at Sef, he still looks sad.

"We used to do that," he says, pointing his biscuit in the direction of the kids. "Uncle Danish used to avoid taking jobs in the summer so he could look after us on the days Mum had to work. He'd bring us here to run wild in the park and the woods while he worked on the caravan. He had a dog whistle he used to call us back for lunch and we'd sit –" Sef turns to point behind us – "up there on tatty beach towels and eat a picnic my mum had made for us. It was the only time she'd make bhajis, because she knew they were my uncle's favourite." He nibbles his biscuit and looks back to where the kids are fighting each other instead of the brambles. "Amir would get angry that we were so much better at everything than he was, then Kam'd take pity on him and the two of them would team up against me."

He rolls up the leg of his jeans and points to a puckered pink scar on his calf.

"One time Amir got carried away and hit me with a post that had a nail in it – he didn't know, was too little to see anything other than a really good sword. We were in the woods and the nail went right into my muscle. I was bleeding all over the place and crying because I couldn't walk. Kam sent Amir running up to tell our uncle and then he piggy-backed me all the way through the woods and up the hill while Amir found Uncle Danish. Didn't put me down once."

It's the most he's ever said about his family and I press myself gently against him in gratitude for this day of firsts. For finally feeling like we're friends.

The stress of the channel and mounting pressure of all the schoolwork I've not been doing make me distant and distracted around Kam, who's clearly in an equally foul mood the way he keeps trying to talk, his intentions coming out as nothing more than a strained moan that frustrates him further. Each time I try to offer him choices as to what to do, he rejects them by turning away and refusing to look, and it would be cruel to force an answer out of him when it's clear he doesn't want to give one.

There's a nurse with us today, although I'm not sure why. He's a young man barely older than me, with no name badge and he keeps calling him Kamran.

"Look," I say to the nurse, hating that I'm talking over the noises Kam's making. "I don't have to read. I've got my laptop. We could watch something on there?"

"There's a private cinema for the residents—"

"I know," I say, glancing at Kam, who still refuses to look this way, but has stopped trying to talk. "But I downloaded *Moon*."

I detect something like interest in the way Kam goes still, but I have to point to the poster on the wall to get the man to understand.

"*Moon* is one of my favourite films too," I say, more for Kam's benefit than the nurse's.

"You could give it a go, I suppose." As the nurse glances out of the door like he's worried someone will tell him off, I catch Kam looking at me and try to give him a conspiratorial smile. He doesn't turn away, but he doesn't look happy either.

My time is up before we can finish the film, but I suggest to Kam that we can watch it again next week and he goes so far as to move his head in a nod. It's the only time he's really engaged with me all session and the whole thing leaves me feeling empty and depressed.

Kam might have a voice, but it's one limited to other people's questions – presenting him with options to choose from, or asking him questions he can answer with a nod or a shake – and I'm quiet on the journey home, contemplating the enormity of living a life like Kam's, having to rely on others because you haven't the tools needed to choose for yourself.

This tiny little taste of what it means to be powerless is too much for me and as soon as I get in, I'm at my laptop, opening up the channel, needing to do something, anything, to feel like I can make a difference. It gives me a lot more sympathy for Sef and the way he invariably turns every conversation I try to have about Kam into a conversation about the channel. The frustration I feel as Kam's friend is nothing compared to what I'd feel if he were family.

We've overhauled all the graphics on our social-media accounts to tie in with our new and improved donation page, where there's now a giant thermometer thingy indicating the amount we need to raise for each of the big dares.

£200: Truth Girl will shave her head.

£500: Dare Boy will streak across a football pitch during a Boxing Day match

£1,000: YOU CHOOSE!!!

I do not permit myself to think of how little £1,700 is compared to what we need, choosing instead to scroll down through the series of stills of Sef piercing his own ear. Although he'd insisted it was because we needed something on the donations page to show we were as good as our word, I can't help thinking that in Sef logic, he was also hoping it'd make me feel better about committing to shave my head. It didn't.

I scroll back up to the top of the page and read the banner:

TELLING TRUTHS, DOING DARES, SAVING LIVES

However much we raise, nothing we do will "save" Kam. This is his life now. There's no cure and the value in him as a person isn't the promise of what he might return to, but what he already is. If Kam is a princess locked in a tower, we're the delivery drivers bringing him whatever it is he needs to live the happiest possible life *in* the tower, not the valiant knights come to break him out.

In real life you can't always write the happy ending you were hoping for and sometimes I worry that Sef has yet to realize the difference between supporting someone and saving them.

DECEMBER

CHAPTER 16

The emotional sucker punch of our new trailer is working. The video has earned tons of new comments, loads of people saying they're sorry to hear about our friend, how they appreciate the fact that we're really in this for someone other than ourselves, that we're keeping it real…

Although once you attract more views, you attract more arseholes.

I smell bullshit.

SOB STORY ALERT.

Is ur "friend" such a state u2 ashamed to show him on film?

Each one makes me wish I could climb into the screen and punch their avatars in the face, but if we want people to set us challenges in the comments, we can't be moderating them.

Staying on-brand, Sef writes the comments up on cards and on Saturday, I pick out one that asks us to confess to crimes we'd rather no one knew about (Sef seemed like he had quite a lot to choose from), before it's Sef's turn to choose.

His grin grows as he scans whatever's written on the card and the tip of his tongue presses mischievously against his teeth when he looks over at me.

"Paperrose348ugh asks, 'Are you guys a couple?'" He delivers it with a slight Californian twang that makes me laugh. "Well, Truth Girl, are we?"

"Is this your way of asking me out?" I play along. "Because it needs work."

In a flash, he's dived down onto one knee, hands clasped as he gazes up at me. "Tell me the truth, fair maiden. Art thou my girlfriend? My snookle noodle? My spunk monkey?"

"Disgusting."

"My sweetest of hearts, my ace of spades, my caddy of clubs, my diamond in the rough—"

"Who are you calling rough?"

"… the apple of my eye, the clementine of my heart, the grape of my wrath—"

And I can't think of any other way of shutting him up than by turning to camera and saying in as loud a voice as possible, "No. We are not a couple."

Sef's up and back on his stool. "She loves me really."

"Like a ship loves a barnacle." I glare at him, desperately trying not to smile as he blows me a kiss.

A rare perfect take.

"What next?" I ask, stopping the camera and heading over to the kitchen, hoping to find a clean mug I can use for a cuppa.

"Well, there's the one with the toothpaste…?" I have my back to him, but his grin's so wide I can *hear* it.

One of our viewers has dared me to lick a toothpaste heart off Dare Boy's chest. I am *not* keen, but I can see the wind is still lashing at the grass and a stray bin bag wafts past the window. Silly-Stringing a car dealer's is a no go for today.

I guess I don't have much choice.

Monday and I'm in the library catching up on the reading I should have done over the weekend. Having intimate knowledge of the cinematography of Joe Wright's *Pride and Prejudice* isn't the same as having read the book and Mr Kontos has been writing pointed comments to "pay attention to the text" on my essays.

Glancing up at the doors, I see Sef walk in and – as always – I get a thrill at seeing him on school premises, as if we're agents in the field pretending not to know each other. An illusion Sef ruins by heading right for where I'm sitting in the comfy chairs by the window. I look around, wondering if there's anyone here to see, but Mr Douglas is in his back room with a cluster of Year 10 library assistants and the only other person around is a tiny little Year 7 hunched over one of the consoles on the far wall.

Sef sits down, sprawling across the two seats opposite me and follows my gaze to the ancient DVD case he's holding.

"Monologues." He holds it up for me to see.

"Any good?"

"Amazing. Having one actor commanding your attention with a single story. Wouldn't cut it on YouTube, though."

Something in the way he's smiling makes me suspicious. "What?"

Looking far too pleased with himself, Sef takes his phone out and comes to sit next to me, his thigh nudging against mine.

"Last night's video was popular," he says, scrolling through the comments for *TRUTH: Coupled up?*

They start off quite innocent:

Too cute!!!

Not a couple. *subtle wink*

S...U....R.....E......

Dareboy is hawt

"I'm so hot right now." I elbow Sef in the side when he says this.

I would

So would truthgirl whatever she says

"I would NOT!" I hiss at the screen, glancing round to check no one heard. "They can't ask for the truth and then call me a liar."

"Methinks the lady doth protest too much..." Sef is insufferably smug.

101

"The lady doth think you're a tosser."

"I've told you before, Claire, all this flirting is unprofessional." His voice has a low pitch to it that sends a forgotten thrill through me. One I try to ignore.

Are they filming in a lab?

...

...?

BECAUSE CHEMISTRY.

Awful

Looooool

How funny would it be to dare them to kiss???

DO IT!

Dare you to kiss Dare Boy/Truth Girl

(on the lips)

Kiss!

Kiss!!!

chants kiss kiss kiss kiss kiss

"I don't care how many people dare us to kiss," I say, pushing his phone away. "I'm not doing it. Not for all the money in the world."

He raises his eyebrows and grins. "Maybe just for free then?"

"Sef." I twist round to look at him, wanting to make sure he gets the message. "You have a girlfriend. Licking toothpaste off –" I can feel the heat rising as I remember tracing a heart on his bare chest and I vaguely wave in his direction rather than say the word – "was bad enough but it wasn't, you know, something people actually do in a relationship."

Or that's how I justified it to myself. Besides, it was the opposite of sexy.

"Kink shamer."

I'm annoyed with him for being so flippant. "Whatever. I don't kiss other people's boyfriends. Not even for a dare."

For the first time since he sat down, Sef breaks eye contact to run his hand up the back of his neck, looking out of the window, then over at the poster advertising an author visit for the Year 8s – anywhere but at me.

"Yeah. Well. I'm pretty sure Laila wouldn't give a shit."

"I'm pretty sure she would." More to the point, *I* would.

Finally his attention settles on me. "And you'd know what my ex wants better than me, would you?"

His *ex*?

"What? When?" And for good measure, another, "What?"

"Broke up with her. Ages ago."

"Define ages." I feel like I've swallowed down a mouthful of food without chewing.

Sef gets extremely fidgety, flapping the DVD case back and forth like an ineffectual fan. "The other week."

"Define. Other." I sound very unimpressed. I *am* very unimpressed.

"I didn't exactly write down the date. 'Dear Diary, today my relationship ended. Sad face.'" He doesn't sound very sad and I feel illogically angry on Laila's behalf.

"And you didn't think to tell me?"

"Any reason I should?" he says, looking across at me, his face pulled into tight, frustrated lines.

Reaching for my bag, I shove my book inside and stand up ready to go. If Sef needs an answer to that question, then we're not the friends I thought we were.

"Just to be very clear," I say, every word accentuated by how annoyed I am, "my position on kissing you remains the same."

CHAPTER 17

Tonight I should be working on the videos for Wednesday, but I'm not in the mood for anything to do with Sef.

Needing a distraction, I log online as myself, trying to remember how long it's been since I waded around the internet wearing my own identity. Truth Girl and Dare Boy have subbed to an incomprehensible number of channels, all middlingly successful – subs in the thousands rather than the millions – but back in the day, Claire Casey liked the big hitters. None of the videos that show up on my home page are familiar, it's mostly Americans adored by millions, but there are also a few choice Brits.

I scroll through them looking for the right flavour vlogger for my angry, bitter palate. No one too sweet – I need someone to cheer me up without actually being cheerful. In the end I click on MozzyMozzaMeepMorp. If Moz could lift my mood during the darkest of #MilkTits times, I'm sure he can do it now.

Pootling round his channel, I discover he's been developing a series of *Rate It or Slate It?* videos, the camera looking over his shoulder as he watches someone else's channel. The guilty pleasure is Moz's playground and his clever and frequently cruel commentary invites you to laugh at the people he's watching. Very meta and very addictive and very much what I'm looking for. I watch quite a few before clicking on the one with the lowest view count, posted earlier today.

"Meep morp, chickadees, anyone else bored of challenge channels? Tired of truths that you know are lies? Dog-tired of dullsville dares? Likewise, my friends, likewise..."

Hearing him say this makes my stomach sink. Moz's video, his cynicism, pushes me too close to believing that we're going to fail and I snap my laptop shut, not wanting to hear him slagging off challenge channels when we're so desperate for people to watch ours.

Down in the sitting room, Mum looks up from the other end of the sofa as I flop onto it and skip restlessly through the programmes recorded on the box. It's supposed to distract me from all the messages Sef's sending me. He's been on overdrive since I left him in the library and it's annoying me – although I accidentally glance down when another flashes up on my phone.

Have you seen how many views have come in on the Toothpaste dare???

Which piques my interest.

No.

Sef sends me a screengrab and despite how annoyed I am with him, my eyes grow wide at the figure. Doesn't change how monosyllabic my reply is.

That's a lot.

UNDERSTATEMENT OF THE CENTURY.

Then:

Fancy going out to celebrate?

I read the message, then turn my phone off without answering. People only try too hard when they know they've done something wrong and until Sef admits what that is, I'm not going to play.

"You all right, Little Bear?" Mum says, surprising me.

"Hm?" I finally pick a BBC wildlife thing on the grounds that the camerawork will be good. "Yeah. Why?"

She shifts in her seat to reach for her wine. "You're always in your bedroom, Dad in his office and me in mine." Mum waves her glass to indicate the sitting room, before taking a sip. "Want to make sure everything's OK. That's all."

Actually I'm annoyed with this boy because he broke up with his girlfriend and didn't tell me.

Aside from the inevitable, *What boy? Where'd you meet him? Is that where you've been going every Saturday? What about your schoolwork?* she might also ask me, *Is it really worth getting this worked up about it?*

"I'm fine, Mum," I tell her.

Rich has noticed I can't stop checking my phone. Although maybe that's just because Gemma has a lunchtime hockey practice and he's actually able to pay attention to me.

"What are you doing?"

"Nothing." I put it back in my pocket and instantly want to take it back out. It's been a week since the popularity of *DARE: Lick toothpaste off Dare Boy's chest!* kicked the donations up the backside and we're very close to the head-shaving target.

"Are you going to finish that pie?" I ask Rich, eyeing his pastry.

Rich ignores me, his fork poised as if using it to hunt. "Gemma has a theory that you've got some secret boyfriend on the go…" He waggles his eyebrows suggestively.

"I don't," I snap and Rich edges away. "Can you answer my question about your pie. I'm hungry."

Rich glances round. "OK, but don't let Gemma know."

"That I ate the leftovers of your pie?" I carefully transfer the crust from his plate to mine. "I wasn't planning on informing her. But why would she care?"

Rich fidgets, looking shifty, and mumbles something into his drink. I frown at him until he repeats it.

"Gemma thinks you should only share food inside a relationship."

There are a lot of expressions trying to happen on my face. "I'm eating a bit of your pie, not sucking up some spaghetti *Lady and the Tramp* style. That's a stupid rule."

"Gemma has a lot of stupid rules," Rich mutters and I check my phone again so he doesn't think I want to hear him talk about them.

Sef has messaged me. Again. Despite having spent three hours filming on Saturday, things still aren't right between us and he's been even more puppy-ish this week than last, bombarding me with questions and GIFs and emojis as if that's the way to fix things.

All I want is for him to apologize for not being honest with me and the longer he leaves it, the grumpier I get.

This time, though, it's to tell me that we've made the

target and a nervous squeak rasps my throat.

"Secret boyfriend or not –" Rich tries to look at my phone and I lock the screen – "something's got you excited."

Scared, I think about correcting him.

I brush my hair out in a sort of farewell gesture on Saturday morning. Soft, fine and slightly mango-scented because I used Mum's nice shampoo, my hair is a rose-gold waterfall plunging down my back to just below my shoulder blades. I twist round to look in the full-length mirror on the back of my door, the flesh beneath my bra folding over on itself. Pale skin, pale hair, freckles bleeding together into a pale-brown blur on my shoulders, peppering what little you can see of my back above my bra.

I feel a bit like I'm some kind of sacrificial offering once I'm dressed, sitting on my bed and plaiting my hair in two long braids so that we can donate it afterwards. When I see Mum on my way out, she tells me my hair looks nice like that and I feel so unbearably guilty that I run down the road, trying to outpace the squirming sense of dread in my guts.

Sef is waiting in Mrs Bennet, her heater going full blast so that it's like stepping inside a hug when I open the door.

I'm greeted with a "Hair looks nice".

"Thanks."

"I'm sorry, OK?" he says out of nowhere and I glance up.

"What for?"

"I'm sorry I didn't tell you that I'd broken up with Laila. You're one of my best friends and…" He lifts his hand to twist the stud in his ear and I wonder if he's secretly quite pleased to have yet another thing to fiddle with when he gets like this.

"And?" I prompt, because I've been waiting nearly two weeks for this and I've no intention of letting him off lightly.

Sef laughs, ducking his head a little before he turns to look at me. "Not going to make this easy for me, are you?"

"Any reason I should?" The same words he said in the library when I'd wanted to know why he'd not told me sooner.

Sef's eyes are all over me and I heat up with more than Mrs B's overactive climate control.

"No," he says quietly. "I'm sorry I hid the truth from you, C. I'll be straight with you from now on. About everything. OK?"

As apologies go, it's acceptable.

CHAPTER 18

Mum bursts into tears and then:

"You look like a CANCER VICTIM!"

We explode into a row so loud that Dad comes hurrying out of his office to break things up. Not that he succeeds.

"What is *wrong* with you? Are you trying to punish me for not paying you enough attention?"

"Oh my God! Listen to yourself – this has nothing to do with you. Literally nothing. It's my hair and my life and I'll do what I want."

Mum's face hardens. "Whose idea was this?"

"Mine."

"Was it Rich's? I'm going to have a word with his mother—"

"I said IT WAS MINE!" I roar, my voice a tidal wave of sound that's rolled in from the furthest corners of my soul. "Do you really think so little of me that you can't possibly believe I might do something for myself? For fun? For charity? For actual 'cancer victims' as you call them?" I hate the words she used, the way she said it, like cancer is something that only happens to people too weak to avoid it.

"How is that your responsibility, Claire?" Mum flails her arms around in frustration.

"There's no need to get hys—" Dad starts, but Mum's not in the mood.

"Oh, don't you even *think* about going there, Connor Casey." Mum swoops her handbag and the car keys from the kitchen counter next to her and leaves the room.

"Where are you going?" Dad starts after her.

"Out."

"Where? Why? We're in the middle of—"

The distant slam of the side door to the garage cuts him off.

"Why is she being so unreasonable?" I mutter, thinking that at least Dad's on my side, until he turns to look at me, finger pointing firmly in my direction to silence whatever I'm about to say.

"That's enough from you." He stares at me, finger still out, indicating I should stay quiet. Dad's scary when he's this angry. "I don't even know you any more."

"Dad—"

His arm relaxes, fist unclenching, whole body sagging before me. "No more, Claire. I can't deal with this right now."

And like Mum, he walks off rather than try and fix his broken relationships.

Sunday is a pleasant reprieve. Kam approves of my new look – his laugh is so loud that the nurse manning the station comes to his room to find out what the joke is – and I wish I could tell him that he's the one I did it for.

My nerves return in full force on Monday, though, and

at the last minute I grab a beanie hat from the miscellaneous accessories box by the front door before I meet Rich at the bus stop. Even though it itches – and smells a bit like head grease – I keep it on long after I've boarded.

"Are you ever going to take that thing off?" Rich asks.

I pull my hat further down over my ears. "Maybe."

"Have you had a haircut you hate or something?"

I nod. Although I actually kind of like it. Zero minutes wasted on washing and drying and brushing and styling.

"Let me see."

Ever so slowly, I lift the hat up off my head, cheeks pink from the heat as much as embarrassment at the way Rich is goggling at me.

"Wha...yyy?" His face is a slow-mo GIF of "horrified reaction".

"For charity." I like how this lie is also the truth.

"You're..." He shakes his head and then strokes mine like I'm a lovable puppy. "A freaky, unknowable human. And a gift. You know I'm going to call you Baldy from now on, right?"

So unimaginative.

I put the hat back on for the walk into school, but I take it off before I walk into the classroom, Rich glued to my side for support.

Vijay sees me first. "Is that Milk Tits?"

But the name is too familiar for it to hurt the way it once did.

There's a swell of noise in the corner, then a collective pause as all attention sweeps across the room straight to where I'm standing. My hand shakes as I run it over my head and try to smile.

"So … I had a haircut at the weekend."

There's another second of silence and then someone laughs. "You are such a weirdo."

And just like that, everyone relaxes back into their conversations. Gemma and Chloe and some of the other girls ask if it was a mistake and whether they can have a feel of it.

When Seren walks in – right on the bell – she pauses, looking at me sitting with Rich on the desk. We lock eyes and then, after a moment's appraisal, a slight smile curls at the corner of her mouth before she nods and turns away.

CHAPTER 19

I've got something to show you.

If this is a surprise picture of your abs again, know that I will not be looking. Things may have been resolved since he apologized for not telling me about Laila, but I'm still resisting Sef's efforts to drive things back to the way they were before. There's no fun in suggestive messaging when you know there's no actual suggestion behind it. When he had a girlfriend, I could allow myself to believe there was a "what if…" air about everything. Now he's single, I'm having a hard time keeping up the delusion.

Something to show you *in person* – meet down in the car park at lunch…

"Perhaps if I spoke to her in English, Claire would deign to give me her undivided attention?"

I'm startled into looking up from the phone on my lap to see Madame Cotterill holding out her hand and looking severe. *"Donne moi ton téléphone."*

Sef's already in the car park when I arrive, late from getting my phone back, complete with a lecture about using it in class.

"What is it, then?" I clamber into the passenger seat of Mrs Bennet, hoping there are no teachers looking out of the staff-room window. You can get into trouble for stuff like this.

Sef's grinning at me and the energy that's rolling off him is electric.

"Three guesses."

"Sef!" But this is exactly the sort of game he will play by the rules. "Fine. Is it an exciting piece of equipment?"

He gives me a very amused look. "I think they frown on that kind of behaviour on school premises."

I shove him in the arm and mumble, "I didn't mean that kind of equipment."

My second and third guesses aren't right either. Sef is not offering me a home-baked cake or a puppy.

"What is it?!"

I didn't know it was possible for him to beam any brighter, but when he shows me what's on his phone, I see why.

There, sent to our Truth or Dare account, addressed to Dare Boy and Truth Girl, is an email. It's only short, but the impact it has is huge:

Hey hey.

So I think your channel is bang. Want to make some noise together?

Moz (meep morp)

The next morning, when Sef picks me up, he's buzzing with excitement while I buzz with something less enjoyable that nags insistently at my insides, churning my stomach, squeezing my bladder and clawing at my throat.

There's a reason I've never skipped school before.

Rich thinks I'm ill. My parents think I'm at school. I think I'm going to faint.

But when MozzyMozzaMeepMorp suggests you meet him for lunch in a swanky London hotel to talk about collaborating with him, you say yes. That *Rate It or Slate It?* video I didn't watch all those weeks ago, that was us doing that stupid toothpaste video and…

If I don't stop staring at my reflection in the mirror and worrying about whether my mum's train has been delayed or something equally awful that could mean we get caught, we're going to miss our own train.

"Will you just chill?" Sef says, when I emerge from the station toilets in my own clothes, uniform stuffed into my rucksack. "It's going to be fine."

"You don't know that."

Sef hooks an arm round me and drags me along the platform towards the gates.

"Trust me," he whispers, his lips close to my ear. "We've already got away with it."

Our T-shirts and jeans earn dismissive glances from the other people in the restaurant, whose shopping bags probably contain socks worth more than the cameras stuffed in my rucksack. Shuffling and awkward, at odds with the opulence of mirrored columns and waterfalls of white crystals hanging from the ceiling, we hunt for Moz, Sef murmuring, "The customers are as white as the tablecloths." Eventually we find Moz in one of the booths, where he glances up from his phone and waves us to sit down, telling us to order something – "They cut the crusts off the sandwiches and everything" – while he deals with an email he's just got from his agent.

He might be rich enough to eat fancy sandwiches, but Moz looks even more out of place than we do with his lip-piercing and cobalt hair. His T-shirt is printed with grainy photos of bums and boobs and he's wearing mismatched Converse.

When he emits a short sharp "Bollocks!" at whatever he's reading on his phone, the couple next to us turn to frown through the row of orchids separating the booths.

Sef and I order tap water, too nervous to actually think of eating. Too scared that we might have to pay for it.

Finally, Moz puts his phone screen-down on the table. The back of the case is a photo of the side of his own face.

"So," he says, "this is what you look like without masks."

He stares at us for an uncomfortable moment, smiling like we're specimens from a zoo. "Cute glasses."

Sef nods.

"Cute face." Moz winks at me. I know he's gay, but *Moz just winked at me!!!*

Over the next half hour, Moz talks. And talks. Mostly about himself, occasionally asking us a question about our own channel, only to try and guess the answer rather than let us provide one. It puts me at ease, him behaving the same way he does online. It's as if I'm watching him onscreen rather than actually sitting at the same table, stuffing my face with the ridiculously delicious circular sandwiches he ordered.

"You want some more?" Moz turns to wave at one of the wait staff. "It's on my publishers."

When I say I didn't know he had a book deal, Moz raises a purple-painted finger to his lips, his smile a sliver of teeth.

"The more money you get, the less you have to spend. World be whack." All his sentences are like this, short statements that sound like you might see them on an inspirational poster across a panoramic photo of that famous rock in Australia. Or a Bart Simpson meme.

"We've a way to go before someone pays for our hotel room," Sef says with enough of a grin to make it cheeky rather than bitter.

"Just the one room?" Moz cocks his eyebrows. "With just the one bed?"

"Er. No." I say and Moz throws his head back in a whoop of a laugh as Sef gives me a faux wounded look.

The conversation has, at least, moved round to the reason we're here and Moz turns serious – or at least, he shuffles to face us instead of sitting sprawled with his crotch out to the whole room.

"So, any questions?"

Neither of us wants to look a gift YouTuber in the mouth, but there is one question that I can't find an answer for.

"Why are you doing this?" I ask. "Why us?"

"I like your channel." He keeps a straight face for all of a second before a wolfish grin emerges. "OK, so here's the deal. I have a massive audience that love me." There's a sardonic twist to Moz's mouth as he says it. "I could write a book, drop a single, advertise an aftershave, print my face on a condom wrapper … whatever. They buy it, I'd make money. Big whoop."

Moz looks deeply unimpressed by the thought of this and I daydream about having so much money you don't care about making any more.

"Money doesn't give me a kick. Do you know what does?"

"Dares?" Sef's guess lacks conviction. He'd take money over dares any day of the week.

"Power. You've seen what a difference it makes featuring a video on *Rate or Slate*, right? Even the ones I slag off see a boost in numbers ... but the few I've rated – the ones like yours?" Moz spirals his finger up into the air. "Got me thinking that maybe it would be fun to see how far I can take things."

"And we're the ones you want to take with you?" It's too good to be true.

Moz shrugs. "You're a bit different. All this secret identity intrigue, the dying friend—"

"He's not dying."

"Whatever. The way you do the dares. It's like *Jackass* – you heard of *Jackass*? Only kinda cute and less gross. And you're not all 'don't try this at home', you're like 'do it do it do it!' and it's refreshing. You're not pranking other people – it's all about you." Moz takes a sip of his drink and keeps going. "And, you know, I could do with people thinking I'm a bit more charitable. Good for the brand."

He stops, looks over. "I get my kicks, you get your money."

I watch Sef, trying to keep my thoughts from my face, but his are scrawled so bold he may as well have written them on his forehead with a Sharpie marker.

And Moz is smiling like that's all the answer he needs.

"Come on," he says, leaping up out of the booth with such vigour the whole seat bounces. "I've got my stuff set up in my room if you want to make it official?"

The luxury upstairs is less in-your-face than the restaurant, but Moz's room is still the size of our open-plan kitchen-diner, the enormous bed made up with a snowdrift duvet. While I'm drawn to the desk to inspect a camera more sleek and sophisticated than mine, Sef asks if he can bounce on the bed and a second later, I turn to find the pair of them leaping around, laughing, whooping and trying to shove each other over.

I get bored of waiting before they tire of messing around and I'm worried we're leaving it too late to get home.

"So what's the plan?" I call out and the bouncing slows to a stop, Moz executing an untidy forwards roll off the bed and onto the carpet, where he lies panting, looking up at me.

"What do you mean?"

"Well – what are we filming exactly? Are you just … introducing us to your audience? Are we playing Truth or Dare…?"

There's a lot of things can come under the term "collaborating".

Moz narrows his eyes and I get the feeling that I'm being measured. "On your donations page there's three dares, right?"

"Right," Sef says from where he's still on the bed, face blotchy from exertion.

"Shaving your head – done," Moz nods at me. "Streaking across a pitch – that's in the bag with the way your donations are going, right?" The glance he gives Sef has an undertone of amusement in it. "Assuming you get away with it."

"And?" I prompt and Moz gives me a wily smile.

"And someone else gets to choose the next one. Right?"

CHAPTER 20

Sorting stuff for Granny's, I heap some warm clothes, my cosiest PJs and an assortment of underwear on my bed before tipping the presents I got today out of my school bag. A neatly wrapped, weighty box from Gemma and Chloe, something no doubt small and silly from Oliver Martinez, whose birthday falls on the twenty-ninth and who sympathizes with me on these things, a rogue Secret Santa gift that I reckon is a bag of chocolates, and a badly wrapped squashy packet that's more Sellotape than paper with "C" written on in black marker pen from Rich.

Nothing from Seren. Not even a card.

Like everyone else in our year, she was in McDonald's this afternoon, but instead of sitting with me and Rich and grumbling about the egg-shaped McChicken fillet in the round bun of the sandwich, she was squashed over on a bench with a couple of girls from the other form. Opposite her, James Blaithe was watching her with the same kind of hunger as I was – like he wished she would notice him.

Obviously we're both going to be disappointed on that front.

Getting out my phone, I scroll through to where we'd last messaged each other.

I'm sorry. Please don't hate me.

I don't hate you, Claire. I just don't want to talk to you. Please stop trying to make me.

That was sent on the twelfth of October. Over two months ago.

I'm still staring at my phone when another message pops up from Sef.

All right, lover?

Too much.

Not really. There. As unflirty as you could possibly be.

Want me to cheer you up?

How?

Birthday surprise. 8 by the bus stop. Dress warm.

Half of me wants to stay home and wrap the emptiness of my house around me like a blanket ahead of facing a week of chaos at Granny's house, but the other half... I can feel an excited sort of sickness twisting my stomach, a tingling in my blood at the thought of a Friday-night adventure with Sef. It's nearly seven now and I'm feeling grubby from wearing the same after-school clothes three evenings in a row. I'd better shower. And eat. Sef seems to live on thin air and biscuits.

"Where are you off to?" Mum catches me in the kitchen in my trainers and coat.

I gesture at the Mini Babybel I've stuffed whole into my mouth, giving me time to think of something. I hadn't realized Mum was even home.

Lying in a note is much easier than lying face to face.

"Film Club. Want to go and test my exciting new camera..."

Sef actually has my new camera to use for Boxing Day.

"Have you packed for Ireland?" she says, frowning. "There won't be time tomorrow…"

"Of course!" I shove more food into my face to prevent further questions and blow her a kiss as I pass her on the way out to the hall. Putting stuff ready on my bed counts as packing, right?

Sef doesn't tell me where he's taking me. We bicker about the secrecy as he drives round the ring road, hand resting on the gearstick like he's been driving a car his whole life. The effect is ruined when he nearly misses his exit and becomes all elbows and muttered curses and anxious glances in all the mirrors.

"Smooth," I say, trying to keep my face straight.

The look he gives me shoots warmth up my body and into my cheeks.

"We're here." Sef pulls over into what passes for a parking space — a slight widening of the road in a narrow country lane.

"We're where?" I ask.

"You'll see." Sef gives me an irritating eyebrow waggle before opening his door. "Come on!"

We follow a sign for what I discover is the Forgotten Footpath. There's no light but for the moon and the sense of an orange glow where the town lights aim for the sky.

"Are we allowed here at night?" I say.

"Why wouldn't we be? It's a public footpath."

"What about murderers?"

"Or stalker weirdos who'll follow you home and watch you sleep?" Sef's teasing me and I give him a shove.

"Shut up. It's dark, we're alone, I've seen enough horror movies to know this isn't going to end well."

When he doesn't reply immediately, I turn and catch him looking down at me.

"Isn't it?"

We're too close for me to be comfortable with the way he says it. Stepping away I call back, "When does anything involving you end well, Yousef Malik?"

Sef hurries after me, giving me a shove and challenging me to race him up the hill. By the time we get to the top, neither of us is travelling at any speed and we collapse onto the grass, too exhausted to care how cold and hard and wet the ground is.

Our breath pools in hot little puffs above us and I enjoy the tingle of cold air on my hot cheeks.

"Thank you," I say, closing my eyes and bathing in the darkness.

"What for?" I feel Sef shift next to me.

"My birthday adventure."

"Is it everything you dreamed of?"

"It'll do." And then, because I don't want to talk about me, worried it will veer into making me sad about Seren, I ask, "When was yours?"

"September."

"I meant what date, Sef."

There's a pause. "The second. The day Kam woke up."

"Oh," I say, because what other response is there?

I reach over and give his hand a squeeze. "Guess there wasn't much time for birthday shenanigans for your seventeenth?"

"Not so much." There's a pause and then a shift in tone when he says, "The birthday *before*, on the other hand…"

"Do I even want to know?"

"Hit the clubs with Finn and Matty. Shenanigans a-plenty." My eyes stay closed, but I know he's smiling.

"Drinking, dancing and kissing all the girls?"

"Two out of three. I don't drink."

"Just dancing and kissing then?"

"And presents. That's the three things birthdays are for, surely?"

"Yours maybe. I usually only manage one of those." Not that I'm complaining. Some people don't even get presents…

There's a rustle of movement next to me before the chime of a piano chord rings out and my eyes flick open to see Sef holding up his phone, the screen displaying the name of the song.

"Moondance" by Van Morrison.

"Let's see if you can manage more than one…" Sef says, standing up and holding out his hand. "Care to dance?"

No one's ever asked me to dance and although I take his hand, I'm not sure what I'm supposed to do with my feet, so when Sef takes a step in time with the beat, I'm half a second behind him. It's not until halfway through the first verse that our feet start to move in roughly the right direction at roughly the right time. At first, I'm looking down at my trainers, then at a button on Sef's jacket, but when the chorus kicks in, he sends me away in a spin and pulls me back so close that there's no space to look anywhere other than at Sef.

"Are you singing?" I say and he nods, smiling as he raises his voice so I can make out the words, but low enough that it feels like he's singing only to me.

It is impossibly romantic.

Every part of me seems more there, more present, more alive than ever before, my skin blazing beneath my clothes, heart beating out of my chest, each breath I take a lungful of cool air, infused with the beauty of the night.

I wish I could tell where flirtation stops and feelings begin, because right now, it seems a lot like we might kiss… The song ends and there's a few seconds of silence in which the mood is preserved, our hands still linked, bodies close.

Then "Uptown Funk" blares out, too loud, too brash and I step back.

"What are you doing?" Sef tugs me gently back towards him.

"You want to dance to this too?" I wrinkle my face up. This song belongs in a nightclub, not a hilltop.

"I thought we were aiming for a hat-trick of birthday goals?" he says, his eyes on my lips a moment before they move up to meet my gaze.

Three months I've known him and I still can't tell when he's serious, but his eyes don't leave mine as he reaches up to my hairline, fingers pressing gently into my scalp as he runs them through the soft fuzz of my hair.

It's unbelievably arousing. I close my eyes, concentrating

on how it feels as he flattens his palms against my skull, his hands running from my crown, down the back of my head, the tips of his fingers pushing against the grain of my hair at the nape of my neck.

I'm left breathless, barely able to open my eyes.

His thumb is brushing down my hairline behind my ear. "I've wanted to do that ever since we shaved your head."

"Head-stroking should definitely be added to the list of things people do on their birthdays…" I murmur, still drunk on the feel of it.

"I'm incorporating it into one of the others."

Gently, carefully, Sef kisses me on the cheek, leaving his lips on my skin for a moment. Then he kisses me again on the curve of my jaw, and on my neck. When he kisses me on the chin, I breathe out in a quiet laugh, my breathing speeding up as I think of where he's sure to kiss me next.

Only he kisses my nose.

"Here." I reach between us and rest an unsteady finger on my mouth. "Birthday kisses go here…"

"Do they now?" he whispers, the breath of his words dusting my skin.

And I catch the familiar, sexy curve emerge at the corners of his lips before he leans in and presses those lips to mine, just for a few seconds.

When he pulls back a fraction I can tell he's still smiling. "Dancing, kisses and what was next? Presents?"

"I don't care about presents," I say, curling my hand round the collar of his jacket. "I want more kisses."

I pull him closer for a series of light, soft, questioning

kisses that grow bolder and more impatient, until our mouths open and I get a taste of ginger biscuits and something that is uniquely and addictively Sef.

His hands are still cradling my head, but mine are free to wander, venturing round his waist and up his back, pulling him ever closer so that our legs and chests and … other parts press together. I'm wrapping myself up in him, losing my doubts and sinking into my dreams of kissing the boy I've been burning for.

It's messy and beautiful and I never want it to end.

CHAPTER 21

Cars, planes, hire cars, Irish roads (or as Mum muttered, Irish drivers), but once we get to Granny's it's cuddling, drinks, nibbles and gossip. Everyone's there and they've all got something to say about my hair while Kathleen, who's only eight, sits on the arm of the sofa and strokes it.

"So nice to see more of your beautiful face."

"Is it cold?"

"I hadn't noticed one of your ears poked out more than the other."

"Never pegged you for a rebel…"

And I smile and say thank you and make jokes about the cold and my rebellious tendencies and my cousin Mark's wonky nose in revenge for the ears comment, all the time itching to check my phone.

In a quiet moment, Mark trades me the Wi-Fi code on the promise I'll load the dishwasher after dinner. There are a few messages from Sef – the kind that should *not* be read casually around my family – and one from Rich grumbling that Gemma wants him to go round and meet her family. I'm a bit jealous of him for that – even if I was spending the holiday at home, would Sef invite me to meet his? Although looking through the door to the kitchen, where Mum is scowling silently in the corner with her third glass of champagne as Dad does the prodigal son thing, I'm not sure I'd be that keen on inviting Sef to meet mine.

Any news on Moz's video??? I ask Sef. Although we only went to London on Wednesday, so much has happened since that it feels distinctly longer.

Moz said it'll drop about 9 tonight.

Then.

It's a boost to my ego to know you're more interested in Moz than me.

I'm typing this in my grandmother's utility room. Your messages are better suited for other locations.

He replies with a photo of him raising his eyebrows suggestively.

"Claire?"

I put my phone away and hurry back to the living room.

After dinner, I sneak up to my room and sit on the bed with my laptop. It's after nine and I tut impatiently as the rubbish internet signal stutters to life and the video buffers on a freeze-frame of Moz's face for about a million years before bursting into action.

"MeepMorp, Mozzy here and…" Moz had his face right up to the camera, but steps back to reveal: mute waving and ridiculous face-pulling from two masked idiots. (Cousin Mark's comment about my ears echoes in my mind and I can't help noticing the one that sticks out more.)

"… Truth Girl and Dare Boy, who you may remember from this video." Moz points to where a thumbnail reminds the viewer of the *Rate It or Slate It?* video in which we starred. *"Two of this old-timer's favourite noobs."*

And he leans back to sling his arms round our shoulders and give each of us a kiss on the cheek.

"*Never washing my face again…*" Dare Boy says with mock reverence as I'm caught wiping it off on the shoulder of my T-shirt.

Moz has inserted a split-second cut of all three of us in hysterics, which actually happened much later in filming, but the effect is instantaneous – this is not staged, not really, we're friends, we make each other laugh, look at the way Moz's hand is on my shoulder as he bends forward, Dare Boy wiping real tears from his eyes and muttering, "*My eyeliner's going to be ruined!*"

"*But don't you crazy kittens be thinking that this here's the collaboration, we're going* Inception *on your asses…*" A black-and-white splice of Moz pretending to be his own viewer, specs drawn on his face in pen, with an overlay thought bubble of someone having a thought bubble of someone having a thought bubble.

"*This is just the trailer for the real collaboration video.*"

"*Dropping when, Moz?*" Sef times it perfectly.

"*Excellent question, Dare Boy – this collab's only going to happen if YOU make it.*" Moz points to his viewers. "*These guys and Mozzy are going to film the best challenge video the internet has ever witnessed, but we need your help. Find these guys' channel –*" he flips his fingers to point at me and I take the cue to say the name of our channel – "*watch their trailer –*" a splice of viewer Moz crying and smudging the drawn-on glasses – "*go through to the donations page and … HIT DONATE.*"

"The target is twenty thousand pounds," Dare Boy says. *"And when we reach that, we're going to hold the mother of all food fights."*

"Where?" I pretend I'm asking.

"Secret," Moz says and there's a cut to all three of us doing the three-monkey "see no evil, hear no evil, speak no evil" pose. *"But I guarantee it is gonna be EPIC!"*

The three of us mess about pulling faces and doing slow-motion firework bursts with our hands and then there's another cut to us in hysterics.

Short, punchy and perfectly edited.

Our golden ticket.

CHAPTER 22

It's New Year's Eve tomorrow and the mood in the Rec is pretty festive.

"Merry Christmas, Kam," I say.

Merry Christmas.

At the start of December, Kam's fine motor skills had developed enough for him to point and press, and before I went away for Christmas, he'd been given an iPad with an app that allows him to choose what to say.

I watch as he presses two short phrases on the screen.

A present. For you.

"You have a present for me?" Kam hoots at my reaction. "Do you need me to get it?"

He makes a noise and moves his hand a little towards the table behind me. There's an envelope on the table and I pick it up.

"This?"

Kam moves his head in a nod. It doesn't feel like there's anything inside and I'm careful as I tuck a thumb under the flap and rip along the edge. Inside, there's a slim piece of laminated paper and I reach to pull it out.

"It's a bookmark?" I whisper, looking up.

From me.

The paper is filled with writing – typed and overlapping,

sentences jumbled up – and I have to concentrate to read them: *Friend. Books. No pirates*. It's become a sort of running joke – if Kam's in a good mood I show him the book and we have a laugh about it – and I smile through the tears that have welled up at the sight of a present that is specific to *us*.

One that I know will have taken *hours* of effort to make.

I step over to his chair. "Can I hug you?"

He nods and I wrap my arms carefully around him. "Thank you for my Christmas present, Kam. Best one I've had this year. Fact."

I can feel him moving for the comms board and I let go to read his response.

That's OK.

"I got you something too." I pull a gift bag out of my rucksack and put it carefully on his tray. Then, making sure Kam's the one directing things, I help him take the present out of the bag.

It's the bowling shirt from *The Big Lebowski*. A hideous yellow and brown that brings an enormous grin to Kam's face.

Totally worth borrowing against my birthday money.

Kam insists I get someone to help him put it on and, as he changes, I give him privacy by turning my back and examining the cards on the chest of drawers. There are loads, but I find the one I gave him before the holidays peeping out behind a photo I've not seen before. It can only have been taken a few days ago, Kam in his wheelchair festooned with tinsel, his parents on either side and Amir leaning in, arms splayed as if mid-photo bomb.

"I like the photo that's up in Kam's room," I tell Sef when I see him. He's on shift and hasn't much time to talk, but this is the first chance I've had to see him since I came back. (I don't count watching the clumsily edited streaking video on my laptop, hands over my face while I died with cringe.)

"What photo?" He's distracted, frowning over my shoulder at some of the kids who are running around the foyer.

"The one you took at Christmas, of your parents and Amir with Kam…"

Sef stands up straighter. "No touching the displays!" he calls over. Then to me, "Sorry."

He looks at me, frowning, like he's trying to work out what we were talking about.

"Thought you didn't take any?" I'd asked Sef if he could send over pics of Kam's Christmas when I sent him the daft selfie I took with the glowing reindeer Granny had up on her back lawn, but he'd replied late at night to say he'd not taken his phone with him.

"They're all on Amir's phone."

"How was it, though? Christmas at the Rec?" It's not something that's easy to ask Kam, whose life is very much about what happens in the present. If anything, mine and Kam's little bubble is even harder to break out of than the one I occupy with his brother.

"As good as could be expected. Tiring for Kam, though— Seriously, those kids…" He points a finger at someone and gives them a death stare. It's hard carrying on a conversation with only half his attention, and I reach for the scarf I left on the counter, thinking it's best if I go.

"What are you doing?"

"Leaving. You're working…"

"I could be on a break?" he suggests quickly.

"You don't have to—"

"I could be kissing you on my break?"

Scarf in hand, I stop to look at the mischievous curve of his lips. Two minutes later and Sef has left a grumpy Mia in charge, holding the door marked STAFF ONLY long enough for me to slip through, before he's pushed it shut behind us and is pulling me gently towards him.

"I'm sorry I was distracted," he says, brushing one hand across my scalp as the other hooks itself through my belt loop. "Gets busy in the holidays."

"I was asking how Christmas went," I say, resting my hands on his chest and looking up at his face, wanting to know the truth. "Was it OK? Not just for Kam, but for you?"

His face is inscrutable for a moment as he looks down at me.

"We can talk about that if you want…" He presses his lips lightly to my forehead. "But there are other things we can do that would make me happier…" He kisses my nose. "Things that I've not been able to do…" My lips. "… without you here."

"Sef…" I say quietly. "You can talk to me about it, you know."

"I know." He buries his face in my neck, lips brushing

against my skin when he says, "I know, C, but I don't want to."

Which I guess I already knew.

"Please just kiss me," Sef whispers into my ear. "I've missed you."

CHAPTER 23

Although I'm sure Rich's mum wouldn't have minded me inviting Sef along to the traditional Richards gathering – the thought of going public is so scary that I don't even mention it to him. Besides, it's not like I'd have had much time for my own relationship given how much of my night is spent counselling Rich and Gemma through theirs.

Sometime approaching midnight, Rich's sister catches me in the hall having a rest. Flo slides down the wall to where I'm sitting and offers me her spare drink.

"What is it?" I frown at the cup and she laughs.

"Non-alcoholic punch. Cheers." Flo taps her cup to mine as we listen to the grown-ups shouting along to "Come On Eileen" in the front room, fuelled by something distinctly stronger than punch.

"Your brother's a pain in the arse," I tell her.

Flo rolls her eyes at me. "I'm related to him. At least you can walk away and leave him to it."

"I'm considering it…"

"Don't." She nudges me gently and stands up. "I like you as my faux big sister."

"I like you as my faux little one."

Whatever Sef gets up to, he doesn't reply to the

message I send of me kissing the camera lens until four o'clock in the afternoon on the first day of the new year.

The last week of the holidays passes in a frenzy of finishing the assignments I've been neglecting around monitoring the channel and squeezing in as much time with Sef as possible – sitting in the back row of the cinema watching obscure films that don't make much sense if you spend more time kissing than reading the subtitles, going for a drive in Mrs Bennet, or just sitting squashed up together on a window seat in his uncle's caravan, talking and kissing and exploring our relationship at a pace we're both comfortable with.

And filming. I want to get a jump on all the challenges that have come flooding in since our collaboration with Moz drove more viewers to our channel. When school starts back up, I'll have more work and less time for editing.

School. The thought worries me. When we were in London, before the video went live, working with Moz didn't seem real, but now it's out there, the view count climbing… People watch Moz's channel. Teenagers. Who might go to my school.

Fear flutters in my throat every time I think about it.

So I don't.

On Saturday, Sef's free for the whole day, having swapped his shift with Mia, and after filming, we Skype Moz as scheduled.

"Hey hey." It might be long after lunch, but it took three

tries for Moz to answer and his face is puffy with sleep.

"Hey," Sef and I chorus together. Below the view of the camera, Sef slides one hand up from my knee to mid-thigh and runs his thumb along the seam of my jeans.

"You scored any more subs?" Moz asks through a yawn and I wonder what it must be like to be such a hit that you don't feel the need to check.

"A few." Sef holds up the scrap of paper on which he's been totting up the increase in traffic, his other hand squeezing my leg gently. It's distracting.

Onscreen, Moz reaches beyond the camera as someone passes him a coffee. There's a tattoo of the Deathly Hallows from Harry Potter with a red Z through it on the coffee guy's wrist and I wonder whether it's Moz's nemesis, ZimBob. A feud as real as an episode of *Made in Chelsea*.

Moz sips his coffee and blows the person who gave it to him a kiss. "Donations are looking a little sluggish, aren't they?"

Comparing the current rate to the old rate is like comparing a peregrine falcon to a beach ball thrown by an incompetent child.

"Yeah … sluggish…" Sef nods as his thumb brushes a little further up my leg so that I'd quite like to both chop it off and let him to keep going.

"So I'm gonna liven things up, OK? Thought I'd film a video saying that anyone donating more than twenty pounds will be entered into a draw from which we'll pick fifty people to join in with the fight. What do you think?"

"Fifty?"

Moz nods, giving me a shrewd look. "Your boyfriend thought it was a good idea when I messaged him about it…"

I dart a glance at Sef, who gives me a sheepish sort of shrug. I don't like the thought of them talking without keeping me in the loop. And I don't like Moz calling him my boyfriend. Whatever we have, it's not something I want Moz to know about.

"Not my boyfriend," I say – although the way Moz eyes me through the screen, it's like he can tell exactly where Sef's hand is on my body. "But if you two think it's a good idea…"

"I think you want this to work fast." Moz raises his eyebrows and I get the feeling I've just been schooled.

"Sure," I say. "Whatever you say, Moz."

Afterwards, when Sef has gone to grab something from the car, I message Moz.

This fight is going to be EPIC.

I figure the more I talk like him, the more likely he is to reply.

Epic to infinity and beyond, TG.

Can I ask a favour?

So long as it's not sexual.

Ew. Gross. I totally walked into that.

If there are going to be other people there, I don't want them to find out who I am.

Privacy is overrated. Says the person who Snapchats while he's on the toilet.

I'm serious, Moz. Online me and offline me are

different people. I want to keep it that way.

Being serious: your secret identity is safe with me.

Locking my phone, I stare out of the window as Sef hurries back from the car. Moz's reassurance at least puts my anxiety of being unmasked by a stranger to rest, but there's nothing he can do about my fears over someone from school recognizing me.

Internet-land is so vast that logic says there's no reason to worry, but then I think of all the conversations I've had with people about our favourite channels, how many times I've recommended Moz's channel… It's not often I actually hope no one was listening to me.

A pale girl with a shaved head is pretty distinctive with or without the eye mask.

There are so many things I'm willing to risk to raise the money for Kam, but the truth isn't one of them. If anyone at school found out I was Truth Girl, how long would it take for them to revive that stupid #MilkTits video? I've felt so strong, so proud, carving a niche for myself on the internet that isn't defined by anything I am at school.

One simple puff and the whole thing could blow down.

Sef and I must have fallen asleep.

"Someone's phone's ringing," he murmurs into my neck. We're curled up together on his uncle's bed, mostly clothed, on top of the sheets.

"Probably yours." I close my eyes and wait for the buzzing to stop, but he's already shifting round to reach for his glasses.

"It's yours," he says, picking it up. Then, "Claire?" The shift in his voice tells me this is a call I want to take. "It's Seren."

Hurrying to answer the phone, I still manage to miss it, but before I can ring back, her name flashes up again and I accept the call.

"Seren?"

"Claire." Then she bursts into tears and I sit up so fast that I knock Sef's glasses askew on his face.

"Seren? Seren? Are you OK? What's wrong?"

"I'm fine, I'm fine." She is not fine.

"Are you OK? Are you hurt?"

"Not really." I wish I knew which question she's answering. "Can you come and get me? I can't call my—"

"Of course," I say immediately, not caring what or why or where.

Seren is hiding in the disabled toilet at the big cinema in the retail park and when she opens the door, she pulls me into a hug, whispering fierce thanks into my shoulder. Even blotchy, she looks beautiful – she's wearing my favourite of her wrap dresses, legs bare because she's wearing a chunky pair of sandals, red-painted nails peeping out of the toes.

"I'm sorry," she says.

"Don't be. What's wrong?"

Pulling away from our hug to splash some water on her face, Seren tells me there were supposed to be a group of them meeting up to watch the film, but when she got here, Chloe had paired off with Oliver Martinez and the other girls were running late, leaving Seren with the Cave Boys for company.

Dread creeps up my skin.

"We couldn't find anywhere to sit with all of us and James…" She pauses, frowning at her own reflection. "I thought it was unusually considerate of him to say he'd sit with me."

She looks so disappointed and her lip trembles a little. I've never seen Seren like this and it scares me.

"What happened?"

"It could have been worse…" She turns to the hand dryer, not looking at me. "He just tried to kiss me and…" With her back to me, Seren gestures below where her dress is tied.

"And what?" I step closer.

Seren waves more frantically in the general area of her crotch. "I shouldn't have worn a dress," she whispers.

Hearing her say this is horrific because it is *so far* from what she believes.

"It's a dress, not an invitation." I echo what she said to Rich about his scrawny torso back when the idea was nothing more than a joke to any of us.

Seren doesn't respond and I want to shake her, I want to cry, I want to shout and I want to find James Blaithe and do something unspeakably violent and definitely beyond my physical capabilities.

"This isn't your fault, Seren." I hug her maybe a little too tight because there's a tiny bit of me that thinks it is mine. That when James called me Milk Tits or grabbed my boobs, I should have drawn a line around my body and told him it wasn't OK to cross it.

I hate having to ask this, but, "Do we need to go to the police or something?"

"God, no." She shudders so violently that my jaw clacks where it's resting on her shoulder. "He didn't do anything. Just tried to."

I want to point out that *trying* still counts as *doing*, but she clearly doesn't want to think about it.

"Come on," I say. "Let's get out of here."

When we approach the car, Seren frowns, as if she didn't really think through how I might have got here. But I hurry the pace up and shovel her into the back before she has a chance to ask too many questions. Sliding in next to her, I watch as Sef turns in his seat to look at us.

"Hi." He grins at Seren – not the usual carefree curve of his lips, but a smaller, more subdued, more sympathetic smile. "I'm Sef, your taxi driver for this evening. Where am I taking you ladies?"

Ignoring her wide-eyed stare that's trying to brand a question mark in the side of my face, I ask Seren if she'd like to stay at mine. She wouldn't – but after only the briefest of pauses, she asks if I'd stay at hers.

There are fresh tears in her eyes when she looks at me. "I'm sorry, Claire."

"Don't be," I say.

It's too awful that something like this is what's brought us back together, but I'm also relieved that when she needs help, Seren knows that she can turn to me and I will be there to give it.

* * *

Later, long after I've pleaded (non-specific/completely misleading) extenuating circumstances to my mother as a reason for a short-notice sleepover, when I'm in the PJs I always used to leave at Seren's house that don't quite fit any more, we lie in her bed, curled up facing each other, knees touching beneath the duvet.

I feel Seren reach for my hand.

"Thank you for coming when I called," she says quietly.

"As if I wouldn't."

She gives my hand a couple of quick squeezes, as if signalling a change in conversation, before she breaks out into a wide smile, eyes sparkling under her bedside light.

"So. Sef Malik. Sexy sixth-former and your own private taxi driver…?"

Sitting here, my best friend back in my life, I find that, in fact, I *don't* want to keep the truth about Sef to myself at all.

"My own private boyfriend? I think?" I scrunch my face up, not quite believing that I really get to say this out loud to her.

"Tell me. All of it. Everything. The whole of your relationship start to finish." Her lip wobbles slightly as she says, "I can't believe I missed it all."

I know that we aren't fixed and there's a conversation to be had about me finally understanding why she was upset with me.

Seren's sexuality isn't an optional add-on – it's part of who she is. But I treated it like it was something *she* was supposed to work around when it was me and Rich who should have put the effort in. I will have to tell her this, offer a hand to help her climb down from the high ground she stranded herself on over the Gemma issue.

But tonight it is enough that when I tell her about Sef, I know she wants to listen.

I know I can tell her the truth. All of it.

CHAPTER 24

Rich's phone has been blinging a ton of messages all the way to school that he's been ignoring, so when he looks up to see Seren standing by the school gate, he's already in such a foul mood that I worry this is all going to go horribly wrong.

"What's she doing there?" Rich mutters.

"Waiting for me."

He grinds to a halt. "What?"

"We made up."

I wait, wondering whether his loyalty to me or the memory of Seren is strong enough to grant the second chance we all deserve.

"So where does that leave me?" Rich looks so lost, so uncertain that I hook my arm through his in a way I've been wary of doing since he started seeing Gemma.

"It leaves you wherever you want to be."

Five long strides along the pavement and up to the gate, Seren watching us, caught between hope and caution.

"Hey," she says.

"Hey," Rich replies.

Rather than go inside, we sit on the wall, ignoring first bell as Seren tells Rich what happened on Saturday, my hands clenched into fists so tight my knuckles turn white. I'm almost as angry now as I was then.

Seren falters when she gets to the bit about James lunging in for a kiss.

"After that he…" She frowns, huffs out an angry little breath and then, "Put his hand where it had no business going. That's when I left. Called Claire – who came."

Rich is staring at her, face hard with rage, his mouth pressed into a lipless line. Until something shifts, eyes glazing over slightly, the blood draining from his face as fast as it rose up.

"What did James try to do?" Rich's voice is tight, his words forced.

Seren's as confused as I am.

"He… You know. Don't make me spell it out."

"Seren…" Rich looks ill as he runs his hand up through his hair. *"Shit."*

A quizzical little frown wrinkles across Seren's forehead. "I know it's pretty sleazy, but he didn't succeed."

"That depends on what he was trying to do."

The way he takes his phone out is ominous, his thumb pausing over the screen for a second before he taps it savagely and hands the phone to Seren.

The last time I was in the head teacher's office was in Year 9 when my mum was upset at the way the options for Year 10 had been timetabled.

"Denver, Seren and … ah…?"

"Claire Casey." You can't really blame Mr Chung for not recognizing someone he last saw over a year and a half ago.

"Sorry, yes, of course. I remember our discussion about

Media Studies – you enjoying it…? Excellent. Please take a seat, the three of you."

Mr Chung folds himself back into his leather throne. His desk is packed with books, trays over-populated with papers, and the keys on his computer are so worn that half the letters have rubbed off.

"Not that I'm not pleased to see three of my less troublesome students, but what is it that brings you to my office when you should be in first period?"

Rich and Seren exchange a glance.

"We're here to report James Blaithe," she says.

A muscle tenses in Mr Chung's jaw and his next blink lasts a little longer than the one before. "Go on."

"Last Saturday, at the cinema, he – well, he made an unwelcome advance."

"At the cinema?" Although what everyone in the room hears is: "Not at the school?"

"Yes. I didn't realize it at the time, but he took a picture up my dress." Her voice is strong and clear, but Seren's fingers are pinching and smoothing and pinching again at the pleats in her skirt.

"Sir," Rich takes over. "James sent a photo to the football team group chat this morning." He holds up his phone with a steady hand. When Rich gets angry, he goes disturbingly calm. "Seren agrees that it's of her. I've screengrabbed the comments beneath the picture so you can see who's involved."

Both of us turn to give him a wide-eyed stare of surprise at this and he swallows as he hands Mr Chung the phone. The plan was to report James, but Rich has effectively turned in half of West Bridge's football team.

"And, Miss Casey, how is it that you're involved? Not on the football team, are you?" Mr Chung is smiling kindly, expecting me to say that I'm here for moral support given the way that I'm now holding hands with Seren.

But it's her giving me strength, not the other way around.

"I should have reported it sooner," I say and Mr Chung's smile turns from kind to weary. "But I believe James was responsible for a video posted online of my ... er ... well, my bikini slipped."

I'm grateful when Mr Chung chooses that moment to break eye contact and straighten a piece of paper on his desk.

"And he's assaulted me on school premises," I whisper, wishing I'd done something sooner and squeezing Seren's hand so tight I can feel her knuckles grind together. "By grabbing me round the chest."

Seren comes round to my house after school like old times. We sit in the kitchen snacking on dry cereal, half doing homework and half chatting about anything and everything except what might have happened after half the football team had been ordered from their lessons to Mr Chung's office.

Particularly what might have happened to the goalie who never came back...

There's supposed to be practice tonight, but Rich rejected our offer to wait for him, telling us we were over-reacting. With James excluded, it wasn't as if anything was going to happen.

Still when the doorbell goes, followed by the sound of Rich tramping in, we both let out a sigh of relief.

It's premature.

"No one's allowed to say 'I told you so'…" Rich's voice is weirdly hoarse and when he rounds the corner from the hall, we find out why.

Rich is habitually slow getting changed and with everyone – even his girlfriend's brother – sore at him for crippling the team ahead of their grudge match with East Bank, all James had to do was wait for the captain to be the last to leave. It seems James hasn't quite taken on board the idea that being excluded means not being on school premises.

If the groundsman hadn't stayed late to put the pitch back to rights, Rich might have more than a black eye and a tender throat to show for his encounter.

Between googling what you're supposed to do with a black eye if you don't have any steaks in the fridge and thrusting tissues at Seren, who's burst into uncharacteristic tears, while *also* trying to stop an argument about whose fault it is, I get very stressed.

When I accidentally drop my phone in the freezer drawer looking for some frozen peas, I yell at them to stop.

"Listen to yourselves, trying to convince the other you're the one to blame. You're *not*, neither of you. It's no one's fault but James Blaithe's." I shove the peas at Rich. This is exactly what I've been trying to tell myself since Saturday. "*James* is the one who mauled you and revenge-posted that picture, *James* is the one who punched you in the face. And *James* is the one who grabbed my boobs."

Maybe I should have reported him for it at the time, but it should never have been down to me to police how James behaves. It should be down to James.

I can feel them both watching me as I set about preparing three deluxe hot chocolates.

"Aren't I supposed to be the bossy one?" Seren says.

"She's been getting uppity for a while now," Rich scrapes out.

Perhaps the stern glare I give them would carry more weight if I wasn't holding a bag of mini marshmallows.

"She didn't use to be like this," Rich murmurs.

"I blame her new boyfriend."

There's a second of silence before I feel a cold, wet slap on my back. Rich just threw the frozen peas at me, didn't he?

"I knew it!" he says, before breaking out into a painful-looking coughing fit, through which he barely manages to add, "Tell me. Immediately."

CHAPTER 25

Sef picks me up from school on Friday and we drive to the caravan. Tomorrow we'll be Dare Boy and Truth Girl, but tonight we're Sef and Claire and we snuggle up against the pillows on the bed, a film on my laptop and a bowl of popcorn between us like a proper couple.

Sef tuts when yet another message buzzes through on his phone. He's been bombarded by them.

"Do you mind if I give my mum a call? She seems to think I said I'd be home for dinner tonight."

"Sure…" I wave him away into the other room and pick up my own phone, tapping through to check for any new comments on the video we posted on Wednesday. I'm hoping to have something easier to film than "Go into a bookshop and turn all the books round so you can't see the spines".

Only, the comments I find aren't challenging. They're just horrid.

Anyone think TG needs to lose a few?

Porker

Don't think his type eat pork

lmao

Do they eat ugly girls???

These aren't people who've commented before and I'm vaguely heartened by one of our regulars telling them to stop being disgusting, but still … *porker, ugly* … and *his type…*

"What's up?" Sef throws himself onto the bed next to me so that my phone bounces out of my hand and onto the floor and before I can stop him, he reaches down for it. "More comments?"

But his smile fades as he reads them.

"Some of our new viewers are delightful, aren't they?" He hands me back my phone and kisses my cheek. "My type likes your type and the rest of them can fuck off."

Sef leans forward and unpauses the film, snuggling into me to watch the screen. His head is resting on my breasts, arm across my stomach, like I'm a giant fleshy pillow.

It's not like these are the first comments I've ever seen about my body, obviously, but there's a part of me that hoped I'd left those behind with Milk Tits, that no one cared what Truth Girl looked like…

Sef's hand moves from where it's resting across me to slide gently up under my top, fingers splayed as if trying to cover as much of my skin as he can.

Those comments make me feel like I should stop him – tug the material down so he can't see what's underneath – but then his weight shifts and Sef's propped up on his elbows, gently lifting my top and dotting a delicate line of kisses across the skin he finds.

It feels beautiful.

"Come here…" I tell him and Sef brings his mouth to mine and we kiss, the film still playing in the background. When our kisses shift gear from welcoming to wanting, my hands run up under his top too.

Sef pulls away to take off his glasses and put them on the table next to the bed then, after a slight hesitation, he pulls his top off and tentatively, he reaches for mine, eyebrows raised in question.

My type likes your type.

It isn't long before we've wriggled out of most of our clothes and under the covers, bodies as tangled together as our breathing and our kisses and the words whispered in each other's ears.

"You're gorgeous…" Sef tells me.

"You're OK," I tease and then, "Ow!" because he bit my shoulder in retaliation.

"So are we doing this?" Sef squints at me.

"Maybe?" I say. "If you want?"

Sef swallows and laughs. "Oh I want…" He runs a finger up under the line of my bra strap and pulls me gently towards him until I'm close enough to kiss.

Then he pings the strap in a decidedly unsexy manner and pulls away.

"It's not something I've done a lot of."

"Really?" I say, tracing the line of his collarbone with my finger, not quite sure what to say to this. Sef's older than me. And a boy. Who's had at least one girlfriend.

He twangs my bra strap a few times and I lift a hand up to stop him because it's starting to hurt.

"I don't like letting people in, you know?" he says eventually.

His face is too gorgeous when he looks at me like that. Open and vulnerable and nothing like the slightly caddish boy he spends most of his time being.

"I've noticed," I say. "But that's OK."

I wind my hands around his body, luxuriating in the heat of having him this close to me, kissing my way to his ear to whisper, "However much I know of you, whether it's the tip of the iceberg or the whole of your soul, I like it a lot."

"Well, then, it's very convenient that I like you back," he says.

When we next kiss, it's with the sort of feeling that wipes away any doubts about how much he likes me, or how sexy my body is, or whatever doubts Sef might have about letting me in. I press my lips, my nose into his skin and breathe him in, thrilled by the soft hum of a suppressed groan. He's tugging at my knickers and I follow his lead so that the pair of us strip naked under the covers, clashing teeth, bumping elbows and shins and giggling and kissing.

We are clumsy. His hands are cold. There is a lot of apologizing and the occasional gasp that comes from discomfort not desire, as he touches me in places I've only ever touched myself.

None of it is how I imagined.

It's not desperately romantic, or even that sexy at certain points. But it is also exciting and comforting, and when my stomach makes a strange noise, Sef doesn't push me away and look repulsed, he just laughs and kisses my belly button. We're both nervous, both happy, both excessively, awkwardly polite at times, hazy on whether we're doing everything the way we're supposed to.

But whether we are or we aren't, it feels right.

Afterwards, when I pull on my T-shirt to run to the loo, I sit there on the toilet and think of the conversations I've heard at school – girls who've been disappointed with whoever they've done it with; or Chloe, who Gemma told me cried when she slept with her boyfriend because she was afraid of what he'd say about her…

But I don't feel like that at all.

I've had sex with someone that I like as much after as I did before. More importantly, I like *myself* as much.

CHAPTER 26

It's D-Day and the messages ahead of meeting up have been flying so fast between the three of us, that the only sleep I get is on the journey there, napping in Mrs B's passenger seat on the way to the biggest shopping centre in the UK.

Moz is waiting for us in a low-key coffee shop, hair hidden by a striped beanie pulled down to his eyebrows.

"Hey hey," he says, attention lingering on Sef a little longer than it does on me.

His morning has been spent meeting and greeting all the winners of the competition. He arranged for them to come in groups of ten to a nearby cafe laid out with brunch. This is something he does whenever he makes public appearances. It's one of the reasons he's got such a devoted following – and why reddit is rife with stories of the subsequent hook-ups.

This time, though, it's all business. He's been handing out T-shirts and masks and very strict instructions about where to sit and what to do (no throwing crockery/glass/cutlery, no hot food, try and aim for each other). And he's made them sign an agreement that if they get caught, they're on their own – all emails and chats were deleted in front of Moz before he'd let them leave.

"Man, it's like we're planning some kind of terrorist

attack." Then he glances at Sef. "No offence."

There's an excruciating second in which Sef looks at Moz – other people's ignorance and fear distilled into one diamond-hard stare.

"If all the most famous serial killers are white, does that mean I should worry about you, Moz?"

"I didn't mean—"

"No one ever does." Sef sighs and says he's going to the toilet.

"Where's he from, anyway?" Moz nods as Sef leaves.

"Britain," I say, the same way I heard Sef say it to someone on the bus once.

"Touchy much?"

"Rude much?" I reply.

You can tell Moz is thinking about pushing it further, but then he bursts out laughing and shakes his head.

"Sorry. I don't mean to be such a dick."

"But you are, Moz." I pat his hand as if I'm joking. "You are..."

Smoothly, Moz lays his other hand on top of mine, trapping it.

"The dick who's handing you your dream on a platinum platter, Truth Girl." But then he's turning to Sef, who's returned from the loo, making the same apology he just made to me. Big grin, expansive gestures, faux humility.

I remind myself: Moz gets the power, we get the money.

The wait until 11.45 is agonizing as I sit at my designated table in the food court, several plates of throwable food in front of me – doughnuts sticky with icing, a plate of chips, little pots of barbecue and tomato sauce with the tops peeled open to detonate on impact, the most aerodynamic vegetables the salad bar had to offer and three paper cups of ice slowly turning to water.

It's down to me to be the first to throw. Apparently our viewers need to see more of my personality.

I think of the crowds around me now, the people who are going to watch me do this in real life as well as online. Would I have been so keen to help Sef if I'd known it would lead me here?

Six minutes to go.

Fear spirals up from the bottom of my gut, swirling through my stomach and stroking the back of my throat. I'm as frightened of succeeding as I am of failing. Getting caught means my parents finding out, getting into actual *real* trouble, but not getting caught… What if this video's as successful as we want it to be?

What then?

A human body shouldn't be allowed to feel all these things at once. It's too confusing to be excited and frightened and anxious and impatient.

There is nothing I want to do less than stand up on this table in … *four minutes'* (oh God…) time.

Every nerve in my body is fired up ready for action and I'm more fidgety than Sef as I glance round, looking to where he's positioned, wishing he was here to tell me that I can do this the way he did in that alley off Covent Garden.

He should have my GoPro rolling to make sure he captures a nice wide shot of the opening scene and I worry briefly about him lining it up perfectly. Sef's not the best when it comes to cinematography…

Two minutes.

You can see Moz on the far side of the food court. He hasn't bothered with a mask or T-shirt – he's confident his fast talk, fame and fortune are enough to get him out of anything.

It's something I've seen echoes of in Sef – hints of recklessness showing through in some of our latest videos and in the way he drove here today…

Seeing Sef acting like Moz, like he too believes nothing can go wrong, makes me wonder what Kam, who's lost so much, would make of the things his brother's doing to help him.

I look down: time to start filming.

Pulling down my mask, I press record on the camera harnessed under my top, then turn to my phone.

"Hey hey." It comes out exactly the way Moz says it. "It's me, Truth Girl. Behold my weapons of mass destruction."

I pick my phone up and scan my arsenal before flipping it back to film me.

"Locked and carb-loaded and ready to go." Unzipping my top, I reveal the rolling camera underneath. My hand is shaking as I hold my fingers up for the final countdown. "Five … four … three … two…"

I don't want to do this.

"… one."

My limbs lock and I stay exactly where I am, frozen to the chair. I can't do this.

I'm back in the park, people turning to look at me, but

before I can fall into that trap, I grasp for memories of Kam, of finally finishing *Moon* last weekend, the bookmark tucked between the pages of the graphic novel we've been reading since someone gave it to him for Christmas, the comms app that allows him to say so much by doing so little.

I will do this for him.

In a series of scrapes and bangs, I clamber onto the table, pick up a doughnut and stand tall, one arm drawn back, ready to fire.

"FOOD FIGHT!" I yell and I throw my doughnut in a perfect lob across the food court, aiming right for Moz's bright blue head.

It is chaos. Stationed all around the tables, people who've paid for the privilege jump up to start hurling foodstuffs. A spring roll sails past and there's a scream as someone slops spaghetti right in one girl's face. Drinks go flying, showering the tables they pass with a rainbow of different slushies. There are kids crying, parents shouting – some of the people who work behind the different counters are yelling at us to get off the tables.

Now it's started, I've no control over the situation. I barely feel in control of myself as I jump down, scooping up my ammunition, and run. Spinning round, I hunt for Sef, but with food flying, surrounded by masked strangers in our TRUTH and DARE T-shirts, it's impossible to tell who's who. My aim is appalling and I'm aware that I've just iced a couple of innocent bystanders too slow to get under their table. Some of them are joining in, though, and I wince as I hear a plate smash.

"FOOD ONLY, YOU TWAT!" Moz yells at the top of his lungs.

An arm snakes out of nowhere and grabs at my T-shirt, but my momentum carries me back out of their grasp.

I'm coated in slops, there's curry in my ear and something cold and wet sliding down into my knickers. All of us draw gradually closer to Moz, who's getting the worst of it, until someone who's standing on the table in a DARE T-shirt shouts from his vantage point, "Get Truth Girl!" and a volley of pizza slices thwap me right in the chest as I throw my arms up *Platoon*-poster style as if I've been shot.

We're laughing, shouting, squealing and I forget why I'm here, what I'm doing, lost in the allure of complete abandon. Enjoying myself.

Until someone blasts a whistle so piercing that everyone – bystanders and participants – pauses.

The signal to get out.

CHAPTER 27

We get away with it. The food fight goes viral. Like *properly* viral. It gets posted onto one of the big share sites – spat out into everyone's feed so that people from all over the internet – the world – come to watch our video.

On Moz's channel.

After all, he's the one who took the risk, the one who thought up the challenge, who got caught. It's his agent who talked the shopping centre out of pressing charges and into hosting an apologetic fundraiser where members of the public can pay to throw foam pies at a penitent Moz as he stands in stocks.

I wonder whether anything has *ever* gone wrong for Moz? But.

The challenge has done something to Sef. Broken him. Made him angry. From the moment he picked me up this morning, his mood has been toxic and we've already had a row about the angry email he sent Moz yesterday, asking if what Moz is paying his agent costs more than the amount we've raised in donations. Now he's returned to grumbling about what we've filmed.

"We're so stupid. We should have done something to tag onto the end of the food-fight video saying what we're going to do next."

"I know, you said." About twenty times already. At least he's stopped grumbling about how long it took Moz to edit and upload the video – if he'd said it one more time, I might have screamed. Moz had so much footage to cut together it must have been a nightmare and it only took him five days to do it. That video is an *incredibly* impressive achievement and Moz is a little bit my new hero for it.

"Everyone's just stopped donating!" Sef sits back down and pulls the laptop over to show me. "Look."

It's not like I need to. Sef might think he's the only one who keeps an eye on these things, but that's not the case.

Miss Stevens once talked us through the take-up ratio of advertising campaigns across different media streams and the figure was shockingly low. We always knew this. It's just that even if it stayed the same percentage, the amount should have increased with the views, right? Like, two per cent of a million is bigger than two per cent of a hundred.

But the point Sef is driving at is that no one donates without an incentive, and we haven't given them one.

"Should we try Skyping Moz?" I suggest.

Sef ignores me and I lie back on the window seat taking in the state of the caravan. The whole place is looking lived in. One of us (Sef) had left a banana skin in the bathroom bin and after a week's missed filming, it has withered to brown and turned the air sweet. Mugs and crummy plates are stacked up by the sink, bits of biscuit and dare debris trodden into the carpet. In the next room, the bed's rumpled, half the covers sliding off onto the floor, the bottom sheet hanging loose in one corner. If Uncle Danish turned up, you couldn't blame him for thinking we'd been using the place as some kind of kinky crack den, what with the handcuffs from one of the dares and the bits of tin foil that drop off every time we move the reflectors.

Next to me, Sef scrolls listlessly through the latest batch of comments.

"Look," I say, reading one of the less pleasant ones over his increasingly tense shoulder. "We can either sit here getting worked up about it, or we can—"

"I'm not in the mood."

I take a second to absorb that verbal slap before carrying on, "... film some dares, or a truth, like we used to." When there's no indication that he's listening, I lean over and push down the lid of the laptop. "Sef. I'm serious. What you're doing won't make you feel better."

"And you'd know?"

I think of all those hours I wasted scrolling through #MilkTits. "Yes, I would."

Sef scowls at me, trying to find something he can fix his anger on.

"What's the point, anyway?" He throws his phone across the room and shoves my laptop roughly off his knee. "We've got about a month to do the impossible. No one gives a shit why we're doing this."

"I do."

"You say that, but it's not your way of life that's at risk." His voice is so bitter it takes me a moment to react.

"No, it's Kam's," I say quietly, hurt when Sef glances away. "I don't know what you want me to say, Sef."

"Why do you always have to say something?"

"So I should just shut up?"

"Sometimes." Sef retreats deeper into himself, folding his arms around his body, slouching into the cushions.

"I can't touch you, can't talk to you. Remind me why I'm here again?"

"You don't have to be."

"Fine. *Fine*. I don't want to spend the day watching you swim about in self-pity when this is exactly what you wanted." I start gathering my stuff together, but Sef's between me and the laptop and he stands up to block me.

"How is this what I want?" he snaps.

"You wanted Moz to help us raise our profile – he has. You wanted him to help us raise money – he has."

I want to shout at him that this has come at a cost to me too – that every night I struggle to sleep because I can't help worrying that the next hit the food fight gets might be someone who knows me. That I'll wake up in the morning to find that it isn't just a few hundred people who know what my boobs look like, but a few hundred thousand. The video has been taken down and James' phone and hard drive wiped by his enraged parents, but I'll bet Isaac or Vijay have a copy stashed somewhere.

Sef puts his hands to his face, roaring into them in frustration before opening them out, his eyes blazing behind his glasses.

"It's still not enough to save him!"

If I wasn't so upset, his words would have made me crumble. But anger makes me strong. Brutal.

"Stop saying we're going to *save* him. That's not what we're doing – Kam had an accident and nothing you do will change that. You know how hard it's been for him to get this far – it's *impossible* for him to recover. You get that, don't you?" I search his face for a comprehension I can't see. "Sef? Tell me you understand."

His eyes flutter closed for a moment before he turns away. "Yeah. Whatever. I know."

The window seat creaks as he collapses onto it, his head falling into his hands and I sit next to him to slide an arm round him. For a moment it seems like he might shrug me off, but then he leans into me, my nose and lips pressed into his hair as I kiss the back of his head.

We've five weeks to make double what we did on the food fight and for the first time since we started, I feel like giving up.

They've mixed up Kam's speech and language therapy over the past few weeks. Although he's still using the app, he's also talking. It's been hard. His words are slurred and ill-formed and he's quick to anger if you take too long to understand, but this is *his voice* and for all it's stressful, it's also kind of wonderful.

We haven't done much reading today, or talking really, but in the months we've been friends, I've learned that Kam's life is less about quantity and more about quality.

"OK?" Kam says, gesturing towards me.

"Yeah, sorry. I'm just…" I was thinking how Kam would react to having to move somewhere new, starting a different programme, working with different therapists.

"Sad." The S is hard for him to get out.

"I am," I say. "Can I have a hug?"

Kam nods.

I lean across and wrap my arms around his shoulders. He smells like a hospital, but also like the person he is underneath.

"Thank you." My voice is strong and true with gratitude for Kam being in my life.

Kam laughs when I let go, and I smile so much that it hurts.

The second I'm out of his door, the smile crumbles into tears and I barely get as far as the closed-off stairs before I have to sit down, head in my hands as I cry from the deepest depths of my soul for everything that Kam's been through. I cry for the accident that happened, the pain he suffers and the fear and darkness and apathy that recovery has brought with it. I want to howl with rage at the thought of him having to face yet another battle that is not of his own making.

I cry because I nearly failed him.

Whatever comes next, I will do it.

It's late on Monday and I've already gone to bed when my phone lights up.

I've made up with Moz.

That's fantastic!!!

The only chance we have – the only way to make the last four months matter – is to keep rolling the dice, and it's Moz who's keeping us at the table. The joy I used to get from planning our dares and editing our videos has drained away since we met him. Neither me nor Sef have ever been in this for the fame and I'm finding the price hard to pay – the pressure to log in every day and interact with everyone, the racist slurs against Sef and the endless comments about my weight that have multiplied with more consistency than the donations.

Moz is a fool's golden ticket, but it's the only one we've got and I'm pleased Sef's made up with him. I wonder how much crawling it took…

My phone flashes again.

And we've settled on a new dare, way bigger than the food fight.

…? It's late and I'm tired and I want him to get to the point.

Moz thinks we should keep it a surprise.

From the viewers?

Yup.

But he's still typing.

And you.

Me???

Trust me, it'll work.

But it's becoming harder to trust Sef the way he's been behaving and rather than reply, I turn my phone off for the first time in months and close my eyes. If he wants an answer from me, he's going to have to wait.

Even if we both already know I'll say yes.

FEBRUARY

CHAPTER 28

The video we cobbled together of Dare Boy and Moz challenging me to a mystery dare has been super popular, but the donations aren't taking off the way they did before, which is a problem.

We're 40k short. Sef typed.

And?

We've been through this and I imagine Moz rolling his eyes.

So we need to do 2 x dares before the end of the month. Not just this one.

Moz is adamant we can't set the target higher than twenty thousand pounds or we won't make it. The problem is that the food fight had a three-week build up and Moz was able to bait people into making larger donations in order to come on board. Not an option for this one, apparently.

Can we get this one out of the way first? I type. I'm sitting next to Sef on the window seat of the caravan and wiggle my feet further under his thigh to keep them warm.

I'm worried about him. Something's not right about this dare, but no matter how hard I push him on it, he won't give in.

Saturday 15th?

Can't. It's my mum's birthday.

Sef tuts.

"Well, it is," I say. "We're going out for dinner that night."

"Means moving my Sunday shift," he grumps, but when Moz agrees to the sixteenth, he doesn't argue.

What if we've not met the target, do we still film?

YES. Sef types, shooting me a furious glare. We've already had this discussion.

"I want Moz's opinion," I say.

We film on schedule, I'll tease the footage and get people to meet the target before we release the full thing.

"See?" Sef mutters and I give him a gentle nudge with my socked foot.

"I wasn't trying to be difficult. I'm pleased there's a solution."

Sef relents and runs a finger down the sole of my foot so that I scream out and try to snatch it back. I send Moz a typo-riddled reply before leaping up and running from the window seat to the bedroom.

When Sef catches up, tickling turns into kissing, which turns into things we don't have the time to be doing when we've filming still to do.

"You can tell me what the dare is, Moz doesn't need to know you've told me," I whisper into Sef's skin. It's not the right time to have brought it up, but I can't seem to let it go.

"Don't do this, Claire. You know I can't…" He kisses me, but I'm no longer comfortable with what we're doing, not when all I can think about is that he's keeping secrets from me.

"Friends are supposed to be straight with each other, Sef," I say, echoing his words back to him.

There's nothing I can think to say that will convince him to choose me over Moz. I get up and start pulling on the clothes I should never have taken off.

Sleep has become so elusive I've barely been able to catch it at all and when I do, my brain can't seem to hold on to it, waking minutes after I'm down, my eyes drawn to check for light beyond my curtains, swinging to the red glare of my alarm clock...

Sunday. All I've done is run through the things I think we might be doing today, only it seems the more I try to stretch my imagination, the more limited it becomes. Whenever I try to talk to Seren and Rich about it, all I get is a lecture on standing up for myself and saying no, but they don't know Kam. To them he's just a boy who went to our school – they don't understand that the Kam they knew isn't the one I'm desperate to help.

At breakfast I'm so clumsy that I can barely coordinate pouring my own cornflakes, let alone adding milk.

"What on earth's wrong with you?" Mum tuts as she mops up the mess rather than risk me making things worse.

"Nothing."

I don't need to look up to know she's exchanging a glance with Dad over the breakfast bar.

"Ready to drive up to the Recreare in fifteen?" he asks, eyeing my pyjamas.

"Sure..." I slurp up some cornflakes and earn a reproving

glare from Mum. "You don't mind me going out later, do you?"

"Where and why?" Mum asks.

"The guys from Film Club want to try getting some night shots of the water. By the river."

If my parents ever string together the weird things I've said we've done at Film Club, they're going to wonder what kind of film we're making. Something avant-garde with no plot and lots of style that I would never actually watch, I reckon.

"So long as you promise to dedicate at least some of this half-term to schoolwork…" Mum warns.

"Cross my heart."

Mum reaches over to take my empty bowl and gives Dad a careless kiss on the shiny skin on the top of his head. There's a tenderness in the gesture that I've not seen around the house for a very long time and I think of how fun last night was, laughing with Dad at Mum's embarrassment over a sparkler-laden tiramisu and a chorus of "Happy Birthday" from the other diners.

Maybe after tonight I should give a little less of myself to the Malik family and give a little more to my own.

The day is bright and warm and when I get to the Rec, the nurse on duty in the Bueller Wing suggests that she wheel Kam out onto the terrace. It bites into the time I'm supposed to read, finding a good spot where the shadows of the trees won't interfere with the heat of the sun.

And there we sit, me next to him, graphic novel propped

open against my knees as my feet rest on the low wall of the terrace. It is a perfect and beautiful hour. The lawns are vast and quiet and in the still of a Sunday morning I can hear birdcall and the faintest rustle of a breeze in the trees. In the cool of the air. I lean in closer to Kam, sharing his heat and his company.

When the nurse returns to help me bring him in, Kam stops her.

"Claire." He nods his head to where I'm already standing behind him. "Push me."

I'm intensely glad that he can't see how hard I'm trying not to cry.

Later, once I have transformed into Truth Girl and the sky is mellowing into dusk, I hurry down my road to find Sef waiting in the layby. When he sees me approach, he winds the window down and leans across from the driver's seat.

"Hey, pretty lady, you need a ride?" The curve of his lips and the mischief in his eyes tugs at my heart and the irritation I've felt these last few weeks dissipates, resurfacing sharply when Sef pulls out into the road where there isn't a gap and a horn blares.

"Could we stay alive long enough to actually do the dare, do you think?"

Sef glances over, scowl replaced with a wolfish grin. "How many times do I have to tell you to trust me?"

I want to tell him that it doesn't matter how many times he tells me, it doesn't mean I can do it. Not when he's driving like this.

"Where's Moz?"

"Meeting us there."

"You're not going to tell me where 'there' is, are you?"

Sef answers with a mirthful, "What do you think?"

We turn into the industrial estate and Sef reaches over to squeeze my hand, the warmth of his skin anchoring my rising anxiety. Sef might get risky with himself, but he wouldn't do that for someone he cares about.

Finally, right on the edge of the estate, where there's as much wasteland as there are warehouses, Sef drives onto a track of land, kills the engine and checks his phone.

"Moz'll be here in five." His leg is jiggling now it's no longer occupied with the accelerator. "Let's get set up."

"What do you mean? Set up where?"

But Sef's already out of his seat and walking round, setting up my camera on the back seat before positioning sandbags on the dashboard and squinting through the viewfinder of the GoPro strapped on top, pointing forward to film out of the windscreen.

"Are we filming in the car?" An unnecessary question, if ever there was one.

"Chill, will you?"

I wasn't aware that I was heating up, but I do as I'm told, sitting in my seat as he looks through the viewfinder of the camera set up in the back, before clipping my phone ("Moz'll call mine – don't want to interrupt filming") into the holder, angling and flipping the view so the screen shows him sitting in the driver's side.

"Very professional," I mutter.

"You're not the only one who knows how to watch a tutorial…" Sef kisses my cheek. "Now, put your mask on and let's do a little filming."

"Where's Moz? Are we racing him?"

"Yeah…" Sef kisses my head. "Put your mask on, please, Truth Girl."

Once the cameras are on, Sef claps to sync the sound and turns to look at me.

"Hey hey, Truth Girl."

"Dare Boy." His mood is infectious and I feel my mouth twitching up into a smile. It has always been impossible to resist the way he makes me feel, his emotions so all-encompassing that they swallow up my own.

"Ready for your surprise?"

"I don't like surprises."

"Not even really good ones?"

"Define good?"

"Exciting."

"You and I have different definitions of exciting. Why don't you tell everyone where we are and why?"

Sef obliges, turning the engine on and revving it, pretending that he's the sort of person who finds the noise a turn-on, when I know full well that the only thing he really cares about is whether there's petrol in the tank.

His phone buzzes and he flips the speaker phone on for Moz.

"Meep morp, Mozzy here. You chickens ready to hatch?"

I pull a face at Sef, but he doesn't see.

"Egg timer's on for one minute." And then he hangs up

and flips the little egg timer that's sitting in the cupholder.

"What?" None of this is making any sense. "How can we race Moz when he isn't here?"

"He will be." Sef's fingers beat a drum roll on the wheel. The egg timer's half empty.

"Tell me what we're doing," I say, frightened now. This is not how races start.

"You'll see."

"I don't want to!" The words burst out of me in a panic. "Tell me what we're doing!"

It's as if my whole body has pins and needles, my hands going numb so that they don't seem to behave as I reach for the door. There's a clunk.

"What are you doing?" Sef yells at me as I yank at the handle and I realize that he's locked the doors. "Calm the fuck down, will you?"

"I can't!" There's a balloon swelling inside me, squashing the air from my lungs.

"Well…" Sef glances at the egg timer, the last few grains of sand sliding from the top to the bottom. "Goddammit, you have to."

And then he turns from me to the windscreen, drawing my attention with it, to see a pair of headlights flare up and flash once, twice, three times at the other end of the track.

This is not a race…

Sef revs the engine once more before leaning over – so fast I don't have time to move – and kissing me.

"We'll be fine, I promise," he whispers into my mouth.

And then he's gone, his reassurance an echo on my lips,

an alarm bell in my mind. Sef slams his foot to the floor, the engine roaring out as loud and terrifying as a dragon, as Mrs Bennet leaps forward, gravel clattering on the car as it snakes to the side.

"SEF!" I yell, no longer caring about the cameras, pressing myself hard back against my seat, my legs braced in the footwell, all my weight pressing down on a pair of imaginary brakes, because we're heading straight for Moz's car.

And Moz's car is heading for ours.

But Sef isn't listening – he's shouting out his own battle-cry, mouth open wide in a smile I don't recognize that makes me hate him and fear for him…

"Stop! Please!" I beg. "This isn't funny!"

My throat hurts, my lungs hurt, my body hurts from bracing itself. The lights ahead are so bright I can't think and I yank on the door handle again even though we're going too fast for me to jump and I've got my belt on. And I'm hopeless and helpless and I lash out at the boy in the driver's seat, thumping his arm with everything I've got.

"Ow! Get off."

"We're going to die! *Please!*" I'm sobbing and begging and he's still driving and my heart is breaking and we're going to die and it's going to hurt…

I squeeze my eyes shut.

There's my mum kissing my dad's head this morning, Seren correcting my French accent and the squashed and crumpled present Rich gave me for my birthday that turned out to be a pair of socks with tapirs' faces on the toes …

and there is Sef, heart-breaking and half-broken, running his hands across my scalp … and there is Kam typing on his new keyboard to tell me I could hug him.

My life is wonderful and I don't want to die.

The scream that feels like it's ruptured my lungs is as much anger as it is fear.

PART TWO: SEF MALIK

When death stares you in the face, you confess.
You're not going to like any of it.
I don't.

AUGUST

CHAPTER 1

Claire might believe I first saw her in the car park of the Rec, but like everyone else, the first time I noticed Claire Casey was because of her tits.

Matty was too busy sniggering into his phone to see Finn walk up behind him and shoot him in the head.

"Aw, mate – we're meant to be on the same team!"

"Pay attention, then." Finn's always taken gaming seriously.

Matty leaned forward off the sofa to show us the clip he'd been watching – some shoddy footage of a bunch of vaguely recognizable people from school messing around in the park.

"And we're watching this because…?" I said, wanting to get back to the game.

"Wait for it." Matty's whole-body grin kept me watching, until one of the girls stood upright and….

"Nip slip!" Matty yelled with the same glee that had gone into editing the video as the action slowed to zoom in on a generous pair of breasts.

Finn shook his head and told Matty not to be such a dick before getting up to fetch another can of pop from the kitchen.

"Give it here." I reached out for Matty's phone and

played the whole thing again. "Do we know who she is?"

"She'll be Milk Tits from now on," Matty said, referring to the title of the video.

"Gross."

"Imagine getting your hands on them."

But she was all flesh and curves and skin that reminded me of raw fish. "I'd rather not."

Matty laughed at the face I was pulling. "How much would I have to pay you to go there?"

"Couldn't afford it, mate."

Matty was still trying to goad me into hooking up with "Milk Tits" when Finn returned.

"Tell me you're not still watching that stupid video."

"Oh, but we are!" Matty crowed.

"You haven't shared it, have you?" Finn was looking at Matty, brows lowered in disapproval, assuming that because it was Matty's phone, he was the one who needed warning. But as Matty widened his eyes in genuine innocence, I was the one hitting share on the link.

All's fair in love and lolz.

That happened before the accident, when I'd no idea what it was like to walk down the corridor, sympathy creasing people's lips as I passed, silent stares gobbed onto the side of my face, pity haunting every conversation.

The girl in the car park knew what it was like to be famous for something you hate.

One little lie. No big deal.

CHAPTER 2

Kam got his results the week before I got mine and Mum went on the offensive, calling every family member, every friend, shouting "He got in!" down the phone at them. She told the woman who knocked on the door asking to read the gas meter. She told the man who always walks his dog past our house. She told the cat.

Kam drew the line when she tried to tell the wait staff at lunch.

"No one cares, Mum."

"I care." She patted and squeezed his hand and beamed around the table at her brood. "Cambridge!"

Uncle Danish hid his amusement behind his menu. Lunch was his treat and he'd taken us to the gourmet diner where the burgers are named after American presidents because he knew it was one of Kam's favourites. Not that this stopped Dad from grumbling at the price of asking for extra cheese on his Nixon.

Afterwards, we split up – Dad had a job on and Uncle D a medical exam for the contract he'd accepted, and Mum wanted to spend her afternoon off uniform shopping with Amir, leaving me to hitch a lift home with the man of the hour.

"Seventeen days till I get behind the wheel..." I patted

Mrs Bennet's dashboard and shot Kam a sly look.

"If you get so much as a scratch on her, I'll kill you. Put your belt on."

"You won't know. Too busy making posh friends at your posh college, spending your free money on liquefied caviar and champagne lollies."

"Think I'll be spending my bursary on things like rent and Sainsbury's Basics, actually."

But it was my way of congratulating him and he knew it.

Pulling out onto the main road, we joined the queue of traffic over the bridge. Sunlight glittered off the surface of the river, so low that the banks had turned a dusty brown.

The drop from the viaduct didn't look so bad from the road bridge, but I knew how much worse it looked from up high, feet planted on the wall ready to jump. Tombstoning off there after I finished my exams was the biggest rush I'd ever had.

"You going out later?" I asked, still looking out the window.

"Going to hang with the lads."

"You really know how to celebrate."

"Some of us can celebrate without trying to shove our tongue down the throat of every girl in a five-mile radius."

"I'll limit myself to one when Laila gets back."

Kam grinned, lopsided, knowing. "Sure…"

It annoyed me.

"So how are you going to celebrate? Paint the town red and watch as it dries?"

He nodded out of the window. "Because getting trashed and leaping off the viaduct is so much cooler."

"I *am* cooler. Face it."

"Stupider."

"Braver."

Kam dropped me home and went round Danny's, leaving me to bum around on the PlayStation without Amir's back-seat commentary. All through the afternoon and on into the evening, Kam messaged me pictures of what he was up to – Hamish hanging upside down from the branch of a tree, his T-shirt slipped down to expose a body hairier than Uncle D's and Danny eating a hot dog suggestively. The same sorts of pictures I'd send him if I was out with Finn and Matty.

The last was a selfie of all three of them squashed together under an almost-blue sky shot through with the rose-gold veins of a perfect summer sunset.

I replied with a photo of me and Amir slobbed on the sofa.

You're the one missing out. Taken's on in half an hour.

Mum and Dad were clattering about in the kitchen when my phone went off at the other end of the sofa.

"Pass it over." I nudged Amir, but the sulky little tit never does what I tell him. By the time I'd clambered across him, angling my knees and elbows to squash the softest parts of his body, my phone had rung out. Frowning down at the screen I saw it was Danny and assumed it was a mistake. Until it rang again.

"Hello?" I answered, slapping Amir on the arm so he'd mute the telly.

"Sef?" There was loads of noise in the background and

I smacked Amir harder when he turned the TV up instead of down. "Are you with your parents?"

"Er … mate, why are you calling my phone and asking for my folks?"

"Shit! I haven't – just – are you with them?"

Which is when I heard the siren.

Hospitals are one of the most confusing places on the planet. Like Ikea, but without the meatballs. I never knew how many ways there are to be sick, every sign pointing to a different "-ology"/"-opathy"/"-otomy" department, wards and units and wings.

Kam was in intensive care: full-on wires and tubes and wash-your-eyeballs-before-you-even-look-at-a-patient scary. I'd sit next to my brother's bed, the wash of whispered conversations flowing in and around the beeps and whirs and whooshes of the machines. Found it impossible to say anything myself – not like Amir, who'd shuffle as close as he could and talk as if Kam lying there with a hole in his head was no different to Kam sitting across the dinner table.

Mum's work gave her leave so she spent mornings at Kam's bedside. Afternoons, Dad would take over Kam duty while Mum went home and read everything the internet had to offer on traumatic brain injuries, gathering lists of questions. Dad took night jobs where he could and slept in the mornings and Uncle Danish left his caravan and came to live on our sofa, ferrying me and Amir over to the hospital whenever we asked.

Ferrying me to West Bridge to get my exam results – the

kind that would have been worth celebrating if everything else hadn't felt so tragic.

For as long as Kam was unconscious, the best was as possible as the worst. We see-sawed between hope and horror: living through hell when Kam had to go back into surgery because of a brain bleed, hearts soaring when he survived.

Seventeen days since the fall.

Seventeen years since I'd been born.

His eyes opened and we thought it was a miracle. Only it wasn't the one we were hoping for.

The impact on his skull and spine had paralysed his left arm, damaged the part of his brain that deals with emotions and communications and left his body unable to regulate bodily functions so basic you never really think about them. Things like swallowing. Going to the loo. Things you never knew had anything to do with your brain. Kam could breathe, but he couldn't speak, couldn't focus, couldn't control his movements.

Once stable, he was moved to a different ward, one in which the focus was on the injuries his body could heal while the doctors assessed the injuries it couldn't, measuring his reflexes, responses, his ability to communicate. Eight or below on the Glasgow Coma Scale means a serious brain injury: Kam wasn't scoring above a five.

Death is an ending, but Kam had been given a beginning.

I didn't want either. All I've ever wanted is my brother back.

SEPTEMBER

CHAPTER 3

Ever since we moved to this house, I'd been jealous of Kam for having a room to himself.

"First thing I'm going to do is repaint." I leaned against the doorframe and surveyed the string-coloured walls. "Something bright and sunny. Like my personality."

"Calm your tits, sunshine," Kam said, not looking up from Mum's laptop. "Maybe wait until I get offered a place before you start *Grand Design*-ing the place."

"You're not the one who has to share with halitosis in human form."

Kam glared up at me a moment.

"He's downstairs," I said. "Smearing pus and misery on the sofa."

Puberty was attacking Amir like a flesh-eating disease – the bin in our room was stuffed with tissues he'd used to mop up the fluid leaking from his face, taking whatever personality he had with it. Me and Amir had never got on, but this spotty, sullen, hormonal version was even more of a ball ache than the little kid who told tales all the time and cried whenever he didn't get his own way.

"Like you were a bundle of laughs."

"I've *always* been a bundle of laughs. That's my role in this family – to bring joy."

Only Kam wasn't really listening. "Shut the door, would you?"

Curious, I did as he said, sitting on the floor, my back against the wall, feet propped up on the bed frame – private it might be, but that room is a shoebox. Kam pushed the computer off his lap to lean forward, elbows resting on his knees, expression as serious as if he was about to answer a question on *University Challenge*.

"Does he ever say anything about school?" he asked.

"Not to me. Why?"

"Hamish said he saw some kid shoving Amir around at breaktime, but Amir got all pissy with me when I asked him about it."

"Amir gets pissy when I ask what cereal he's having."

Kam frowned. "This was different. Angry, like I was sticking my nose in…"

I shoved him gently with my foot and he swatted it away. "That's *your* role in the family, Kam. To be a bundle of sticking your nose in."

"I'm looking out for him!"

"Amir needs to look out for himself," I said, bored of the conversation. "Stop babying him."

Kam shrugged and stood up to kick me out, wanting to get back to geeking over gas giants or red dwarves or pink midgets. Space spunk stuff.

"Family take care of each other, Sef," he said, eyes wide and solemn. "When I'm not here, I need to know you'll look out for Amir the way I've always looked out for you, yeah?"

"Do I have to inherit your responsibilities, too? Can't I just have the room?"

"It's a package deal. Now get out."

Redecorating was the last thing on my mind when me and Mum packed up Kam's stuff to take to the Rec. Mum was relentless, her conversation a stream of positive thinking at how lucky we were for him to move somewhere so good, so close, as I stood on the bed untacking his posters.

I should have known she was faking it. We all were.

Mum pulled open his chest of drawers and stared down at a jumble of T-shirts, shut it, opened the next and started taking out all his sweaters and hoodies, tutting and throwing them onto the bed until she pulled one from the back of the drawer and held it up.

Rust-coloured, faded, with one of the ties starting to fray at the end.

"He hates that one," I said.

"I know my own son, thank you, Yousef! But it's the only one with a zip!" She gestured wildly as if I couldn't see for myself. "And I don't see how I'm going to pull all those other ones over his head—" Her face crumpled in on itself and she bent her head into Kam's hoodie, a fist of material bunched over her mouth, muffling the wail that tried to escape.

I tripped over all the crap on the floor as I went to wrap my arms round her, squeezing her in a hug. Mum's sobs sent shock waves of despair through me, the pair of us folding onto the bed, my arms glued round her like she'd fall apart

if I let go. And we stayed there, that stupid scrunched-up hoodie pressed over my mum's face as if she couldn't bear for me to see her cry.

"I'm sorry," she said eventually, sitting away from me. "You didn't need to see that."

"It's OK…" I stroked her arm the way she does to us when we're upset.

"It's not, Sef." She lifted my hand away to sandwich it between palms smaller than mine. "You have your own burden to bear – there's no need for you to carry mine, too."

"You don't have to hide the fact you're sad, Mum."

Her smile was as sorrowful as her tears. "My son is alive. There are worse things to be sad about." She gave my hand a purposeful pat as if she was done with her woes and stood up to get on with things.

The pile of clothes to take to the Rec was pitifully small by the time we were through. I couldn't even suggest giving him any of mine – Kam's built like a tank. Or he was. Mum wasn't prepared to throw away what was left and I helped her bag it up for the loft, neither of us admitting Kam might never be in a position to need it.

The room looked wrong stripped bare like that.

Still looks wrong, my clothes spilling out the drawers, shelves crammed with Penguin classics and bound scripts, walls a jumble of newspaper clippings and ticket stubs.

The only thing that belongs is the chalkboard hanging on the outside of the door that still says FOUR A*s, BABY!!!

CHAPTER 4

The first full week of sixth form interfered with going to the hospital, but what felt like a relief for me was torture for Amir. Every day he would plough through the front door and bombard whichever parent he found with questions, trailing them round the house the way the cat does when it's her teatime. He'd even follow Dad upstairs to interrogate him through the bathroom door while he was on the loo.

But once Kam moved to the Rec, it was me who got offered the first visit.

"It's tomorrow you have the test, isn't it?" Mum asked while I was sitting in Dad's armchair practising theory tests on my phone.

"Nine in the morning." Roll on driving licence…

"Would you like to drive to the Recreare afterwards?" Mum has an uncanny ability to memorize our timetables faster than any of her three sons and she knew I didn't have any lessons until after lunch.

I looked up from my phone.

"What about Amir?" He'd be narked if we went without him.

"I want to see how Kam is with you before we take Amir." Aware of the look I was giving her, she added, "It's difficult for him, Sef. Kam isn't…" She struggled with finding the

right words, like they might not exist. "He's not good with visitors."

I passed my theory. Booked my practical.

None of it felt real. Unease churned insistently through my mind and my stomach, growing more insistent as we approached the Rec, Mum wincing when I took the speed bump at the gate too quickly. We were welcomed by the brown-brick walls, windows flashing gold in the mid-morning sun as I swung into a parking space.

In reception, Mum signed us in as I stared around at the framed certificates hanging behind the desk. Along the corridors, bland awards gave way to photos of the people who stayed here. People in wheelchairs and walking frames, their crossed-eyes and twisted limbs made more obvious by the able-bodied councillors and celebrities posing with them for a photo op. There were more casual, less posed pictures too – residents and their helpers next to rows of raised flower beds or watching a string quartet in the lounge.

Those pictures stirred something inside me – I'd call it fear, but that makes it sound simple, something that could be tamed and labelled. There was no taming the nightmare I could feel swallowing me up, my body being ingested by something so incomprehensibly terrifying it was nothing but a feeling – a numbness in my fingers, a chill in my blood.

We took the lift up to his floor and dread soaked deeper into the marrow of my bones.

"He'll be pleased to see you," Mum said.

"Will he?" The words came out on a belch of panic.

"Of course he will." A reassurance for her not me.

The lift stopped. Doors opened. Mum walked out.

"Sef?"

I stared at her. The pale yellow walls of the ward loomed large, like a hand reaching out to grasp me, and I could hear someone approaching, the whine of wheels on lino. I couldn't bear the thought of seeing one of those people from the pictures.

Couldn't bear the thought of seeing my brother – *He's not good with visitors.*

"I can't!" I slammed my palm on the button to close the doors before Mum could talk me out of it.

When she came to find me, I was sitting curled up on the wall where I'd met Claire, my head pressed into my knees and my hands over my head.

"I'm so sorry," I whispered as my mum put her arms round me and kissed my head. "I don't think I can see him."

"It's OK," she said and I knew she was crying too.

Friday afternoon Dad cornered me in the kitchen. It was the afternoon and he was still in his work clothes, old shirt and tatty cords, frayed and faded from lifting and carrying and sitting for hours in his van.

"You have to visit your brother."

Ever one to be sensitive.

"I have." Technically. I opened the fridge, blocking Dad out.

"I meant at the home. He'll want to see you."

I said nothing, scanning the contents of the fridge and seeing nothing.

"So?" Dad peered round the fridge door. "Are you coming with us tomorrow?"

We'd planned to go as a family mid-morning, when they said Kam was at his best. The thought made me feel sick.

"I…" (wanted to say yes) "… don't… I'll try."

"What is there to *try?*"

I shut the fridge, hands empty. "It's hard, Dad—"

"You think it is *easy* for me? For your mother? *Easy* for Amir?"

We were standing in the arch between the lounge and the dining area and my gaze drifted to the table, where Amir had put an old poster frame. He'd been printing out pictures and digging out photos from albums and frames to arrange inside. A project for Kam's room at the Rec. A room I'd not seen, but Amir had visited without difficulty the day before.

It *did* seem easy for Amir.

But Dad hadn't finished. "And what about Kamran, do you not think it is harder for him than for any of us?"

I couldn't even look at him when he said that, shame stinging me to tears.

All evening I worried about it, the pressure building in my chest until something would burst and I'd start to shake so much that I'd have to put down whatever it was I was trying to concentrate on – a book, the PlayStation controller, the can I was about to sip from. What little I could stomach of my tea came right back up half an hour later.

When Mum came up the stairs carrying the clean

laundry everyone else had forgotten existed, she found me draped over the toilet seat spitting the last of my meal into the bowl.

"Sef..." She poured cold water onto a clean flannel and laid it gently over the back of my neck.

"I'm fine," I said.

"You're sick."

I was spared the visit to the Rec. Hadn't meant to fall asleep.

The bang of the front door woke me up, so drunk on deep sleep that the room span as I heard the familiar double-time of Amir thumping up the stairs and into the bathroom with a slam.

Amir's never done anything delicately.

Used to drive Kam mad when he'd lend Amir something that got returned in pieces...

More stomping along the landing into the room next door and, without wanting to, I pulled myself up and out of bed. The door to our old room was wide open. In the time he'd had it to himself, Amir had set about redoing the place in the style of the local tip.

"How was your visit?" I asked from the landing, not wanting to go any further in case some tentacled beast lurked beneath the layer of crap on the floor.

Amir ignored me, yanking the cupboard open to look for something.

"How's Kam?"

Amir's jaw tightened. "Like you care."

I sighed and went into my room, picking up a script

from where it had slid onto the floor. I read the title – *A View from the Bridge* – and put it down.

"Why haven't you seen him?" Amir had followed me as far as the door, not able to set foot in the room he still felt was Kam's.

"I have." I don't even know why I said it.

"Don't lie. I heard Dad talking." Of course he had. "You're not really sick – so why didn't you come today?"

"I can't explain…"

"*Try!*" he shouted.

"Why? What good's an explanation going to do anyone?"

"Then just go and visit."

"I can't!" I felt trapped. "I tried… It – I couldn't…" That all-consuming fear reached out from my memory, the lift doors opening, the sound of wheels on lino, Mum walking out…

"He's your brother, doesn't that mean *anything*?" Amir was yelling louder now and someone downstairs had opened the lounge door – "What's going on up there?" – but Amir didn't notice. "Why are you being so selfish?"

I stepped over to move him out of the doorway so I could shut the door, shut out the noise, but Amir reacted like I was coming for him and swung for my face.

It wasn't hard to block.

"Fucking hell, Amir! Don't be a dick."

"*You're the dick!*" And he lunged at me.

"Amir!" I wrestled to pin his arms to his sides. "Chill out, will you?"

He was squirming, angry as a pit bull with a bag on

its head, jackknifing his body so that I lost my grip and he brought his head back, smacking me on the chin and knocking me loose. The scrawny little shit piled into me, scrapping and slapping.

"Why won't you see him? Why are you such a coward?"

Someone was coming up the stairs.

"Tell me!"

I couldn't talk, wouldn't fight back, just let myself be pushed to the floor, taking all the flailing, the smacks to my head and chest and arms.

"He's family!" Smack, punch, kick. "GO AND SEE HIM."

"I can't," I whispered.

"WHY NOT?" Amir screeched in my face, spit flying out of his mouth and onto my glasses.

But Dad was there, pulling off my sobbing, struggling little brother, his face webbed with snot.

"It should have been you!"

"Amir!" Dad looked horrified and glanced to where Mum was on the landing, mouth open in shock. "That's enough."

Our parents bundled him away from me and into his room to calm down as I curled up tighter against the corner of my bed.

It should have been you.

I couldn't be in the house the next day, but I'd lost shifts when Kam was in hospital. Brian was still covering my Sundays, and for all Finn would have had me round, I needed to be somewhere I wouldn't have to explain myself. So I messaged Uncle Danish – and because he's my Uncle D, he came to my rescue without question. Took me driving and spent the whole time discussing my technique, the traffic, his caravan, the job he was supposed to leave for that would take him away for the next six months.

207

"Do you have to go?" I glanced over at him, the car wobbling slightly.

"Relax your shoulders, Sef. Take the first exit at the round-about," he said as I slowed to join the queue, indicator ticking. We drove on for a bit longer, until Uncle D directed me to an empty enough road, where we practised manoeuvres.

My turn in the road was near perfect.

"Beginner's luck," Uncle D teased as we pulled over to the kerb for a rest. "When is your test?"

"Seventeenth of October." A month away. "Think I'll pass?"

"You're better than your brother was." He faltered. "At this stage, I mean."

No one likes to talk about Kam in the past tense.

Uncle D took his wallet out of his back pocket, opening up the creased brown leather. "I was going to do this with a little more ceremony, but…" He handed me about eighty quid in twenties. "Book yourself some lessons the week before your test. Make sure you pass."

Kam had taken his twice and it felt wrong to want to beat him, but I accepted the money and thanked my uncle.

"I wish you were staying," I said, pretending it was still about the driving.

"I know." My uncle rested a heavy hand on my shoulder. "Farah told me what happened."

"Dad won't look at me, Amir hates me—"

"Amir *loves* you."

But Uncle D hadn't seen the look that accompanied the words.

"Siblings fight, Sef." His eyes lost focus for a second, like he was remembering long-distant arguments with Mum and Auntie Iffat. "We fight because we love. We struggle because we love."

We weren't talking about me and Amir any more and I studied the wiry white hairs emerging from the black of his eyebrows, avoiding the tenderness in my uncle's gaze.

"Please stay," I whispered. Begged. Prayed.

"I wish I could—"

"You can!"

"This family needs…"

"This family needs *you*." *I* needed him.

"… money."

I frowned down at the wodge of notes in my hand.

"What? We've enough, haven't we?"

"Not if your brother needs to stay where he is."

My attention sharpened. "What do you mean?"

"I shouldn't be talking to you about this—"

"Please. Tell me – no one else will." I sounded so desperate, wanting to be treated with the same respect, the same confidence as Kam would have been.

Uncle D sighed, sinking back into Mrs Bennet's seat and staring out at a ginger cat ambling across the empty road.

"I don't know how much your parents would like me to tell you…" Almost nothing, but I didn't say so. "The first six months of your brother's care is covered by the NHS, but after that, it changes."

"Changes how?"

"I don't even know if I've got this right. It's complicated." Uncle D's hands opened out in his lap in a shrug.

"Do the government stop paying? Just like that?"

"Funding for the next level of care must come from the local health authority. There isn't much to go round and the Recreare is one of the best of its kind, which means a place there is expensive. Perhaps if we had a compensation claim—"

"And we don't?"

"Your brother was trespassing. He ignored the wire and the warning signs on the bridge." His expression was the same I'd seen my parents wear. One of sorrow and sickness that there is nothing to be done about the past.

"What sign?" Mentally I was scrambling up the bank

to the top with Matty and some of the others from school, holding the wire wider for them to get through…

There hadn't been any sign – I was sure of it.

"… notice warning anyone stepping beyond of the risks they face. You ignore the warning, you forfeit liability." As my uncle rubbed his eyes, I tried to process what he'd told me. "Something like that, anyway. I'm not a lawyer. Your mother is talking to people, but…"

There was no hope in the way he said it.

"Why does that mean you have to leave?"

Uncle D turned to look at me once more. "Your brother needs two things, Sef: family and money. Kam has his family. He has his parents, his brothers. Of all of you, I'm the only one in a position to choose to provide the other. This contract in Oman is a good one."

"How much does he need?"

"More than I can earn." Obviously I'd reached the limit of his trust. "But still I must try. And so must you."

But I couldn't. That night, I lay awake, thinking about seeing Kam in intensive care. That whole time felt like a stare-out with death and if we so much as blinked, death would win. Every second I spent away from his bed would have me panicking. Sleep was the only time I got a break, my brain shutting down so effectively that I didn't even dream, waking instead to the nightmare of what had happened. I'd bolt my cereal (breakfast, lunch, tea, each meal the same), barely shower long enough to get wet and I'd sit by the door, like a dog pining for a walk. I'd mentally run through

red lights and straight-line roundabouts on the journey there, walk so fast along the corridors that if Mum was with me she'd have to jog to keep up. And then I'd get to his bedside, watching, waiting and hoping with everything I had that Kam would live.

When I thought he was dying the only place I wanted to be was by my brother's side. Now he was alive, I'd rather be anywhere else.

Amir's disappointment was something I felt in every sullen look over breakfast, every slammed door, every second of the silent car ride to West Bridge. I wanted to tell him that I was disappointed too. That no one could be as ashamed as I was.

The day after I saw Uncle D, I left my stuff and walked up to the Rec from school. With every step, my blood grew thicker, legs and heart and soul heavier. I waded through the weight of my shame and the depths of my fears until I reached the glass doors of the Rec.

Breathing was hard, and it felt like the world was contracting around me. All I had to do was push.

But I couldn't. Instead I sat on the wall for a long, long time, thinking about everything my uncle had said, piecing together an ugly truth.

Back at the start of summer, when my jump off the bridge made the front page of the local paper, there'd been no sign to stop me – but there had been one by the end.

It doesn't take a Cambridge-bound brainbox to work out why. Not only was I a failure as his brother; I was the reason he needed the money.

Your brother needs two things, Sef: family and money.
If I couldn't provide one, I would do anything to provide
the other.

CHAPTER 6

Post was piling up on the top of the radiator next to the front door but the most urgent would make it through to the dining table, where Mum (never Dad) would read it over breakfast before dropping it in the bowl on the sideboard to be dealt with later. Didn't take me long to find the correspondence from the Rec, letters stamped with the logo of a pair of hands cradling the top of a person's head, but these letters were less helpful than I'd hoped. I needed a firm figure.

The best way to get an answer for something is to ask, but there was no way I could ask my parents. Not with things as they were. I'd have to go straight to the source.

Taking a breath and slipping into character, I dialled the number on the letterhead.

Five minutes later and I'd been put through to a very helpful lady who seemed keen to set up a meeting to discuss my fictional mother's care following her stroke.

"Let me get this straight –" my voice smooth and smarmy – "the cost is two thousand five hundred per week?"

"Thereabouts, as I explained, Mr Bibi."

"And you only accept residents whose costs can be covered for how long?"

"Six months, but that shouldn't be a problem if your mother has private healthcare."

I'd said this so they'd take me seriously, but Imaginary Mum's insurance had become more of a hindrance than a help.

"And if I'm wrong and she doesn't?"

"We still need six months guaranteed in advance. The Recreare takes continuity of long-term care seriously."

After ending the call, I tapped the figures into the calculator on my phone, a violent flutter of blind panic breaking out in my chest at the figure I kept getting.

My nerve has always been something I've had going for me.

"Oh my God!"

Kam grabbed my leg and practically hung off me to stop me from climbing over the fence. He was heavy enough that it worked and I scraped my shins and elbows as I slid back down.

"What did you do that for?" I yelled at him, stung at my brother embarrassing me in front of my friends. Izzy Khan and Declan Summers were smirking at each other behind his back.

"What were you doing?"

"Getting our ball back." I shot a shifty look at my friends.

"Have you got a death wish?!" On the other side of the fence, the dog that lived at Number 71 was barking and snarling, the panels of the fence shivering as it threw its body against the wood.

"It's just a dog."

"With teeth!"

"I'm not scared of it..." I turned round as if to try and climb back up, but Kam had me by the collar and yanked me back. This time when I stumbled round, Izzy and Declan weren't looking so smug. No one likes seeing another family row.

"You're an idiot then – that dog wears a muzzle in the park."

In truth, I'd thought all dogs did.

"I'm still not scared," I said resolutely.

Kam wasn't listening. He dragged me round to the front of the house – my friends following like puzzled shadows – and pressed the doorbell, holding me until the woman who lived there answered the door with a scowl, revealing a gold tooth and a bad temper.

"Excuse me," Kam said, perfectly polite. "My brother accidentally kicked his ball into your garden. Can we go and collect it, please?"

Only she told us to fuck off. We'd probably done it on purpose and if we didn't get off her doorstep, she'd set her dog on us. As lessons went, it wasn't the one Kam intended.

Later, after tea, while Amir was in the bath and we were allowed an extra hour of telly, Kam turned to me with a grin and asked who'd dared me.

After a pause, I said, "Izzy."

"How much for?"

"Offered me some Lego she got for her birthday."

Kam grunted. "Charge cash next time."

And from then on, I did.

* * *

When I went up to the Media Suite, it wasn't with any particular plan in mind. I'd heard about challenge channels, watched a few, found them pretty lame, and figured I'd see if I could do better. Since the video on my old phone was bust, I thought I'd try my luck with Miss Stevens.

Finding Claire there kind of surprised the truth out of me. One I regretted revealing almost as soon as it was out. Sweet as it was that she wanted to help, I was only humouring her when I agreed to meet up.

I didn't want her help, just her camera.

When she turned up at the cinema, I couldn't help checking out just how low the neckline sat on her infamous breasts and decided to put at least a little effort in.

"So I buy you a drink and you lend me your camera, deal?" I looked at her like it was a joke, but that's pretty much how I expected it to play out.

"I made some notes," she said, her embarrassment blossoming up from her neck. I reached over, deliberately brushing her arm.

They were surprisingly good. Reading them through gave me ideas and I had fun making her laugh, enjoyed the way she sparred back. I've always fed off the energy of my audience and I could feel my character taking shape around the way her eyes would meet mine before darting away as if she'd been caught, the way certain jokes would bring out the hint of a dimple in her left cheek.

It wasn't until I flipped over another page of her notes that I discovered what role she really had in mind for me.

"Ignore that." Claire tried to turn back the page, but I

pinned it down, intrigued by all the little doodles between her brainstorming – funky little tapirs peeking out from behind the boxes she'd drawn around the ideas she liked best, a galaxy of stars crammed into the margin and two figures at the bottom of the page, lines so sharp they could have come from the pages of one of Amir's comics. But their stance, their figures, the way she'd styled their hair … their identity was unmistakable.

TRUTH GIRL and DARE BOY.

The sentiment behind it punched me in the heart.

Claire was serious about helping me – and in a moment of weakness, I was willing to accept that help.

"It's good!" I looked up, cocking my eyebrows and giving her the grin. "We should do this."

"Are you serious?" Claire looked wary.

"Why not?"

"It's just … you're an actor and stuff. Don't you want to be the star?"

But that's never what it's been about.

"I'm better with someone to spark off –" I glanced at her lips for a second, just to suggest – "and me and you, I reckon there's a spark."

"Is there?"

"You don't think so? And you say in your notes that we need a good brand…"

"It doesn't say anywhere that *I'm* a part of that brand!"

For a moment I wondered if I was being too pushy. But there was something in Claire when I looked for it.

"But you could be," I said.

Like everyone else, all Claire has ever wanted is to be noticed.

Once she'd left, I slid round behind the counter and thanked Mia for covering for me.

Mia's always been my favourite to work with and since the accident I liked her even more. Nothing in the way she treated me had changed. She'd asked me about Kam exactly once and when I'd told her, she'd said, "These things are shit, aren't they?" and offered me the other half of the misshaped cookie she'd been eating.

Major film geek.

"You know that scene in *Galaxy Quest*?" she said.

"Nope." I've always avoided space stuff to piss Kam off.

"Well –" Mia followed me along to where the tills were – "there's this magnetic minefield and the pilot flies the spaceship so close to all the mines that they become magnetically attracted to the ship. When it leaves the minefield, this big-ass spaceship has a trail of activated space mines trailing after it ready to blow up the second they hit something."

"Sounds shit. Do you think we need more tens?"

"No, we don't, there's a bag under the drawer there. My point is, Spaceship Sef, why are you flying so close to yet another lady-shaped mine when you've already got so many trailing after you?"

She leaned on the counter, arms crossed, eyebrows arched towards her tiny hipster fringe.

I didn't really get what she was on about.

"You mean my own special brand of customer service?" Not that I'd had a chance to serve any customers yet.

"Well, there is that…" Last week Mia had fielded two questions about whether I was seeing anyone. "But I meant that girl just now."

"Claire?" I closed the till and logged off.

"If that's her name."

"She's helping me out with something." Mia pursed her lips sceptically. "Get your mind out of the gutter."

"Wow. It's like you don't even know you're doing it." Mia slid along the counter towards me, pressing near as she pretended to be very interested in what I was doing. "I mean, look how close you have to be to see the same piece of paper … and –" looking up at me through her eyelashes – "how playful it is when someone looks at you like this and touches you when they want your attention…"

"Get off!" I twitched my arm away. Mia's one of the few people on this planet I don't flirt with. "I was being friendly."

"It's not friendly if they fancy you."

"It's friendly if I don't fancy her. I've got standards, you know."

"You're a dick, Sef." The colour had drained out of her mood and when she turned away, Mia added, "I'd have thought the fact that you have *a girlfriend* might have been more important than your so-called standards."

OCTOBER

CHAPTER 7

We moved to the area during the summer holidays before I turned eleven and I'd been at school exactly three weeks when I found out Milla Stenner fancied me.

Despite caring more about collecting Pokémon than girls, I was very pleased about this and made the mistake of bragging about it to Mum. Mostly because no one else would have listened.

"Helen Thompson says Milla wants to kiss me if we all go to the cinema on Saturday."

"And what are you going to do about it?" Ever pragmatic, Mum took advantage of me being in the kitchen and nodded at me to open the oven door for her.

"Nothing." I was more interested in hanging out with Finn Gardner, who had recently acquired the latest *Fallout*, a game Mum wouldn't let in the house. "Milla's not very pretty."

Mum had given me a shrewd look, ditched the oven mitts and guided me out to the dining table.

"I'm going to talk to you about—"

"NO! PLEASE!" I pinned my hands over my ears. "School covers that stuff!"

Mum laughed and gently reached out to lower my hands, holding them in hers so I couldn't escape.

"This is not that talk, Yousef – although that will come,

once you're mature enough not to behave like a child."
Mum has always known where to apply pressure. "This is
a talk about respect."

I'd frowned.

"Whoever this Milla is, she is no worse for not being
pretty than you are better for being handsome."

I missed the point and she tutted at the way I puffed up
at being called handsome.

"Goodness, where did all your ego come from? It's not
something to be proud of, one way or the other."

"I don't get it."

Mum took a moment, staring over my shoulder to where
Amir was hitting a tennis ball against the back wall with a
cricket bat. I could hear the uneven slaps of success and
growls of frustration when he missed.

"Do not judge people on the things they cannot choose
for themself," Mum said, as much of her attention on Amir as
on me. "A person cannot choose pretty. They cannot choose
the colour of their skin or the fact that they need glasses."

"They could wear contacts." I was trying to be clever.

"But they cannot choose that they need help to see." She
looked at me very seriously then. "Judge people on what
they have control over. Judge them on the way they treat
their friends, or whether they persevere when they can't do
something." We listened to Amir outside – slap … smack
… frustrated growl … slap… "Be careful not to confuse a
beautiful face with a beautiful heart." She'd kissed my head
as she stood up. "Not everyone is blessed with both."

* * *

"Did we settle on a sum?" Matty said after he'd caught me talking to Claire in the corridor.

The only one that sprang to mind was how much we needed for the Rec.

"What are you on about?" I muttered, logging on to a PC and clicking through to where I'd saved my work from last lesson.

"For you to pull Milk Tits."

I closed my eyes for a moment, reliving the split second I'd decided to keep up the act, so convincing I'd thought she might self-combust from embarrassment as she spelled it out for me. Worth it, though, for the way she'd looked at me like I was too good to be true...

Too good to be trusted.

Matty was still going on about it, slapping me on the arm, face lit up with mischief. "Ha! As if you would. I'm only messing with you."

So I laughed too, at Matty, at myself – at the thought of me and Claire – and it was there, then, I realized that there would never be any going back to how I was before. All I could do was pretend, perform yet another part in the play that was my life. I couldn't share my problems with my friends, couldn't give them a window into what sort of person I really was, skiving off the brotherly duties they assumed took up all the time I told them I was too busy to hang out.

If I didn't pretend to share Matty's jokes, what else was there left?

"Pretty tacky pimping me out like this when I've got a girlfriend, Matty," I said.

But he shot me a look with the piercing baby blues that all the girls go on about without knowing it's down to his contacts. "Laila's punching well below her weight with you. There's already a queue around the block – you'd be doing the girl a favour."

Something I found hard to deny. It had been difficult for us since the accident, with me blowing hot and cold and confused. One minute I'd be calling round Laila's house for nothing more than the peace of resting my head on her knee and having her stroke my hair, the next I was cancelling plans, avoiding the intimacy that comes from revealing what's on your mind as much as what's inside your pants.

Friday night I realized I'd sent Claire more messages in the last three hours than I'd sent to Laila in the last three days, the girl I'd been joking about with Matty slowly creeping into my confidence ahead of the girl I was supposed to be going out with.

It was all too easy to see the effect it was having on Claire when I met up with her the next morning, reminding me of what Mia had said at the cinema: *It's not friendly if they fancy you.*

Claire was my cake and if I wanted to keep her, I couldn't keep nibbling at her like this. Flirting had to be guilt-free for me to enjoy it and I needed to draw a line where Dare Boy left off and Sef started.

No idea why I decided to draw that line using the word "babe".

"What did you just call me?" Laila sounded both bemused and revolted.

"Babe." I lowered my voice a little.

"How many girls do you have on the go that you have to refer to us generically?" Laila might have laughed, but I was glancing back towards the other room thinking of Claire. "Where are you, anyway? I called in on your house on my way past with Helen this morning and your mum practically cried when she had to tell me you weren't in."

"I'm with one of those generic girls you mentioned."

"Ha ha."

Would she have laughed if she knew I wasn't joking? "I might have to bail on seeing you later."

The silence that followed spoke volumes.

"I'm sorry," I said.

"It's OK, Sef. I'm here when you need me as well as when you don't."

"Thank you. If it makes you feel any better, I'm sure my mum would have you over whether I'm home or not."

Her laugh in reply was forced and when I ended the call, I slapped the screen of my phone to my forehead, feeling like the shit that I was.

CHAPTER 8

By the end of our session, Claire and I had clicked awkwardly back into the groove we'd carved for ourselves before Laila's call.

After filming, we talked about setting targets and Claire wrote down a figure of how many subs we should aim to get before the end of the month. A figure too low to make a difference, too high to be achievable. A figure that levered open the door to doubt.

"OK," I said, slamming shut that particular door. "How do we get there, oh media marketing guru?"

Claire tutted away the compliment, and I enjoyed watching her colour rise to a petal-pink flush as she wrote some more numbers down on the sheet.

"This is the formula Miss Stevens used for the ratio of views to take-up for online advertising."

"I love it when you talk dirty."

"Shut up." She was turning crimson.

"Make me." I'd leaned in then, elbow propped on the fold-out table in the caravan so I could rest my chin on my fist.

Too much, too soon – and Claire sat up, leaning back to reclaim the space I'd invaded.

"Are you like this with all girls, or just the ones you aren't going out with?"

"Charming, you mean?"

Claire levelled me with a look.

"I'd have used the word 'shameless', myself."

Running late for work, I asked Claire if she could email me what she wanted me to do on the social-media side of things and, like the conscientious student she is, I got an email breaking it down into chunks like a map to internet fame and fortune, with targets for finding and watching videos, commenting and building relationships with other YouTubers. She arranged them into categories: people who were starting out like we were; people who were already immersed in the community; rising stars to keep an eye on. Stars like Moz. She supplemented this with a list of tags then told me how many videos she'd watched when she was doing research into her plan for the channel.

Challenged me to beat it.

Kam was always the brainiac. Dad used to mutter that this was because he knew how to listen – a skill Dad thinks I lack because of how many times he and Mum have had to hear teachers say that I never sit still in class. For weeks afterwards, Mum would spend her evenings sitting over me as I fidgeted in my seat, finding it hard to concentrate. Whenever I gazed out of the window too long, Mum would poke me none too gently in the arm with the end of her pencil and tap it three times on the textbook or screen I was supposed to be looking at.

"Work first, play later."

"The sooner this gets done, the sooner you can do something else."

"I'm not putting the tea on until you've finished, Yousef Malik. We'll be eating at midnight at this rate!"

"For the love of all that is holy. Pay. Attention."

Reckon they should have been thanking me: if I hadn't been so flaky about schoolwork, Amir wouldn't have been such a keener. He's a contrary little uglyfruit and working hard was something he'd proved time and again he could beat me at.

So when I started spending every evening set up with Mum's ancient laptop at the dining-room table, or on Dad's armchair by the window – anywhere that wasn't Kam's old room – it got noticed.

"It's good to see you working so hard." Mum sat down opposite me at the dining table and I pushed the laptop shut as she passed me a glass of water so fresh that the limescale hadn't yet settled. She was always going on at us about staying hydrated and keeping our brains sharp. "But you're not the only one with homework."

"Amir said he didn't need it."

"I wasn't talking about your brother – I meant me." Mum smiled wearily and rubbed at her wrist where she'd taken her watch off. She was still in her work clothes, eye make-up faded from a day of meetings and interviews. A few weeks later and I'd hear her arguing with Dad about how much longer she'd be able to keep working if she had to hold everything else together as well.

"Oh. I'm sorry – I…"

Mum laughed and reached over to lay a hand on my cheek. "No need to apologize, Sef. I've been meaning to talk to you about this, I just…" She closed her eyes for a beat and sighed. "The computer we bought your brother, to take to university—"

"Mum…"

"He doesn't need it any more. Seems such a waste."

I wasn't able to look at her. "Couldn't we sell it, use the money for the things he does need?"

It was the closest I'd come to asking about our money problems, opening a door to invite Mum to treat me the way she would have treated Kam if he'd asked.

Instead, she brushed her hand down my cheek. "There are some things you need too, Sef."

I nodded and stared at my water glass until she got up, kissed my head and left.

Later that night, Cheddar nudged open the door to the bedroom and settled into a bony little tea cosy on my sternum, her paws tucked away under her chest. It was the first time she'd been in there since I'd moved in. The last of Kam's things left to inherit.

"Is it because I'm the one giving you biscuits now?" I rubbed a finger behind her ear and the cat blinked at me, a phlegmy purr rattling in her throat.

There was a noise out on the landing as Amir padded back from the bathroom. The look he gave the pair of us was one of complete betrayal before he went into his room and shut the door.

So much for Kam's idea of a package deal.

Finn was my first passenger after I passed my test. We both had a free before lunch and I drove him home, the way I'd always imagined doing, music blaring, windows down. And yet I felt hollow.

Claire had messaged me.

How'd it go?

For some reason this had pleased me more than Matty letting off a party popper in the common room.

Only three minors, baby!!! I replied, adding every emoji applicable and some that weren't.

Does this mean I don't have to get the bus up to the caravan?

Only if you upgrade your congratulations.

WELL DONE. DRIVING A CAR IS AS IMPRESSIVE AS DRIVING A ROCKET.

You're surprisingly sarcastic in text form.

Sorry. Have a biscuit. Complete with emoji.

I tapped out a reply: **Didn't say I didn't like it...**

"All right, trippy – you paying attention over there?" Finn threw a Mini Babybel at my head as I sat on the kitchen counter looking at my phone instead of answering his questions about what I wanted to eat.

"You're gonna regret that." I deleted my message and went

for Finn, pushing him into the fridge and trying to shut the door on him, the jars in the door rattling as he fought back.

Ten minutes later, we were sitting at the table as I fed his dog slices of ham from the packet. She'd been young when we were first getting to know each other, but now there were flecks of grey in her muzzle and a portliness to her middle.

"So, congrats on the test." Finn raised his can. "What else has been going on?"

"You mean with Kam?" I just assumed that's what everyone meant.

"With you." Finn tipped his head back to drain the can before looking at me again. "Seems like when you're not with family, you've not got much time for anyone from school."

He picked the ring pull off, pushing it into the can and rattling it a little before putting it back on the table, avoiding looking at me.

"What are you trying to say?" I asked.

"That we don't see you much. This is the first time you've been round in ages."

"I see you in school."

"I see my teachers in school. Doesn't make them my friends." Finn still wouldn't look at me. He doesn't like confrontation and I can count on one hand the number of times he's been pissed at me. For him to have said any of this meant it was a big deal.

"I'm sorry," I said. "It's been hard, you know, with Kam and stuff."

"I get it – and I'm not having a go – it's just, we're here,

OK? Me and Matty." There was a pause as he screwed his mouth to the side, chewing on his next word. "Laila."

I flicked my head up and down in a nod. "I've been round to see her a few times."

"I know." Something about the way he said it made me think he knew more than just that. "She's worried about you, mate. We all are."

"Talk about me lots when I'm not around, do you?" Words frosted with hurt.

"We get stuck for topics of conversation without you yakking twenty-four seven." Finn has always known how to defuse an argument and he lifted his foot to give me a gentle shove in the side, the smell of his socks wafting towards me. "You should probably come out with us tomorrow, stop us from talking about you then."

There's no mirror in Kam's room, so I'd been checking myself out in the mirrored wardrobe next door the way he always used to do. I'd tried two tops already, and grown bored by number three. It would do. I've always been someone who takes care of how they look, but I could barely summon the energy needed to go out, let alone give a shit about what I wore to do it.

I'd rather have stayed home and hung out on the internet with strangers than hang out with the people I called friends.

Thumping on the stairs and Amir walked in before I could leave.

"Get out of my room," he said, and I couldn't tell if that was a reflex at finding someone in his room or seeing me.

"Already gone."

I could feel the heat of his glare on the back of my head as I left, refracting round the corner to follow me to the room I was supposed to call mine, wondering whether I would ever belong there. Whether I belonged anywhere any more.

After I picked the lads up, we headed to meet some girls from school. Girls that included Laila. We'd been messaging a bit beforehand and she'd sent me a couple of pictures of what she was planning on wearing, camera held high, angled down for a view of what I could look forward to.

There were hints in those messages. When Laila broke up with her nice boyfriend to hook up with me, it had been for more than kisses and flirty messages.

"Hey, stranger," she said, sidling up to me at the bar.

"Looking good." I flicked a gaze down the full length of her outfit, kissed her cheek and murmured, "Beautiful, in fact."

It wasn't a line.

"Likewise." That was. She gave my third-choice T-shirt a dubious look. "How you feeling?"

I didn't want her to ask so I pretended she hadn't. Bought her a Coke – Finn and Matty had given me excess petrol money and I felt bad about it. A feeling that only grew worse the more the night went on, squashed on the sofa with Laila pressed against me on one side and Helen on the other.

We moved from the pub and Laila fell into step beside

me. As we turned the corner, the wind funnelled up the high street to hit us with a slap so strong it felt as if we'd been blown into that darkened doorway rather than stepped in there ourselves. Beyond, the others carried on towards the club, Matty's drunken attempt at beatboxing echoing round the square.

And we kissed, because what else are you supposed to do?

"This is nice," Laila whispered, running the flat of her palm up my chest, smoothing the scratch of stubble on my jaw and running her fingers through my hair.

Something inside me had died the night of my brother's accident, and it had taken my feelings for Laila with it, but I carried on kissing her anyway. That's what you do in darkened doorways with girls you think are beautiful.

CHAPTER 10

"Ow! Get off! Mum – tell him to sit on his own seat…"

Mum looked across the table at us with a serene smile and shrugged. She'd made Kam sit next to me on the train and we'd had a fight about who got the window seat. He won, but the way I was clambering all over him made it seem like he'd lost. Amir was across the aisle with Dad, the pair of them oblivious to the backs of the houses marching past the window as our train slowed through the city, too busy playing cards.

Not like me. I loved coming to the city, the ceremony of catching the train, the buffet trolley where I was allowed to pick one thing for the journey, the blocks of flats and converted warehouses, offices and houses an incomplete jigsaw against the sky, the announcement that we were coming into *London*…

No matter how many times I'd been before, London was the city I wanted to go to again and again.

Being there with Claire fired me up, the tall buildings narrowing the roads and pushing the sky higher above our heads, stepping out of the Underground into a city that was both past and future. By the time we got to Covent Garden, I was buzzing off the energy of the crowds and the promise

of being watched, too caught up in the thrill of it to realize the effect it was having on Claire.

First I knew of it was when she made a bolt for it down one of the little alleys. Surprisingly quickly.

"Claire! Stop! Please. What's going on?"

"I can't do this. Not in front of an audience." Her head was down the way it was whenever she thought someone was looking at her, but with her hair tied up into Truth Girl's twisty little buns, there was nothing for her to hide behind.

"But all the stuff we've filmed—" I began.

"… has been in the safety of the caravan."

"And recorded for the whole world to watch." I waved her own camera at her like she might need reminding of what it did.

"We have thirty-one subs, Sef." She didn't smile, knowing there wasn't anything good to be taken from that fact.

Because there wasn't. All those hours she'd spent twiddling the videos and I'd spent watching vloggers I wasn't sure I really liked, all for thirty-fucking-one subscribers. I'd have had a better result if I'd just sent an email to all my contacts and asked nicely.

It wasn't enough.

It didn't matter what Claire wanted, not now.

Claire's eyes are the grey-green type that change with the light, her make-up and her moods and I stared at the sunburst of deep green bleaching to grey round the edges of her irises. "We don't have enough subscribers. We don't have enough donations. But you made me think we could do this and we can. *You* can."

"I can't." And I could hear it then, the same doubt I'd been shutting out every time I looked at our donations page, the prelude to a failure I couldn't face.

"We came to London because we need to be seen to be taking more risks. So why are you here if you aren't even prepared to try?"

The look I pinned her with was fierce, frustrated. This girl had thrown me a rope and now she was threatening to let go of her end at the point when I needed her to pull hardest.

I wouldn't let her do this to me, wouldn't let her do it to Kam.

I needed her. He needed her. *We* needed her.

We got home late that night and for all I teased Claire for being anxious about her parents catching her, I was too. My parents had so much on, they barely seemed to care where I was or what I was doing half the time, but I'd rejected a flurry of calls from my mum when we were on the train home and ignored whatever messages she'd sent, not wanting to get it in the neck for missing tea (and then some).

Slipping carefully into the hall, I pushed my hand through my hair to shake the rain from the ends. My trainers squelched and my jacket was drenched. Everyone on our street parks their car on the road and I always have to leave mine miles away when I get in late. Cheddar came trotting in from the lounge, squeaking a welcome and I picked her up and flipped her over in my arms so I could scritch my fingers through her tummy fur.

"You look happy," I whispered as she smiled at me with

her eyes and her big orange-fur chin.

Only then did I clock how quiet the house was, despite the glow coming from the front room.

Stepping into the lounge was like walking into a horror-film tableau. The telly on mute in the corner, light on over the dining table down the far end, where Mum's computer was surrounded by printouts of spreadsheets, Dad's padded lap-tray on the floor by his armchair, beans congealing on the plate, a fork with a bite of lamb still on it. The cat had obviously been at the rest of the chop, dragging it from the plate and halfway across the carpet.

No wonder she looked so pleased with herself.

In the kitchen, I found the oven still on, some indeterminate fruit dish dried and shrivelled on the second shelf, but when I called up the stairs and out of the back door, there was no one there to answer.

All those calls I'd been ignoring from my mum hadn't been her wanting to know where I was or what I'd been doing.

They'd been about Kam.

CHAPTER 11

Now Amir's a teenager, his face excretes excess fluid via his spots, but as a kid, it mostly came out of his nose. Comic-book nerd from birth, Amir always wanted to talk about what superpower he'd choose – conversations that would end in tears after I'd wind him up by calling him names like Mucus Man, Goo Goblin and Snot Gobbler.

Until the day his snot turned serious.

He was only five. All three of us shared a room in the old flat and he kept me up for most of the night, coughing and complaining he was hot. By the morning, he had a fever and all the symptoms of pneumonia.

Within the day, he got bad enough that Mum overrode her usual protocol of bedrest, fluids and Calpol, and packed the lot of us into her car to drive him to hospital, messaging Dad, who was away on a job, to let him know what was happening. In the back, I let my little brother slide sideways in his seat belt and rest his head on my knee and, when I knew no one was looking, Amir too delirious to hear it, I told him that I hoped he wouldn't die.

Hospitals are quieter at night. Not that there aren't people there, patients, staff – a subdued A & E. But it's easier to find a parking space.

I spent a long time sitting in the car, waiting for my body to move without me having to tell it why. In the end, I got out of the car because I'd had a drink before I'd left the house and I couldn't hold it in any longer.

After the toilet, I headed for the ward that felt the most familiar: intensive care.

Stupid, because that wasn't where he was now.

I got to the doors and stopped.

This time round, Kam had been taken to hospital with a UTI – urinary tract infection – an infection that came with a fever. When your brain has a hard time regulating anything, a spike in temperature is a bigger deal than it would be for anyone else. But by the time I got hold of Mum on her mobile, they were coming home. Kam was being treated for the infection and the pain that came with it. A new catheter fitted.

None of them knew I was here.

The doors in front of me opened and one of the night duty nurses came out.

"You all right?" he asked, a twang to his vowels.

I lifted my glasses to wipe my eyes. "I came… I wanted…" I couldn't really say, to be honest.

"You know someone in there?"

I shook my head and told him the name of the ward written on the note I'd found on the fridge.

"Well, visiting hours are over for the wards…" It was past midnight, but there must have been something in the way I looked, because "Guy" led me along another corridor, down some stairs to a different set of doors. He

talked quietly to the nurse on the desk, leaning round to look at something. "You can't go in, people are sleeping, but Kamran Malik is in the third bed on the right."

Being told I couldn't go in was a relief.

Cupping my hands round my glasses to keep out the light in the corridor, I peered into the darkened ward at the lump Kam's feet made in the bed.

"Live," I whispered, knowing no one could hear me.

My family didn't know I'd been to see Kam in the hospital, the same way they knew nothing of the Saturdays I spent in the caravan and the hours I'd waste driving up to the lookout, where I'd park the car and sit staring out across the valley, rain or sun, day or night. Somewhere to be that wasn't my home. Somewhere I couldn't be found. Not by my parents, my friends or my girlfriend.

I'd been cut a length of freedom so long I could wander as far as I liked, but the UTI stretched my father's patience too far. He's always had less for me than for my brothers.

The Monday of half-term, while Mum was at work and Amir had gone out with his friends, Dad marched into where I was eating breakfast on the bed.

"This is ridiculous. You'll see your brother whether you want to or not."

Barely enough warning for me to put my plate down before he was wrestling me out of the room and down the stairs and into the van, me flailing and yelling and pulling every step of the way, until, in a melee of limbs, the pair of us toppled down the front steps and into the garden.

Outside, as I nursed a graze that ran from my elbow to my little finger and Dad a twisted ankle, we stood across the path from each other, panting, not saying a word. Inside, there'd been no one to see us fight, but now, out in the street, I could sense net curtains twitching, the old man out with his dog crossing the road to avoid our house.

Dad might be harder to read than Mum, but even I could see the moment the fight left him.

He didn't say anything. Just got in his van and left me there, blood beading along my arm as I watched him drive off to see Kam without me.

Shutting the door, I went up to the bathroom to check out my arm, rinsing it, not showing the pain, imagining Kam mocking me for feeling it. Back in the bedroom, leaning against the wall to finish my breakfast, I thought about him sitting there with me, telling me not to get crumbs on his bed, taking my juice from where it was propped between my knees because he didn't trust me not to spill it.

"I miss you," I told the room.

Don't be so soft, he'd say. Then, *Seriously, stop getting crumbs on the bed, you fucker.*

This was stupid. Kam was *alive*. He was *there*. And yet there I was, sitting in an empty room, haunted by a ghost of someone who hadn't died.

NOVEMBER

CHAPTER 12

"Hey, there," I said when Claire got into the car two weeks after she'd last got out of it.

"Hey yourself. Miss me?"

I had. More than I'd have thought given all the messaging we'd been doing.

"How was your grandad's?" I asked, pulling out into the road, wondering whether to risk the traffic in town or take the ring road.

"Was my blow-by-blow account not enough information for you?"

"Not enough if you did, in fact, blow someone…"

"SEF!" Claire punched me in the arm.

She'd have handled that perfectly well in a message, but being suggestive IRL overloads Claire's system.

"I'll take that as a yes," I said with a knowing grin, knowing full well Claire hadn't done anything of the kind during her half-term. Or ever, maybe.

"You're so unprofessional," Claire muttered, sinking down into her seat as we slowed to join the queue of cars edging towards the high street.

"So that's Devon covered. What about that gig on Sunday?"

"Hell." I'd guessed as much – crowds aren't Claire's thing – but as she chatted more about it, I realized it wasn't just

about that, but about her friend Rich getting with this girl.

"You and Rich close then?" It was the first time I'd ever properly asked about her mates. Not thought about them existing really.

"He's my best friend." Her tone emphasized the subtext: nothing romantic. "My only friend at the moment."

"Don't I count?" I pretended to be offended, but for once, Claire took me seriously.

"I've known you two months, Sef. Rich and Seren and me have been friends for years."

"Who's Seren?"

"The friend who isn't." Claire angled her gaze firmly out of the window.

"What happened?"

She left it long enough that I thought she might not want to answer, until I saw she was trying not to cry. Trying and succeeding, actually, given how steady her voice was.

"Rich messed up. I took his side. Seren isn't forgiving us."

A succinct way to sum up something that obviously felt a lot bigger. I reached over to give her arm a squeezy sort of a stroke. "That sounds shit."

She laughed, then, "It is."

We cruised along on the clutch for a few shop-lengths, me searching for something to make the stranger in my car see me as a friend.

"You can talk to me, you know, about this stuff."

Claire smiled – a different sort of sad this time. "Your problems are bigger than mine."

"It's not a competition."

"Thought everything was a competition with you?"

I resisted her tease, wanting her to take me seriously. Wondering whether my performance as Dare Boy was so convincing that she really believed that's all I was.

"It doesn't matter how big someone else's problems are, doesn't mean yours don't count. Or that if that someone wants to be your friend, you have to hide them from him…" We were stopped at the lights and I looked across to Claire, but within a split second her eyes widened and she was slithering awkwardly down her seat until half of her was in the footwell.

"Drive!" she hissed.

I looked at the brake lights of the car in front.

"Where? Off across the market? This isn't a Bourne film, C."

"It's your friend! The nice one."

I glanced out the car to catch sight of Finn standing at the bus stop, headphones on, attention firmly fixed on his phone. Something like excitement flared up at the thought of him seeing us, but the lights were changing and only a few seconds later Finn was receding in my mirror, my thrill a spent firework.

"You can get up now," I told Claire, looking down to where she was bundled up and giggling to herself in the footwell. "What's so funny?"

"The whole, you don't have to hide from your friends and I'm…" She couldn't seem to get out. "*Literally* hiding from your friend … and now –" she gave up wriggling – "I'm stuck."

Pulling over, I went round to move the seat back, half in

hysterics myself as I helped her unwedge until she tumbled out onto the pavement.

Looking at her sprawled and giggling on the floor, I held my hand out to pull her up.

"I've missed you," I said.

They say pride comes before a fall, but there's no pride in running away, is there? The channel had become a way out for more than my guilt over Kam – it had become a way out of being me. At night, Sef Malik could be sitting in the room with his folks, living another life as Dare Boy through the computer on his lap.

Over a month from when we'd started and I'd fallen down a rabbit hole of my own making, lost in an online wonderland. The comments I made and the ones that came back harnessed a community spirit that spread right across the world and I discovered you can flirt all you like behind an avatar without worrying about hurting people's feelings. Made me wonder why anyone bothered trolling when being nice felt so much better…

Until it didn't.

We'd had a few little back-and-forths where people had copied our dares like we wanted them to. Some stoner students ate cat biscuits out of a cereal bowl and there was a mini domino effect of people filming themselves licking slugs – all newbies with hardly any followers. Not enough momentum to get our dares out into the mainstream.

Then came the two girls. The Merry Cherries, they called themselves, and there they were on my computer screen,

trying to catch some pigeons in the park. Everything about it had been ripped off our dare in Trafalgar Square, right down to the music. No credit. No link. *Nothing*.

I combed the donations records, looking for a way to let them off – to let myself off for being so naive as to think the internet was a Utopia populated by cupcakes and rainbows and altruists. There was no way around it.

Those girls had watched the video, liked the idea, copied the dare.

All for nothing.

So I did one of the many things I'd been too cowardly to face until that point and wrote down all the stuff we'd spent money on. Our outfits, food and props, petrol and train tickets. London was supposed to get us more comments, more likes. More money.

But Kam's donation fund was well into the red.

"Fuck!"

The pad I'd been scribbling on made a satisfying smack as it hit the bedroom wall and I picked up the calculator to see if it would do the same.

Better.

"Sef?" Kam's door swings inwards and Mum pushed it open to find me picking up the shattered case from the floor. "What's all this?"

"Computing's stressing me out." I cast a furtive glance to check the laptop had faded to screensaver, taking the pigeon video with it.

"Is this something I need to worry about?" She stood there, dressing gown on over the blouse and skirt she'd

worn to work, looking like she could barely support the weight of the worries she already carried.

"I'll work it out," I said, my mind already backtracking the steps that had led me down this dead end, hunting for a way out. A way to make it right.

"OK then." But she didn't move. "I came to say I've made an appointment for you with Dr Garrison."

"Why?" Before the accident that would have me a reproving, "Tone, Yousef!" But Mum had no energy for fighting battles like that any more.

"I want you to go to the doctor because I'm worried about how you're coping with what's happened to Kam."

My hand closed round the remains of my calculator, the plastic biting into my skin. Everything about the way I was tensed, breathing too hard, was the same as I'd been in the garden after I'd fought with Dad, but Mum's gentle touch was harder to resist than Dad's force.

I relaxed my grip. "What's Dr Garrison going to do?"

"If you can't talk to your family, maybe you can talk to him. Yes?"

It hurt too much to hear the hope in her voice and I concentrated on one of the stars on the chalkboard, dusty and faded.

"OK," I said.

"I've written the appointment on the calendar – do you need me to come with you?"

"No."

"But you'll go?"

"Yes," I lied.

CHAPTER 13

When we were younger, summers were spent at Uncle D's caravan and Easters at Auntie Iffat's – where I'd been sent to my room, or rather, Zahid's. Little Parveen never had to share with anyone, Amir and Kam got the spare room, and because Zahid and I are about the same age, I got a fold-out camp bed on his floor.

I was intent on the perfectly constructed Lego on his shelves and executing my revenge.

At the click of the door, I collapsed onto the camp bed with an ominous creak.

"All right." Kam shut the door behind him and I flicked him a mutinous look. "Came to find out what happened."

I redirected my gaze to the Lego. "Nothing." Having just been royally roasted for fighting with my cousin, I wasn't in the mood for Kam's wise older brother act.

We were ten and twelve and the gap between us had stretched the furthest I'd ever felt. Kam had spent two years in a different school to me, his friends strangers, interests narrowing along lines I didn't want to follow. Amir was too little, too weird for me to feel close to him and Kam was leaving me behind.

"What did Zahid do?" Kam asked.

"Nothing." But Kam sensed this was a different sort

of nothing from the previous one. A nothing that meant everything.

"What did Parveen's rabbit have to do with it?"

Auntie Iffat had found us wrestling out in the garden by the rabbit hutch at the unfortunate moment that I'd grabbed one of Zahid's temptingly large ears and given it a good yank.

"Nothing." But I couldn't suppress the ripple of amusement.

Kam sighed and shook his head like he was too old for all this, but he plopped down on the beanbag opposite and raised his eyebrows.

"OK. So now I'm curious."

And I grinned then, in spite of myself.

"Zahid said there was no way I'd eat Bumpkin's poo."

Kam's expression was the reward I was looking for, his whole face wrinkling up in disgusted disbelief. "Oh my God, *you didn't!*"

But he knew I had.

"Zahid didn't think I'd do it. Bet me ten quid and everything."

"A tenner?!" Kam was right to question that part of the story. I stopped smiling and went back to contemplating the Lego. "Zahid probably doesn't even *have* ten pounds. Or if he does, he has to give Auntie Iffat a receipt for whatever he spends it on. You were stupid to take the bet."

I scowled, annoyed with him now he wasn't on my side.

"He didn't think I would do it."

"Come on – Zahid knew full well you'd do it." Kam

threw a pair of balled-up socks at my face and I batted them away.

"Yeah, well, then he should have been prepared to pay!" The promise of hard cash was what got me through ingesting those dusty little rabbit turds.

"When are you going to learn?" Kam shook his head. "The only person you can trust to be honourable is yourself, Sef. Zahid's as trustworthy as a vegan shark."

He stood up and frowned at the shelf next to him, where the crew of the Lego pirate ship were artfully arranged in the sort of debauchery that Auntie Iffat would not approve of when she came up here to clean.

"Next time –" Kam adjusted the angle of the broom the deckhand was holding – "get your payment up front."

Everything we'd filmed for the channel had been daft stuff almost anyone could copy if they wanted. As Claire had said way back when we set the terms and conditions: that was the point.

Now we needed to change the model, a promise of something our audience *wouldn't* dare to do themselves … something more daring than firing jelly beans at each other from our mouths or telling people what colour underwear we had on.

The problem was that the only decent (legal) dares I could think of were either dangerous or involved nudity. Or pain. There was no way Claire would agree to any of them without having a London-sized freak-out about it.

That's the problem with people who think too much

about things – in front of the camera I could goad Claire into doing almost anything, but I needed leverage to get her there.

Frustrated, I clicked back through our videos, reading the comments, not knowing what I was looking for until I started to see it. The comments about us, our chemistry, the "Are you guys a couple?" question...

It's not like I'm some stage actor with a weird hang-up about watching myself onscreen, but I'd never felt the need to do more than give Claire's edit a cursory once-over before posting. After posting, all I cared about were the comments, the shares and the views and likes. I had enough of other people's videos to watch without wasting time on our own.

But in doing so, I'd missed what the magic was. I'd always thought it was about what we did, but watching *TRUTH: What colour is your underwear?* I realized it wasn't what we did, but the way we did it.

Claire looked horrified as I stood to pull up the waistband of my knock-off Calvins, before – as was the way with our truths – she had to answer too.

"*Black pants. And before you ask, I'm not showing anyone. You'll just have to trust me.*"

"*Always, Truth Girl.*" Then, with a wicked grin, "*I believe the phrase 'underwear' refers to more than just your pants...*"

Blushing furiously through her smile, she pulled the neck out on her T-shirt to glance down, her other hand stretched out to keep me at bay, even though all I'm doing is giving the camera a meaningful look.

251

"*Purple. With a turquoise trim,*" she confirmed.

"*Sexy.*"

"*Shut up.*"

Dare Boy and Truth Girl had as much, if not more, of the same chemistry that Claire and I had in our messages. As I watched with a clear head and honest eyes, I saw things I missed during filming – things that couldn't be edited out. The veiled looks Claire gave me when she thought I wasn't looking, or how much we touched each other, nudging each other's thighs with our knees – hugs and shoves – both of us talking with our hands as much as our mouths, Claire's gestures mirroring mine.

Onscreen, she pushed me playfully off my stool as she told me to shut up about her bra being sexy, her ears bright red and a grin a mile wide on her face.

This was gold and we were wasting it on stuff people could copy when we should have been spending it on something better. Something bigger.

I was prepared to do almost *anything* to help Kam – all I had to do was convince Claire that she was prepared to do the same.

Her scarf was ridiculous. Fifty metres long and knitted from the sort of colours you'd find in the bargain bin. When Claire finally emerged, her nose was pink and her cheeks flushed.

"You quite finished there?" I said, enjoying the side-eye she gave me and the indignant, "It's cold out."

I took her to Cine Obscura because that's where we'd

met before and for all Mia radiated disapproval so tangible I could feel it all the way across the foyer, it was still the place I felt safest outside our caravan.

Uncle D's caravan.

Only, once I got her there, I didn't know how to start, my fingers almost as busy as my brain as I tried to work out what I wanted to say, lining up all the arguments I had in my arsenal.

"So. Here's the thing. We do the dares and ask people to pay to copy us. But that's all the wrong way round. People need to pay first, then see the dares."

"Why would they pay, though?" Voice set to sceptical.

"We give them an incentive…"

"What kind of an incentive?"

"Offer up dares worth paying for." I glanced up from where I'd been spinning my can around on its coaster, knowing she wouldn't like what I was saying.

"Sef…"

I rushed in too soon, too desperate to convince her.

"The amount we've raised averages out at fifty-four pence per video. The money you're planning on spending on a GoPro is more than we're ever likely to make if we carry on like this."

I regretted mentioning it the second the sentence came out. Claire's loaded compared to me, but it's not something we'd actually discussed – she just quietly left petrol money in the change pot in the central console, offered to sort out train tickets and never asked me to pay her back… The GoPro thing might not have been fair, but it was also true.

"I don't mind *you* doing dares…" she started to say.

"People want to see *both* of us doing them – we're a team." It was what I'd been waiting for. I read the comments from my phone. *"OMG – you guys are adorbs. Freshest vid I've seen this week. Truth Girl's such a little cutie. Anyone else totally shipping these two?"* I looked up to see her squirming in her seat and skipped the one that said, *Has anyone dared them to kiss? "Love your channel – have you thought about opening up to challenges in the comments?"*

"So you're saying they have to pay to challenge us?"

"No." This wasn't going the way I'd planned – I was going to tackle the money issue separately. "But we should do this anyway, take up challenges from our viewers. You always said audience involvement was the key to getting people to come back – and what better reason to come back than to check to see if we've done their dare?"

"How does that—"

I could tell she wasn't getting on board.

"Two different things: accept challenges as part of our regular posts and make it just about growing the audience. No donations." I boxed off the words with my hands and pushed them to the side. "To make money, we offer up something big – a series of proper dares set up so that we have to reach a target amount of donations before we perform."

"What do you mean by 'proper' dares?"

I shrugged.

"Things people want to see other people do that they wouldn't do themselves." I was losing patience, needing

her to agree, to trust me on this one. "Please, Claire."

And before I could check myself, decide whether what I was doing was fair, I was leaning in sliding my fingers a little way up the smooth skin of her forearm. I didn't know how much Claire might be prepared to do for Kam, but perhaps she would do it for me.

"I can't do this without you."

CHAPTER 14

Just you, looking at the camera, while we hear a VO of you talking about Kam. Our viewers need to know why this matters.

I'd pushed Claire further than she was comfortable with on the dares, now she was pushing me on the truth.

After my Thursday night shift at the cinema, I drove over the bridge, the arches of the viaduct following my progress like three hooded eyes and took the road up to the lookout,

past the school and into the countryside beyond the lights of the town.

Truths slip out more easily when there's no light to see them by.

Felt stupid the first time I tried.

"Hi, so, it's me and…"

Sounded like I was leaving an answerphone message. Never was any good at those.

"This is me. Dare Boy." That wasn't right either. This truth belonged to me, not Dare Boy.

"I hate this." I didn't know who I was really talking to until I felt the familiar heat in my eyes, guilt creeping out as tears. "I hate that I can't talk to you. Why aren't you here? Kam? I love you. I'm sorry. I'm so sorry…" I could barely breathe for the misery clogging my throat. "*Fuck*."

Brought my fist down too hard on the wheel and Mrs Bennet let out an indignant little "Peep!"

"I don't want your stupid fucking *car!*" I hit her again. "Or your fucking computer or your fucking *room*..." Didn't mention Cheddar. Of all the things that had once been Kam's, his ugly little cat was the only one that brought me comfort.

"I want my brother back!" I screamed at the ceiling, at the night outside and the silence inside and I was sobbing so hard I thought I'd choke as I collapsed forward, pressing my forehead against the wheel until it hurt.

"I'm doing this for you," I told the speedometer.

All for someone who didn't know. Did he?

But the only way Kam would know about the problems we were having paying for his care would be if someone told him. And who would do that? What kind of monstrous parents would pass problems like that on to the son they're trying to protect?

"I'm trying to protect you too," I said. "I'm sorry. I love you. Let me help, let me make up for it..."

And I scrunched my eyes tight and cried into the night as I whispered the truth into my phone. "This is all my fault."

Whatever barriers I'd put up fell away as I sat with Claire on the step of the caravan and told her about the summer I got my scar. Dare Boy and Yousef Malik no longer seemed like separate performances so much as two halves of the same whole.

A whole that only Claire would ever see.

"So we gonna film you saying you'll shave your head?" It was the only dare we'd been able to come up with that met my criteria for being interesting and Claire's for being "safe". Even so, you could see she was on edge about it.

"Do I have to?"

"Film the video or shave your head?"

"Either. Both." But she'd already got up from the step, ready to re-enter the studio. "I really don't want to do this, you know."

I did know. "You think I want to streak across a football pitch on Boxing Day?"

"Yes. Absolutely. You're obsessed with getting naked."

"Am I now?" And I pulled up the hem of my T-shirt as I followed her inside. "You think the world isn't dying to get a load of this?"

"The world might be. I'm not." She turned away to fiddle with the camera and I ducked round to make sure she could see me.

"You can totally pull off a shaved head."

"Really?" She did that disbelieving little head-roll-chin-tuck thing at me.

"Yes. Really. You have a beautiful skull."

"Creepy."

"And a beautiful face."

"Now I know you're lying."

"Fine. Your skull is kind of average and your face is funky-looking." She fought back a smile. "But bald girls are sexy, so deal with it."

But the way she was fiddling with the settings on the

camera, adjusting the reflectors that were already perfectly angled, was all just a way to stall filming the appeal and I nudged her gently on the arm.

"How about we film something else first? That proves we're worth our words."

"Like what?"

I frowned, thinking of something that would show her I was willing to do something that would last beyond the time it took to film, something I couldn't hide from everyone else. Something to show solidarity.

CHAPTER 15

It's quite hard to hide the fact you've pierced your ear when:

   A) You wear your hair short and sharp round the sides
      like I do

   B) Your ear swells up and starts leaking pus

and

   C) Your little tit of a brother draws your mum's attention
      to it

She wasn't very sympathetic to the infection.

"Invent a time machine and go back and stop yourself from doing something so stupid." Mum stared at me with crossed arms and a disapproving stare before relenting. "There's some TCP in the bathroom cupboard. If you get it, I'll bathe your ear."

Amir sniggered into his cereal as I winced and yelped at how rough she was.

"Be glad your father's not here."

"Why?"

"He doesn't like this sort of thing."

"What sort of thing?"

But she got very evasive. "Let me talk to him before you see him later, yes?"

It wasn't much easier going to school, where Matty led the charge on ripping the piss out of me so loud that

everyone within earshot joined in.

"I thought you'd back me up!" I slapped Finn on the arm – he'd been gently stretching his ear for the last six months.

"Yeah, but mine's on brand... Yours makes you look like—"

"A twat?" Matty.

"A poser?" Helen.

"A wide boy!" One of the lads from my Drama class pitched in.

"A moron?" Laila – who was looking *seriously* annoyed with me.

Finn grinned at the others and then at me. "Take your pick."

When the bell went for next lesson, Laila pushed on ahead of me and went to sit with Helen, leaving me to Matty's mercy. All lesson I watched the back of her head, wondering when she'd turn round.

She never did.

When I first started at Cine Obscura, before the novelty wore off, Finn and Matty would come and find me on a Saturday night once they'd got bored of bumming around town.

"Didn't know you two were such a fan of Hungarian cinema," I said looking up to see them approach. It was May, it was wet and I wasn't surprised to see them.

"What?" Matty screwed up his face as he studied the listings behind me while I wiped down the counter.

"Thought this was Coen brothers week?" Finn pointed at one of the posters.

"Next week," I said. "And before you ask, no, you can't get a discount."

"Not even for your oldest friends?" Matty tried for puppy-dog eyes and I slapped him in the face with the cloth I'd been using.

"That rules you out then." I only started hanging out with Matty at the end of Year 10.

"Bet he'd answer different if someone else was doing the asking," Finn said with a lazy drawl as he leaned back on my clean counter and eyed up the empty foyer.

"You mean someone prettier?" Matty joined in.

"Someone more female."

"Someone called Laila Jalil," Matty finished, his grin wide and knowing.

"Fuck off." I wrung my cloth out in the sink with my back to them.

The week before, things had shifted gear with Laila. We'd always been friendly, but a load of us had been round at Bradley Summers' house for a barbecue and all I could remember of the night was lying squashed next to Laila on a sunlounger left out on the lawn, talking with our heads bent close and me playing with a strand of her hair that kept falling from where she'd tucked it behind her ear.

"You know she's seeing someone," I said, trying not to think of how I'd been noticing the way her school shirt gaped open a bit and daydreaming away the lessons we shared wondering what it would be like if she undid all the buttons down to that point...

I had a feeling Laila might have been noticing my noticing.

"Whatever," Matty said. "We'll see how long that lasts."

So far most of my encounters had been limited to one-off kisses with nameless girls in nightclubs or something a little fumblier with girls I knew from school who got bold with booze at a house party, but Laila was cut from the cloth of girlfriend material.

By the time we broke off for study leave, my head was filled with thoughts of her when it should have been filled with facts about the impact the Industrial Revolution had on the standard of living among the working classes. There wasn't a day that passed when I didn't send her a sneaky Snapchat, starting off a spiral of flirty messages until she'd tell me to get back to work. That I was distracting her.

The night our exams ended, everyone in our year descended on the high street, fake IDs at the ready, sequinned skirts and shiny shirts shimmering like a shoal of fish as we moved from pub to bar to club. Everyone was hugging and kissing each other on the cheeks the drunker they got, although Laila and me were both sober and she seemed to be saving all her hugs for me. But then she pulled me close and shouted in my ear, "I didn't break up with my very nice boyfriend just for hugs, you know…"

Four weeks we'd had, spending all our free time together without either of us being fully committed. When Laila left to go travelling with her family, we suspended our relationship on the understanding that things would turn serious once she got back.

Neither of us banked on the kind of serious it turned into, though.

I owed Laila more of an effort than I'd been putting in.

"Do you want to come over to mine for a bit?" Both of us had frees and it was likely to be quiet at mine for once – Mum would see Kam straight from work, then pick up Amir from Nerd Club, and Dad was working so many jobs the chance of him being home was pretty slim.

Laila had her books open on the table by the common-room window and when she looked up, it was with the kind of smile I should have taken as a warning.

"Sure," she said.

Things started out OK. I offered her a drink, we sat on the sofa. We kissed. Only our kissing soon moved from vertical to horizontal, Laila's hands running up under my T-shirt, her pressing herself into me so that I couldn't help but notice the feel of her body against mine.

"Shall we go up to your room?" Laila whispered, glancing at the huge front window. Our house is set back from the street enough that Mum has refused Dad's repeated request to put nets up, but it's still pretty exposed.

Once we were in my room – Kam's room – it felt all wrong. A girl kicking her shoes off to climb on the bed, kissing me, touching me, should have brought with it the thrill of doing something my parents would thoroughly disapprove of.

It didn't. Instead it seemed as if I could only experience it through some internal narrator.

Kissing, kissing, pause for heavy breathing...

Rubbing up against each other.

Careful now, that's how fires start…

Laila getting impatient as she tried to guide my hands.

That's a breast and … roll to disengage. Well played, sir.

Laila, however, has never been content to be passive. Of the two of us, she was the one who knew how to have a relationship.

What? No, not there. Oh, well… Yes, but … no. No, no, no.

Every time she made a move for my flies, I shifted so she couldn't get a grip. By the third time, it had become ridiculous, as my girlfriend attempted to wrestle me round the bed while we remained locked at the mouth. Laughter bubbled up in my throat, but there was nothing about this that felt funny.

"This is stupid. What's going on?" Laila sat up, her lips a little darker from all the kissing, hair rucked up and tangled. She'd never looked more beautiful and I'd never wanted her less.

"I'm sorry." I tilted my head back against the wall, my eyes closed. I didn't really have anything else to offer. I *was* sorry.

"Is that it?" I couldn't tell what question she was really asking, so I didn't answer. "Look at me, Sef."

But I kept my eyes closed. I didn't want to see myself reflected in her eyes. Someone supposed to be much more than I was.

"Look at me." Her voice was softer now, she was closer and her fingers were on my chin, turning me to face her. "Please, just talk to me."

"I don't want to talk," I whispered.

There was the softest possible sigh as she let go and leaned away. "You never do, but if you can't talk to me, can't touch me, what are we going to do together?"

I looked at her then, with a weak sort of smile: "Watch films and cuddle?"

"I'm not in this for films and cuddles. You can get those from Finn. Or your mother." She traced a pattern on the thigh of her leggings. "Limping on like this is making it harder for both of us."

"Are you breaking up with me?" I asked.

"I think you want me to."

I didn't say anything, but that was an answer in itself.

Laila slid off the bed and pulled on her shoes and jacket as I sat watching her. Before she left, she leaned over, one knee resting on the bed, and stroked my hair.

"I'm so sorry this happened, Sef." She kissed my forehead. I think she might have been crying. "If you ever change your mind about talking, I'll still be here to listen."

I stayed where I was on the bed, sitting in silence, dusk turning to dark outside my window.

The only person I wanted to talk to was Kam.

CHAPTER 16

Want to wake up to something sexy?

Claire replied with a photo of her peeking through her fingers as if frightened of what I might send, but for once I played it straight and sent her a screengrab of the number of views last night's video had gathered overnight.

Seriously sexy.

I've more where that came from…

There was actually some cash in the donation fund. Quite a lot, actually.

PHWOAR.

And saving the best till last…

I pulled down my duvet and tried to tense what little I had in the way of abs.

YOU TRICKED ME! NOW MY EYES ARE BURNING.

I replied with a little kissy emoji.

I hate you.

Which made me laugh as I hurried down the stairs to where I was already late for breakfast.

Smiling to myself, I replied. **You love me.**

"What's so funny?" Dad asked as I sat down and grabbed the cereal box. We were talking again now I'd agreed to seek medical help and Mum'd had a go at him for being aggressive.

"Nothing," I told him, but my phone went again and Amir snatched it from where I'd put it on the table, not yet faded to lock screen.

"Ooh…" He'd already scrambled out of his chair and was dodging around the table, keeping it between me and him as I lunged for my phone.

"Don't you dare—"

"Who's C-l-a-i-r-e?" He dragged it out with so much relish you could have put it in a jar and sold it at a farmers' market.

"No one – give it back, you little c—"

"Yousef!" Dad snapped, anticipating the abuse. It's what Kam used to yell at me when I did this to him.

Mum stepped in from the kitchen, where she'd been brewing a coffee to take on the train rather than risk being tempted by a Costa she couldn't afford at the station.

"What's all this? We live in a house not a zoo." She glared at me in particular and I sunk back into my chair.

"Tell Amir to stop reading my messages."

Mum plucked the phone from his grasp to hand to me, giving Dad a withering look like maybe he should have tried doing the same.

"Sef's cheating on his girlfriend," Amir piped up.

"No, I'm not!"

"With someone called Claire." His greasy little face had oozed into a repugnant grin.

"I raised my sons to treat girls better than that!"

It always made me uncomfortable when Mum commented on relationship stuff. Kam hadn't ever had one and

the only thing willing to date Amir is his left hand and a box of tissues – I was her test case.

"I—" I darted a look of white-hot hate at my brother for forcing me into doing it like this. "I'm not cheating on Laila. We broke up."

Mum's vague interest crystallized into disapproval. "For this Claire girl?"

"No! Claire's got nothing to do with it."

"Says on your phone that you love her…" And Amir caught my eye as he made to lift up the front of his shirt, enjoying the look of outright horror on my face at how much of my conversation he'd seen.

"Who – Laila?" Dad wanted in too. Brilliant.

"He means Claire." Mum did not approve.

"No!" I was stressed with all the questions, the three of them interrogating me. "This is a violation of my privacy."

"Your family wanting to know about this new girlfriend?" Mum uses "this" to indicate her disdain for whatever follows.

"I haven't got one! She's just a friend."

"That you love," Amir added.

"Learn to read, dipwank. I'm telling her she loves *me* – and it's a joke."

"Don't call your brother a … whatever it was that you said."

Dad's reprimand was half-hearted because all three of them were laughing at me as I growled into my soggy cereal. No good wishing Kam was there – it's not like he wouldn't have been ripping into me worst of all.

"So what *did* happen with Laila?" Mum asked on the

way to the station. Although Amir had his headphones in, I caught sight of him in the rearview mirror looking up like he knew what we were talking about.

"Nothing." That was the whole problem, wasn't it?

"Sef. Indulge your mother. Talk to me."

Mum had been excited when she found out I was seeing Laila at the start of summer. Demanded I bring her over for tea and afterwards I'd heard her on the phone to Auntie Iffat saying I was dating "a nice Pakistani girl". I don't like it when Mum gets into that kind of mentality, but I figured she was allowed one free pass to Auntie Iffat since they're engaged in some kind of nuclear arms race when it comes to their teen sons' accomplishments. Me picking a palatable girlfriend was definitely one up on Zahid, who'd recently been in trouble for sharing a porno link on the school network.

It's not like she thought we were going to get married or anything, but I still hadn't wanted to tell her it was over. Didn't want to disappoint her on this, too.

"I wasn't being a very good boyfriend."

Mum tutted and I could tell she was about to bring up Claire, thinking of all the lectures she'd given me on treating girls with respect.

"I wasn't cheating on her, Mum. I just wasn't the person she started going out with. Laila was the one who ended it." *Are you breaking up with me? I think you want me to…* "We're still friends."

I didn't even know if that was true – of Laila, or any of the people who'd once been so important to me.

When I pulled over by the station, Mum leaned across to stroke my face, guiding me to look at her.

"Perhaps it's best for you to take some time to be yourself for now," she said, her face softened by love and grief. "You've been through a lot."

She kissed my cheek amid the brief bustle of her leaving and Amir getting in the front. Both of us sat there in the car, engine idling as we watched Mum march towards the station, Thermos in one hand, overstuffed handbag in the other.

"Thanks for dropping me in it, you lumpy dumpling," I said to Amir once I'd pulled back into the traffic.

"Like Kam wouldn't have done the same if he'd caught you sexting someone."

"Mate. It wasn't sexting."

"Sure. All my selfies look like sleazy Tinder profile rejects."

"You're too young for Tinder. And sleaze. And sexting. Not that what you saw on my phone was sexting."

The way Amir was looking at me made me so twitchy I nearly missed a light turning red and had to step on the brakes.

"Was that you giving me a big-brother lecture?" he said after he'd bounced back into his seat.

"Might have been." I frowned at the road ahead, not entirely sure that's what I'd intended. "Did it work?"

Amir laughed and looked down at his phone, slipping his earphones back in. "Like I'm ever going to listen to *you*."

Which is exactly what I'd have said to Kam.

DECEMBER

CHAPTER 17

PabloPickaxo had dared Truth Girl to draw a toothpaste heart on Dare Boy's chest and lick it off. It was one of the racier dares that had come in through the comments, but I was game. It wasn't like the weather gave us much of an option on Silly-Stringing a car dealer.

Claire stared out of the window at where the wind was whipping through Sunny Slopes so violently that there were flowerpots all over the place and someone's picnic table had wedged its legs around the corner of Uncle D's caravan.

"OK..." She turned to look at me, eyes narrowed cautiously. "Off your T-shirt, right?"

"It says chest." I waved my phone, where I'd been logging all the dares that came in. "I'm freshly waxed and everything."

I'd just done a dare, waxing a strip of hair from my chest and nibbling the hair from the waxing strip.

"And this isn't, you know, *weird*?"

I knew what she was referring to. Dodged it.

"No weirder than anything else we've done."

"I meant—"

"I know." I turned away from her to fiddle with the tripod, bending down to check the camera was in position. "You meant about Laila?"

Even though I wasn't looking at her, I sensed the awkward way she shrugged.

"I don't think she'd care, Claire, or I wouldn't have suggested it."

Both one hundred per cent true and one hundred per cent lie depending on how my answer was interpreted. I'd already decided things would be easier if Claire carried on believing I still had a girlfriend. Things would be different if Claire was updated on my relationship status, but I didn't want to give her false hope and I didn't want to have to change the way I behaved around her – it was too much fun.

When the edited video came through, I got the all-over skin tingle that comes from knowing you're watching something special.

She's so awkward that this in itself was enough to get me grinning. The pair of us argue about the best way to apply toothpaste to my naked chest, then the video cuts to several short shots of us actually trying to get it on, ridiculous muzak playing in the background, pausing every so often to allow the viewer to hear how much we're laughing – toothpaste *everywhere*, dropping off my body, smeared all over Claire's hands and arms – until we finish with me holding my mask on and saying, *"I think I'm about to cry this thing off."*

Claire's giggling too much to get started and even once she does, she keeps stopping every two seconds.

"This is the worst thing I've ever had to do." "What if I overdose on fluoride?" "Stay still! You're making it harder."

Which was too easy.

"*I'm making what harder now?*"

And she slaps me right in the middle of my chest, leaving behind a toothpaste palm print.

"*Making more work for yourself there…*" I tell her.

The video cuts from that to when I started letting out groans and gasps, whispering, "*Yeah … that's the spot.*"

"*I hate you.*"

"*You hate PabloPickaxo.*"

"*No. It's definitely you I hate. Pablo never said anything about simulating sex noises.*"

My whip-fast "*Oh, these aren't my sex noises.*" Accompanied by a neat little cut of me giving the camera a salacious look.

Didn't know it would take off the way it did, but looking back I can see why. It was a sharp contrast to the video we filmed the following week after I'd wound her up about kissing me and fallen flat on my arse about breaking up with Laila.

I'd not wanted to click on the file she sent through, remembering how awkward it had been to film, Claire folded up, keeping her hands and her smiles and her thoughts to herself and me overcompensating, filling the space between us with noise. I'd left myself at the mercy of whatever edits she chose to make and it would have been very easy to make me look like an utter twat.

I wasn't sure that I wasn't one.

But Claire is nothing if not fair and the cut she sent over was fine.

Fine. A word that doesn't do what it says on the tin. Watching it through, there was none of the buzz of our old videos. The argument we'd had was there, in the thin line of her mouth, the studious concentration on the dare at hand.

I clicked back to the toothpaste video, where the pair of us look like we're friends who might be something more, having the kind of fun people want to be a part of. The internet loves a good ship and the views on that particular video had rocketed up, dragging the donations with it. And the subs.

I rewatched the video she'd just edited.

Truth Girl and Dare Boy had all the rapport of a dog chasing a car.

Banter was part of our brand – if we couldn't get it back we'd lose the audience I was so excited to finally start getting.

We'd fail. *I'd* fail.

But Claire had cooled off so fast that our friendship had turned frigid. I charted it in her messages – the brevity of each one inversely proportional to how long it would take for her to reply. I'd never had to go longer than the length of a lesson before and all the waiting made me restless, forever checking my phone in case she'd sent me something. One morning, Matty got halfway through telling me about some epic night out before I realized he was making the whole thing up when he uttered the sentence "… so then I asked a giant badger where was the best place to score some crack and he told me DiMaggio's." Finn just laughed at me and

teased me for being a space cake, but you could tell Matty took it personally. I'd been phasing out during a lot of our conversations.

The one and only time Claire responded with her usual speed was when I sent her a message during lunchbreak to say we'd met the target for shaving her head. Even then, her single thumbs-up emoji lacked enthusiasm.

I tried to type a thousand and one different messages that might encourage another rapid response, but in the end, all I sent was a string of excitable emojis. Rockets and stars and a fried egg.

"Don't you have Drama now?" Finn nudged me as he plopped down onto the common-room sofa next to me.

Glancing at the clock, I realized the bell must have gone fifteen minutes ago.

"Shit." I got up and grabbed my bag, hoping I had everything packed already, then paused a moment. I needed to get hold of some clippers if we were going to cut Claire's hair at the weekend.

"Do you want a lift home this evening?" I asked Finn.

CHAPTER 18

Finn had stopped shaving his head a while ago and went to the barber with Matty like someone bothered about his looks. Years he'd been ripping into me for taking care of myself but three months of sixth form and he'd turned dandy.

"Who they for?" he asked after he'd dug them out of the bottom of his wardrobe.

"Would you believe me if I said they were for me?"

Finn smiled. "I'd offer to do it for you and call your bluff."

I handed them back. "Go on then."

He just laughed, shaking his head at me. Known me too long. "If you wanted them for yourself, you'd have asked me to do it straight off."

"Thanks." I took the clippers. "I'll bring them back once I'm done."

"You can come round any time, you know. Not just when I ask." He nodded at the clippers. "Or when you want something."

I stared down at the clippers in my hand trying to think back to the last time I'd called round on my best mate without him inviting me. Finn waited, his careful stare asking me the questions he knew I wouldn't want turned into words,

wanting me to know he was there, that he'd listen.

I wished there was something I could tell him.

"Thanks, mate," I said, turning away. "For everything."

"Sure." One thing Finn would never do is pry.

Things still weren't right when I picked Claire up on Saturday.

"Hair looks nice," I said, my fingers tapping on the wheel. I was almost sorry we were going to cut it off. She looked cute with plaits.

"Thanks." She was already drawn into herself and I hated the way it felt like I was losing her the way I was losing everyone else. I didn't want to carry on like that. Couldn't.

"I'm sorry, OK?"

"What for?"

"I'm sorry I didn't tell you that I'd broken up with Laila. You're one of my best friends and…" I didn't want to be there, confessing this much to her, but what choice did I have?

"And?"

I turned to look at her, relieved to see the first smile I'd witnessed in a while breaking through her mood.

"Not going to make this easy for me, are you?"

"Any reason I should?"

"No. I'm sorry I hid the truth from you, C. I'll be straight with you from now on. About everything." Except Kam. Except the guilt I felt for what happened. Except, except except… "OK?"

"You're forgiven," she said.

* * *

Up at the caravan we set things up quickly and it hardly seemed any time at all before I was standing, revving the clippers like we were about to start a race and asking Claire if she was ready.

She gave me a baleful look. "I'm going to get into so much trouble over this."

I put the clippers down to lay my hand on her shoulder, pleased to feel her lean into me, rather than away.

"If it makes you feel any better, my dad has some very outdated views on boys who wear earrings."

A laugh puffed out of her. "That doesn't exactly make me feel better…"

"But it cheered you up, right?" I grinned at her then, and she flickered her gaze up to my eyes for a moment before looking away.

"A bit." She sucked in a long breath, holding it there as if the oxygen was enough to make her brave. "Let's do this."

Claire had used double-sided tape to fix her eye mask directly onto her skin so there'd be no straps to get in the way and plaited her hair into two long braids to make it easier to cut. Which might have worked if the scissors hadn't been so blunt that I had to hack and saw through each plait like I was chopping off a branch. Once they were off, I tried to raise a smile by wriggling her plaits around, hissing, "It's alive!" but all Claire managed was a weak little wibble of her lips before she turned to stare at the camera again, her hand going up to where her hair now hung, hacked jagged along her jaw.

I flicked on the clippers again, their high-pitched buzz piercing the bubble of anticipation in the air.

Claire met my gaze and locked her jaw.

In the edit, Claire sped the footage up and ran some music over it. It's a trick she uses on the videos with less banter and more action. If you watched it, you'd think it was funny.

But that's what editing is for. That's how our channel – any channel – operates. Show people only what you want them to see. It's why I have a hard time watching traditional vlogs. I can't believe they're real. Claire believes what people present to her, but I can't, because I *know*.

Running those clippers over Claire's head wasn't funny. It wasn't horrific or awkward, or any of those emotions that can be added in the edit.

It was intimate, pressing the blades into her head, feeling the give of her skin, the meagre cushion of flesh on bone, running the clippers over with one hand, the other brushing away the hair I'd shorn off, feeling the prickle of loose hair and the velveteen fuzz left behind.

Thinking back to my balls-up in the library, I ran my hands over her scalp one last time, dusting off any loose hairs, seeing her face bared, her ears and eyebrows and jawline all at once. As I looked at her, I thought about kissing Claire for real.

How much would I have to pay you to go there?

I didn't know which of us would carry the cost – Claire, who deserved something more than a boy who fed her

nothing but a lie, or me, too broken to be able to tell the difference between wanting to kiss a girl because I liked her, or because I needed her.

CHAPTER 19

It was a slow day. The last week of term and all anyone could think about was when it would end, even the teachers. For English, Kontos had scheduled a library lesson where we were supposed to be researching Chaucer's historical context. I was on my phone.

The donations were climbing up towards the target needed for me to do my streaking dare on Boxing Day. Whether they'd make it there before the twenty-sixth was another matter – and I'd have to film the dare on faith. And on my own. Claire was off to Ireland and already I was stressing out about what I was going to do with all the time that left me with…

I tapped subtly through the usual cycle – Twitter, Instagram, the channel itself and, just for good measure, just because I was avoiding having to actually read anything in Middle English, I checked our email.

And found the one from Moz.

"Where'd you get to yesterday?" Finn asked, sliding onto the common-room sofa. He'd messaged me a couple of times while Claire and I were with Moz in London, but I'd ignored them until later and fobbed him off with an excuse about my phone being out of battery.

"Coursework," I lied, surprised he'd even noticed I'd been gone. We don't have any subjects in common and we only sync on a few of our frees.

Finn stared at me for a very long moment, elbow propped on the back of the sofa as he gently tugged at the ear he was stretching.

"The kind of coursework that takes place in London?"

I was so unprepared that there was no way of styling out the way my head snapped up and my mouth started forming a horrified "What?"

"Mum was at a nursing conference in London yesterday. She left early. Same train as you, it turned out, same carriage."

Finn was looking at me closely, daring me to deny it.

"Said you were with a girl with very short hair." Finn's brows lowered a fraction. "That it looked like you were close…"

I turned away to dodge the disappointment in the way he was looking at me.

"So," Finn said. "Who is she?"

"Claire Casey." Finn frowned like the name might mean something and I added, "She's in the year below. We're just friends."

"Is she the reason for what happened with Laila?" The way he said it, the look he gave me, you'd think I'd done something wrong.

"Laila broke up with me, remember?"

"How would I remember when you never talked to me about it?" He sounded like Claire. Finn muttered something that sounded like "fuck" and he sagged forwards, letting out

a sigh strong enough to blow my discarded sweet wrappers off the table next to us. "Why couldn't you just be straight about it?"

"What? I am—"

"Seriously. Just stop. I was the person whose clippers you borrowed to cut her hair. Or are you so wrapped up in whatever this is that you forgot?"

He looked up to see from my expression that this was exactly what had happened.

"All this time I've been giving you space, backing you up when Matty bitches on about you cutting us out of your life. Him and then Laila – and I tell him the same thing I've been telling myself, that we need to let you work through what's happening with your family and…" He shook his head, mouth twisted in distaste. "I thought that maybe you might drift away from Matty for a bit, that Laila was a good girlfriend at a bad time, but you and me, Sef…"

Mild Finn Gardner, my best and oldest friend, was calling me out.

"You and me are mates, Finn."

"Mates *talk* to each other. When was the last time you were straight with me about anything that's going on in your life?"

I couldn't answer that.

"You don't need to say anything, Sef – I wouldn't be able to believe you anyway." He got up to leave, not even bothering to turn round when he said, "If you could give my clippers back, that'd be great."

CHAPTER 20

I had no one left but Claire and things there were still precarious. My apology over the Laila situation had patched things up enough for us to work on camera, but that wasn't enough. Not any more.

The next day, Claire was off for her Christmas break with her family and although we'd talked about meeting up for me to give her a birthday present, we'd not actually sorted anything out. Took me a while to work out that if I was waiting for her to suggest it, then it wouldn't happen and the relief I felt when she agreed was scary.

It wasn't until she got into the passenger seat that I knew what would happen. That I needed her to be more than whatever it was we'd become. This girl, with a shaved head and a hole in the knee of her leggings, whose body I'd once wrinkled my nose at…

I was going to kiss her.

We drove to the Forgotten Footpath, following it to where there's a bridge that crosses one of the streams that feeds into the Lay. Uncle D used to take us there on hot summer's days when we'd grown bored of the park. Felt nice to share something more of myself with her, something I didn't have to put into words.

Lying on the hilltop, I thought more and more about how

much I'd miss her over the holidays. Claire had become my escape from the world and all I wanted to do was hold her so close she couldn't leave. When we danced, I wondered if she could tell, with how tight I held her hand or the way that I looked at her, what it was I was feeling.

I don't dance on a hilltop with just anyone. I mean, who does?

When the song stopped, that should have been my moment, only she pulled away before I had a chance.

"What are you doing?" I pulled her towards me, my fingers knotting a little tighter around hers.

"You want to dance to this too?"

The way she wrinkled her nose wasn't pretty and yet…

"I thought we were aiming for a hat-trick of birthday goals?"

… I'd never wanted to kiss someone more than I did Claire.

I know the moves – I've kissed girls in clubs and house parties and on dark nights down by the river – but I've never touched a girl and watched her melt beneath my fingers the way Claire did, pushing her head against my hand, closing her eyes, drunk on touch.

"I've wanted to do that ever since we shaved your head."

"Head-stroking should definitely be added to the list of things people do on their birthdays…" I had her.

"I'm incorporating it into one of the others," I said.

I kissed her cheek, her jaw, the soft, pale skin of her neck, where she smelled like soap and tasted like comfort. Her chin. Her nose.

I felt like I was on fire for her by the time our lips met, everything sensible burned away by the feel of her mouth on mine, my hands in her hair, my body wrapped up in hers.

It was dangerous to let Claire get this close to me – as much for her as it was for me – but I've never let that stop me from doing something.

CHAPTER 21

We've always done Christmases well. Nan and Paps were never ones to turn down the opportunity to squash too many people around their dining-room table and talk over the top of them, whatever the holiday. Once they died – within a devastating three months of each other five years ago – Mum took over: Easter for Auntie Iffat, summer with Uncle D, Christmas at ours.

Not this year. Not with things the way they were between Auntie Iffat and Mum.

After the accident, me and Amir and Mum and Dad had lived in a bubble pierced only by visits from Uncle D and phone calls from Auntie Iffat. Living so far away, she was desperate to help. She'd order online shopping to be delivered to our house and call every evening to check in on Kam's progress.

For the first month or so, she was everything Mum needed in a sister. Until they talked about her coming to visit Kam.

I only caught the gist of it. Mum's voice was raised loud enough that the sound carried up the stairwell to where I was in Kam's room putting away the laundry I was proud to have washed myself.

"… how can you say that?" A pause. "Well, it's not helpful.

If you can't—" Interrupted. "I can't talk to you about this. Tell your husband to keep his opinions to himself!" I wondered what Uncle Ali had said. "No, Iffat, I'm not having anyone with that attitude come to visit. I'm sorry." That sounded ominous. "You think about that. I've got to go... OK ... well, bye then." And the conversation ended with the sound of the house phone clattering back onto the cradle.

Dad was there before I was and I stood, hidden from view, and listened to Mum tell him that Uncle Ali had said that we get what the world gives us for a reason.

"As if this is Kam's fault!" *No. Mine.*

Dad's voice was muffled when he spoke and I imagined him leaning over Mum and kissing her head. "You know how Ali thinks about these things."

"I know, but *my sister*..."

"It does not mean she does not love Kam."

"I can't have her visit knowing she thinks like this, I'm sorry."

The calls resumed after that – less frequent and shorter – and although the Christmas holiday was the first chance that all of them could visit, no one said anything about it happening, my parents throwing themselves into very different distractions. Dad took every job he could – it's a busy time of year for deliveries and if the law hadn't said otherwise, he'd have been driving twenty-four seven. Mum was the opposite. As her office wound down, she'd been spending more time at home, batch-cooking dishes to replenish the freezer stocks and teaching Amir how to make stuff like chicken biryani and shepherd's pie – the

same recipes she'd talked Kam through in preparation for uni, worried he'd fall into the typical student diet of baked beans and takeaway burgers.

For Amir, the problem was too much free time.

"What do you want?" I didn't even bother looking up from my laptop. Didn't need to, I could see him out of the corner of my eye, lurking in the doorway like a pungent shadow.

"I wouldn't ask, but…"

I paused the video I was watching and looked up at his ferrety little face, waiting for him to say it.

"Could you give me a lift?"

"Depends." I was only messing, but Amir looked crestfallen.

290

"Doesn't matter." The words practically fell out of his mouth, his lips were so slack and sullen.

"Oh, come on, you doughball. I'm not serious." I pushed the computer off my knee and got up, ready to go, but Amir stayed where he was, wary.

"It's to go see Kam."

My heart turned into a vortex, sucking any feeling into a black hole and leaving my insides cold.

"OK," I said. "I can drive you there."

He didn't trust what he'd heard, waiting for me to go first down the stairs and out of the door. Neither of us said anything in the car, the radio masking the suspicion that hung so heavy in the air around us, the DJ's inane banter providing the backdrop for the moment we both glanced, ever so slightly, to where the outline of the viaduct was

sharpened by crisp white winter light.

"Are you even allowed to come here without, like, booking?" I asked, eyeing up the front of the building.

Amir nodded. "So long as it's within a certain slot in his schedule."

The schedule had been pinned to the fridge by lumpy magnets made in art classes gone by, but of everyone in the house, I was the only one who'd have to look at it to know what Kam was up to. The rest of them had absorbed his routine into their psyche with the same ease as if he were living under our roof.

The thought of Kam being somewhere so far that Amir wouldn't be able to drop by for a visit like this twanged at my fears about the channel. No one would know about Moz being on board until he'd edited and uploaded the video and we'd not yet reached the target for my streaking video…

"Sef?" Amir had opened the door and was looking across at me. His expression was one I'd not seen for so long that it took me a moment to decode it. "Do you want to come in?"

Hope slipped from his face the longer it took me to answer.

"I can't, Amir."

And I waited for him to say something, to call me selfish or tell me he hated me, his anger my penance for being so weak.

I waited like I wanted it.

"Maybe next time," he said.

* * *

But next time was Christmas Day, and I didn't go then, either. I gave Amir Kam's present wrapped in newspaper because I hadn't been able to find where Mum had put the Christmas paper.

"What is it?"

"A photo."

"Who of?"

"Me. Blowing a kiss to the camera like I'm Marilyn fucking Monroe." I shoved the picture at him. "I'm assuming you'll be there when he opens it. See for yourself."

Amir grunted then gave me a look. "You could be there too, you know."

"Don't…" I said, squeezing my eyes shut and feeling sick with sadness.

"Is talking to the doctor helping?"

I kept my eyes shut so he wouldn't know the depth of the truth.

"No." Although I'm sure it might have done if I'd actually been to see him.

I Skyped Uncle D for the four hours they were gone. Although I'd been messaging him regularly, I'd not really been involved in the family Skype chats. Even from the screen of my laptop I could feel the warmth coming off him like he'd trapped the sun in his smile. Despite the different time zones, we ate our dinner together – Uncle D eating vicariously as I showed him all the party food I'd bought from Aldi.

"What's that you've got there?" he asked, leaning close enough to the webcam that I could see up his nose.

"Profiteroles."

Uncle D held up some greasy-looking pastry thing and grimaced. "I don't even like almonds."

It seemed so unfair that the only other person I felt like I could talk to was a four-hour time difference and over 4,500 miles away. Four hours and the only time we were silent was when either of us had to go to the loo.

"Thank you," I said after Dad's van pulled up outside.

"You don't have to thank me for loving you, Sef. Merry Christmas."

Christmas last year. We were four of us, sitting under the stars in plastic chairs intended for warmer conditions than approaching freezing on a midwinter's night. My brothers sitting either side of me, Zahid lounging opposite, feet propped on the table where we'd put our drinks. I studied the soles of his trainers enviously. If he hadn't been two sizes smaller than me, I'd have tried hiding them when it came time for him to pack up and go home.

"If you could buy one person one thing – *anything* – in the world, who would it be and what?" Kam tipped his head back and puffed his breath into the air, before adding, "Anyone except the four of us."

Our street was still soused with the Christmas spirit and I idly counted the number of houses backing onto ours that still had lights in the windows.

"I'd buy my girlfriend something," Zahid said with a grin, interrupting me at house number eight.

Neither Uncle Ali nor Auntie Iffat knew about the

girlfriend, but Zahid had shown us pictures on his phone as evidence. Nothing too racy, but enough to convince even me that Kayleigh existed.

"What would you buy her?" Amir was enjoying being too old to be considered a child, unlike Parveen, who'd been sent to bed in a rage at not being allowed to stay up with the rest of us.

"Money's no object?" Zahid asked and we all looked to Kam for the ruling.

"None at all."

"There's this handbag all the girls at school want," he said. "Designer. Kayleigh's got, like, a knock-off from the market or whatever, but I'd buy her the real thing."

None of us teased him for it, because it was obvious he was serious. That he liked Kayleigh enough to notice her handbag and refrain from showing us the photos he had of her in her bra.

I was almost as jealous of him for that as I was for the trainers. Almost.

"What about you?" Kam asked Amir, who was obviously itching to get his answer out.

"A car for Mum. Nothing too fancy, or she wouldn't want to drive it anywhere. Just a Mercedes or something."

I huffed out a laugh as I sipped my drink. *Just a Mercedes.*

"Good gift," said Kam. "Leaves me with Mrs B all to myself."

"Who the fuck is Mrs B?" asked Zahid.

"*Our* car," I said, giving Kam a meaningful look. "September the second and she'll be mine…"

"*Half* yours."

"So who are you buying a present for, then?" I asked him.

Kam narrowed his eyes, thinking, although I reckoned he'd already thought of someone since he was the one who'd asked the question.

"I'd buy Dad a really expensive tailored suit."

I pulled a face. "What for? So he could look like a chauffeur when he's driving around in his van?"

"For no reason at all. Just because it's nice, isn't it? Having one expensive thing."

"Wouldn't know…" Although even as I said it, I thought of all the stuff I had – my phone, my watch, even my shoes – all of them more expensive than what Dad would choose for himself.

"What'd you buy?" Zahid flicked something at me that missed.

I glanced back towards the house, to where I could see all the parents with Uncle D playing Trivial Pursuit round the dining table.

"I'd buy Uncle D a house," I said. "One so nice he'd never want to leave it."

And I'd buy it as close to ours as I could.

CHAPTER 22

When someone knocked on the bedroom door on Boxing Day, I wasn't expecting it to be Amir.

"What's up?" I said, bouncing on the balls of my feet as I looked out the window, too jittery to stay still. For the first time since we started the channel, I was nervous about doing a dare. Moz's video had gone live and even with it being Christmas – perhaps *because* of it being Christmas and people wanting to escape their families – the numbers on our channel had rocketed, and we'd smashed the target.

And the first video we'd be uploading for our new audience would be of me streaking at a football match. (Sort of – I had a jock strap. You can get charged with indecency if you go full monty.) Waiting for my performance, I was starting to get an inkling of how Claire had felt before we took a razor to her head...

"Wanted to see if you were OK," Amir said.

The night before I'd had a massive row with Dad and the house hadn't yet recovered. We'd both said some pretty unforgivable things.

"I'm fine." I puffed a breath onto the glass and drew a little smiley face in the condensation before it faded to nothing.

"Actually, I wondered if you wanted to talk about it..."

"Why do you all think it's that easy?"

"I don't!" He laughed then and I turned round in surprise. "It's not always about you... I meant, did you want me to talk to you about Kam? About yesterday and what it was like?"

I watched him, wary of the offer, wondering if it was a trick to get me to open up about what was wrong with me, but Amir just stood there, not hopeful, not anything. Waiting.

"OK then..." My worries about the dare had faded away, replaced with the swell of fear I felt whenever I thought about Kam, but I sat down on my bed, knees bent, as I watched Amir sit on the floor opposite, mirroring my posture.

How I used to sit in here and talk to Kam.

"How was it?" My throat felt dry and my heart stuttered over every beat.

"Nice. You've been inside, right?" I nodded, one swift, shameful duck of the head. "They'd hung fairy lights along the ceiling so you felt a bit like you were walking into a grotto and one of the nurses and some of the other staff had helped him decorate his room."

"Helped him?" I asked, confused.

Amir gave a hint of a shrug. "Showed him the decorations they had, let him pick the ones they put up."

My parents talked about how much better it was once Kam had enough control over his muscles to point. *Pointing*. A skill so basic babies learn it without anyone teaching them, but for my brother it had taken hours of

physio across *weeks* of his life to learn how to make his muscles obey his brain, to teach his brain to understand what was being asked of it.

"What did it look like, the room?" I asked, my attention focused on a crease in my duvet.

"Would you like to see a picture?" Amir pulled his phone from his pocket. "I took a few."

"Just of the room?" I said, not sure I was ready to see a picture of the person who lived in it.

"OK." Amir tapped open one of them and got up to pass me his phone. Through the starburst of his cracked screen I could see Kam's room, his home, the bed he slept on with its metal mechanisms, the drip stands and other miscellaneous equipment that I couldn't identify. Beyond that the walls were lined with familiar posters and pictures, the globe on his windowsill masked by a line of Christmas cards. Garlands of silver and green tinsel hung in ungainly loops from the ceiling.

"Our dinner slot was one of the early ones, so we ate first," Amir said.

"I didn't think Kam ate solids?"

Amir shrugged. "He doesn't. But he can eat potatoes mashed up with gravy and there was trifle for pudding."

"But he can't…?"

"He needs help getting the food into his mouth."

I didn't understand how matter-of-fact Amir was about all this.

"And that's not…" I couldn't really put it into words. "Is that, you know, hard to watch?"

Amir looked across at me as if I was the one who was difficult to understand. "Does it matter if it is? Cutting up turkey with a knife and fork isn't as important as being able to eat together."

I looked down at the phone I was still holding, wondering what other pictures were on there.

"What did you do after dinner?"

"Presents."

He was waiting for me to say it.

"Did you give him mine?"

"Uh-huh."

"Did he open it?"

"No," Amir said quietly. "He only wanted to open presents with the people who were there." I closed my eyes, tears leaking out through my lashes. "We put yours with the ones the rest of the family sent over. He might change his mind next time – Kam's not always consistent about what he wants."

"Sure." I blinked away my misery and looked at Amir. "So, did he like what you gave him?"

He grinned then. "I bought him a Lego rocket and we made part of it together – want to see?"

Once I nodded, Amir leaned over and swiped through to a picture of him and Kam leaning over a tray of Lego. My fingers hurt from how tight I was gripping the phone and I leaned into my first sight of Kam in four months. The photo had been taken from over Kam's shoulder and all I could see was his right ear, the vague hint of a smiling profile and the scar on his head.

"How far did you get?" I asked.

"Not far. But it's something we can keep working on together every time I visit."

"Did you—?" I faltered. "Did he have a good Christmas?"

Amir took the phone from me and swiped along a bit, keeping the screen hidden. "I think so. He got tired towards the end, though. Started shouting at us."

"What was he saying?"

"Wasn't using the app, so we don't know." He looked up and I saw the hand holding the phone was trembling slightly. "Do you want to see a picture of him? A proper one?"

CHAPTER 23

Everyone at West Bridge might have liked Kam, but there were only ever two people that mattered – Danny and Hamish.

He didn't even like them at first. Danny and Hamish were already tight by the time Kam joined in Year 9 – Danny was sharp and sarcastic, as smart as Kam and twice as cutting with it, and Hamish acted like his bodyguard. But slowly, as they grew older, the three of them grew closer. Hamish stopped caring about throwing his weight around and Danny mellowed to the point where he became one of the funniest people I knew. Even Dad liked him enough that when Kam let slip Danny was bisexual, Dad just muttered, "Some people are, I suppose" and carried on laughing at his jokes.

Late one Saturday, when there was only me and Mum still awake, watching trash TV and eating chocolate buttons on the sofa together – Kam stumbled in through the door, blood all over his best T-shirt and his hand over his nose so that he had to say it twice before we heard: "I might have been in a fight."

Never one to panic, Mum sent me upstairs to get the first-aid kit and led Kam into the kitchen. When I came back down, she was tilting his head all around under the fluorescent lights, frowning and poking him.

"Ow!"

"It's just bruising. You'll be fine. Let's get you cleaned up."

As Kam sat on a chair I brought in from the dining table, Mum washed him off with warm water and TCP, tutting every time he winced. He'd been queuing with Hamish in the Chicken Shop on the parade while Danny was on the phone outside. Some drunk bloke started throwing chips at Danny and calling him names.

Mum asked what names and Kam met my eyes where I was standing behind her wrapping the frozen peas in a tea towel. She wouldn't have asked if Danny wasn't white, but there are some prejudices Mum doesn't see.

"Nasty names, Mum. The sort you don't want me repeating."

"Oh," she'd said. "And Danny retaliated."

"He told the guy to perform an impossible sexual act…"

Mum rolled her eyes.

"… and the guy objected. Physically."

"And you thought the best way to help Danny was to rush face-first into that person's fist?"

"Danny's my friend, Mum."

"Your friends will be the death of you, Kamran Malik." She held out her hand to me. "Pass me the peas, Sef."

New Year's Eve I got a message from Danny.

I don't know what to do with myself tonight. You?

We had stayed in touch since he went to uni – me drawing comfort from knowing there was someone else

who felt responsible for what happened, him needing someone who would tell him about Kam.

No idea, mate. I replied. **Hamish not around?**

But I knew he wasn't because I'd seen the postcards that came through the door from all the places Hamish had been travelling, all addressed to Kam. All stacked neatly on the radiator, as if denying Kam access to the postcards was a way to punish Hamish for sending them. Punishing him for being able to go on with his life when Kam couldn't.

My parents were punishing Danny, too. Whenever anyone (who hadn't made the mistake of saying the wrong thing) wanted to visit Kam, Mum would arrange for them to come on a Sunday afternoon and escort them to the Rec herself – a trickle of aunties and uncles and cousins, family friends and our next-door neighbour – but not Danny. When he'd emailed me to ask if he could see Kam when he came home for Christmas, I'd forwarded it to Mum.

Her reply had been succinct: *Here are the best times for Kamran to receive visitors. I'm sure Daniel will understand that he'll have to arrange this himself.*

Kamran and Daniel. Mum only uses long names when she's too upset to think informally.

When Danny asked me if I wanted to hang out with him for New Year, I said yes. Claire wasn't free and I'd pushed my own friends too far to call them back.

University had changed Danny. He looked softer, like he might have been living on the diet of burgers and beans that my mum was so disparaging about. His shirt wasn't ironed, either – another thing she'd insisted Kam learn how

to do. But Danny also seemed older – not cocky, like the students at Cine Obscura, but more mature. Wiser.

Or maybe that was just the accident. This was the first time I'd seen him since I'd run into A & E to find him sitting white and shaking on one of the plastic chairs by the entrance, the phone he'd used to call me still clutched in his hand as Hamish shouted at the people on reception.

Danny was surprised when I asked for a JD and coke at the bar. A double.

"Didn't think you drank…"

"Not often." Or ever, as far as my family are concerned, but other people drown their sorrows – thought I might give it a go. New experiences for a new year.

"Thanks for the emails, Sef." Danny lifted his glass and chinked it against mine. "It meant a lot."

I shrugged, like it was no big deal and took a swig of my drink. Couldn't tell him that they meant a lot to me, too.

My drink wasn't pleasant, but the more I drank, the less it mattered, and for the first couple of rounds we talked about university – Danny's Psychology course, the halls he was living in, a boy he'd hooked up with who refused to acknowledge anything had happened because he had a girlfriend back home. Kam was always talking about Danny's doomed crushes, using him as an example of why it was better to avoid relationships altogether.

By number three the alcohol had loosened us enough to talk about the one person we had in common.

"It's not as bad as I thought it'd be, that place," Danny said, studying the ice in his gin and tonic.

"Great facilities," I said. I knew more about the Recreare than the person I supposedly visited there. "Nice staff. They've got a pool."

"Kam seems happy, I guess. Do you think?"

"I do think." I chucked back the rest of my drink and shook my glass to make the ice tinkle. "You want another?"

Danny checked his watch. "Not yet. Need to pace myself."

There was a suggestion in the way he looked at me that I should do likewise, but the girl behind the bar was already taking my money.

"But he is happy, right?" Danny repeated, like my answer mattered.

"Did I tell you they have a pool?"

"You did." Danny was looking at me funny and I felt like poking him on the nose. Managed to refrain.

"Sef." He laid a hand on my shoulder.

"Danny." I laid my hand over his and grinned.

"I'm serious. Do you think Kam's happy?"

My hand slid away. "I don't know. Ask Amir."

"You what? Why?"

"Amir's the mind-reader, the boy who talks to vegetables."

Danny's confusion turned to disgust. "Fucking hell, Sef!" He shoved me away. "What the – how – you can't talk like that!"

"Is a joke."

"I don't care, it's not fucking funny! It's—"

"I know." The stupid smile I'd plastered on fell away. "None of it is. I don't know why I said it. I'm sorry."

"I'm not the one you should say it to."

"Apologies mean nothing." I banged my glass down to make my point and the guy next to me told me to watch it. "Sorry changes *nothing*."

"I know, Sef, all right." He apologized to the man I'd swayed into before turning his attention back to me. "Nothing can change what happened, I know..." It still seemed like he might be talking to someone else, maybe not the man, though, given how Danny's eyes seemed small and pink and sad as he stared at the floor.

"Why didn't you?" I asked.

"Didn't I what?"

"Change things. If you hadn't been up there..." But that hadn't been Danny's fault... "If I hadn't gone on at him about it..."

"Slow down, all right?" Danny laid a hand on my arm and I stared at the chapped skin of his knuckles. "What are you on about? This isn't anyone's fault."

"You saying it's his?!" Was Danny pulling an Auntie Iffat? I tried to stand up and failed, got my legs tangled in the bar stool.

"No, that's not—"

But anything Danny was saying had stopped making sense, like I could only hear the things I expected him to say, my own guilt projected onto one of the two people in the world who might know what it felt like.

"I'm the one. Me." I still couldn't disentangle myself from the bar stool. "Didn't you see the sign?"

"You're not making any sense, mate – shit – I knew

I shouldn't have let you have another. Sef?"

"You should have stopped him!" I yelled.

"Sef – stop shouting."

"It's my fault!" I finally broke free of my stupid bar stool and stumbled forward, arm out to balance – I'd fallen off a cliff. A bridge. Alcohol impacting on my brain the same way the rocks had smashed into Kam's…

I felt hands pulling me up and I was yelling at Danny to stop him – them – me? – finding myself bundled outside, my arms wrapped round his neck so that I was sobbing into his shoulder.

"I'm sorry, I'm sorry, I'm so sorry…"

As the words looped in my ears, around my brain, out my mouth, I cried harder and harder until I had to push away from Danny to throw up in one of the beer-barrel planters by the door.

Apologies mean nothing.

JANUARY

CHAPTER 24

So much of my holiday had been spent on the same circuit: Instagram, Twitter, our channel, Moz's video, the donations page, Instagram, Twitter… The only time I felt like I could relax was once Claire was back. As if being with her gave me permission to stop.

Whereas school got in the way.

"I've been standing here for thirty seconds, you know."

I assumed whoever it was couldn't have been talking to me.

"Hello…? Sef?" A hand swept back and forth between my gaze and the screen. Small. Brown. Gold rings and red nails. Laila.

"What?" I looked up fast enough to catch the disapproval she tried to hide.

"We've got English."

"Have we?"

This time she let her exasperation show. "It's been the same time every Thursday since September. Come on."

I looked at my phone. Moz had posted the second video to bait his viewers into donating more for a chance to be part of the food fight and I hit refresh on the donations page – to find it snatched from my hand. Laila took a step back, fingers wrapped round my phone casing as she

waggled it, like a bone to a dog.

"Give it back, Laila." I held out my hand, barely able to keep the irritation from my voice.

"No … you have to –" she glanced over her shoulder to navigate her way across the room – "come with me to lessons."

"What are you, my mum?"

That hit its target. She stopped smiling, her arm slowly coming down. The look on her face wasn't one I recognized, not even after years of being friends, months of being something more. Puzzled and hurt. Embarrassed. We weren't the only people in the common room – other people who had frees were still there, some bell-stallers for the next lesson. Helen, who had English too, waited by the door, shaking her head.

"I'm just trying to get you to come to English, Sef."

"Why?"

"Because that's where you're supposed to be."

"So? Isn't it up to me to decide whether I go to lessons?" I snapped my fingers for my phone. "Give. It. Back."

"Come to English." Laila tightened her grip on my phone, hugging it to her chest.

"Give me the phone, Laila." I stepped over and she stepped back – a parody of the sort of fight I might have had with Kam or Amir – and I darted in to snatch it back.

Missed.

"What's wrong with you?" Every last trace of humour had drained from her face, eyes wide, not quite believing what she was seeing.

"Nothing! Just give me my phone and fuck off to your lesson." I was shouting now, the whole room stopping what they were doing to stare as I told one of the most loyal friends I'd ever had to fuck off.

"Fine." Laila's voice was quieter than mine, but it hurt so much more to hear. She held out my phone and, without hesitation, I plucked it from her grasp, tapping in my passcode to check for views.

When I looked up, she'd gone.

Fame brings misfortune more assuredly than it brings anything else and as the comments multiplied on our channel, so did the venom. Cruel comments on Claire's body and her face, stuff that she showed a remarkable resilience to until the cinema incident with her friend Seren reminded me that Claire had already had practice at this. Practice at *pretending* – didn't mean it wasn't cutting her beneath the surface and I took every care to make sure she knew that whatever was being said, it wasn't real. I'd kiss the skin that winked between her T-shirt and her jeans, tell her that she was gorgeous.

Show her what I meant by that.

It was a surprise, up in the caravan, my hands all over Claire's body, taking things so much further than I'd felt comfortable doing with Laila. A surprise at how easy it was. How enjoyable. How having Claire that close felt safe when the thought of letting anyone else in felt so dangerous.

But there were other dangers out there. Comments that couldn't be kissed away. Not about her, but about me.

Claire called me in tears during my shift and I had to sneak into the staff room to take it, pissing off the guy I was working with.

"What is it? Are you OK?"

"No…" She just kept crying, worrying me with every sniffle until she blurted out, "Someone's left some more horrid comments on the *TRUTH: Coupled Up?* video."

I didn't understand. I'd done a comment sweep a few hours ago and there'd not been anything to raise the alarm.

"About you," she whispered.

"Oh," I said, staring at the broken padlock that hangs off my locker. She meant those ones. "That. Racist troll in internet shocker. Be sure to get the *Daily Mail* on that, yeah?"

I was surprised it had taken this long.

"It's *awful*." I could picture her then, knew exactly what Claire looked like when she was appalled by something.

"I know, but I'm at work, so…" I could feel myself getting irritated.

"I was worried you might have seen it."

"Of course I've seen it." I rolled my eyes and started pacing the room. "It's not the first time I've been called those things, Claire."

Diet, heritage, birthplace. Terrorist leanings. All fair game for bigots.

An anonymous weasel bashing away at a keyboard bothered me a lot less than an angry mob of snot-nosed runts following me down the street. Or an old lady shouting

at my mum in Tesco. Or the people in my class who shouted up to defend free speech while shouting down my right to be offended by it.

Claire was asking if I was OK, annoying me because it wasn't really about me being OK at all, it was about making her feel OK.

"People are racist. Shit happens."

"I'm not racist," she said in a small voice. But whatever Claire wanted not to be, she couldn't help being privileged. Couldn't help but see something awful aimed at me and feel upset about it herself.

"I know," I said, trying to be patient. "But I've had a lot of practice at this, OK? So ... can you maybe let me get back to work before Brian starts hurling justified abuse at me for being a skiving bastard?"

It wasn't the funniest of jokes, but it got her off the line.

CHAPTER 25

It was Moz who decided that Claire should kick things off for the food fight.

Me???

You. Viewers have seen more (too much) – winky face – *of Dare Boy. Time we saw Truth Girl get her hands dirty.*

We'd been on a group chat, but Claire was sitting curled into the crook of my body as we lay on the bed in the caravan, not-quite-watching a movie on her laptop, and I recognized the panic burning in her eyes as she showed me the message on her phone.

"You'll be fine…" I'd murmured. Jealous as I was, there's never been any point arguing with Moz. What Moz wants, Moz gets.

I'd kissed her bare shoulder, pressed my face into her skin and wrapped my arms around her body, wondering whether I could make her feel safe too, or whether it only worked one way.

I felt so proud of her when she clambered up onto the table, fist raised like she was starting a revolution, but as soon as the first bun was fired, I lost sight of her, too immersed in my own battles, my arms aching from throwing food at my ten-second friends, people whose names I didn't need to

know to get off on the high of fighting with them.

When the whistle went, Moz was near enough to slip across the spaghetti-strewn floor to deliver a straight-to-camera shot, his hair matted with what looked like ice cream, a tomato-sauce handprint smeared across the side of his face like sweet and sticky blood.

"And so the fun begins…" He blew a kiss to the camera, winked at me and ran.

I waited until the last possible second to run so that it felt more like fleeing, a rocket of adrenalin tearing through my body, burning brighter, hotter, faster than anything I'd felt before – on the car roof in London or even on Valley FC's frosted football pitch. It was the closest the dares had brought me to the rush I'd felt the moment I stepped off the viaduct. I wondered if this was the last thing Kam had experienced before his life crashed in on him.

The world flipped the wrong way up and I exploded on impact, my armour blasted off to leave me bare.

Driving back, I found it hard to keep within the speed limit, the need to escape weighing down my foot as it rested on the accelerator, making me impulsive as I pulled in front of that car or tried to make it through those lights…

Claire might have asked me to slow down but I'm not sure I heard her until she let out a frightened little squeak when I misjudged the roundabout leading off the motorway.

"I'm sorry…" I'd barely remembered she was there.

The girl who'd brought me hope.

When I met her, Claire had turned down going "For a ride in a strange car driven by someone yet to pass their

test" – she'd been someone who sculpted her life around doing things right, pleasing other people, avoiding getting into trouble. If you watch the early videos, you can see it there, under the smiles and the jokes, the banter we've got, a tremble of fear that she is doing something wrong.

The channel had made her bolder, brought her strength, whereas I felt it was about to bring me face to face with my weakness.

The food fight was the biggest dare we'd done, but the thing I was running from now was the fear – the certainty – that it wasn't going to be enough.

When I pulled over, Claire was out before I had a chance to say anything in reply to her goodbye, but when she walked round to my side of the car, I wound the window down in time to catch the sleeve of her coat.

"Come here…"

"What?" She leaned on the sill of my window, hat pulled down over her ears, skimming the line of her eyebrows. Her nose was red from the cold and there was a rash of small red spots on her chin that had flared up from under her foundation.

"Thank you," I said.

"What for?"

"For all this."

"You don't need to thank me."

"I'm sorry." I kissed her on the lips, more desperate than tender.

"Sef…" She stroked my face, her thumb tracing in the wake of my tear. "Are you all right?"

I shook my head. "I'm frightened. What if he can't stay there? What will happen? Where will he go?"

"I get it." She kissed me on the forehead. "I'm frightened too."

"We're not going to make it."

"Shush now." She kissed the tears from my cheeks, the words from my lips. "We still have time."

I shook my head, but she reached in and cradled my head in her hands.

"Let's just see, OK? No giving up. Not yet." Her eyes were as gentle as her hands. "We're going to do this. It's not going to happen. Kam will be safe, I promise."

CHAPTER 26

Back in September, I'd thought we could raise over sixty thousand pounds in the time we had. The page for the Rec says it takes *millions* to run – compared to that, sixty grand isn't that much, but compare it to the amounts of money people raise on the internet for charity and sixty thousand pounds is *huge*.

I'd been kidding myself, hiking my hopes up to match the amount.

Our idea wasn't original, but our brand was. Claire's talent for tech and mine for messing around, multiplied by our onscreen chemistry, that was our magic formula. We'd go viral within weeks…

Equation not working? Change the formula. Add a Moz-shaped catalyst.

We'd had until March to make a difference and all of a sudden it was February.

With nothing doing on the channel, I was downstairs writing an essay when the phone rang. I yelled for Amir three times before I gave up and ran to catch the house phone on the last ring.

"Hello?"

"Hello, please can I speak to Omar or Farah Malik?"

I was surprised it was actually a human – most of the

317

house calls are robot voices talking about insurance claims and stuff.

I slipped automatically into being a kid, when I'd race for the phone to play at being grown-up and important. "Can I ask who's calling?"

"It's Genevieve Tatlock, from the Recreare, regarding their son, Kamran."

"Oh." And without hesitation, I told her, "This is Omar."

My best Dad voice is usually reserved for taking the piss, but there are other benefits.

"Of course, didn't recognize you on the phone for a moment there!" Her voice thawed a little. "It's about the directors' meeting. I'm afraid that things haven't worked out the way we'd hoped."

"How do you mean?" You have to be so careful, pretending to be someone else. Would my dad say that?

Apparently he would. "I was hoping we could talk about this all together, rather than over the phone."

"Please…" My voice was my own, but she didn't seem to notice.

"I'm really sorry to have to tell you this, but I've spoken with the long-term care team and although I made the case for Kam to continue his stay on a rolling basis, I'm afraid without guaranteed funding, he'll need to be moved by the end of this—"

"No."

"I'm sorry?"

"No, no, he has to stay."

"Omar?"

"How much do you need?"

"Is everything OK?"

"HOW. MUCH." I screamed into the handset.

"Who is this? I need to speak to—"

But I missed the end of her question as the phone smashed against the opposite wall, the battery case falling open. I picked up other things, anything. Throwing them across the room and shouting. Pictures and trophies and DVD cases – a vase, the clock...

Amir was thundering down the stairs and flew through the door. "What the—"

Olympus Has Fallen caught him across the forehead and he ducked back into the hall.

"Sef! Stop it! Stop throwing stuff."

"MAKE ME!"

But he didn't. He just waited outside in the hall as I threw everything I could around the front room, rampant in my rage, powerless to stop what was happening to Kam. I swept my arm along the shelves, sending the remaining plastic cases flying, the atlas Mum gave Dad for his fortieth knocking over the big lamp. I hurled a set of coasters at the window and reached for the last thing left standing on the mantelpiece.

A photo of Kam. One they took at Christmas with him wearing a flashing Rudolph badge and a massive smile – one that is *really* his, not just a projection of what other people want to see when they look at him.

I smashed it into the marble ledge, the glass shattering in my grip, cutting deep into the flesh of my palm, my fingers

still wrapped round the picture inside, as if by clinging on to this, I could cling on to Kam.

There was a noise by the door into the hall and Amir peered round the doorframe, gazing at the mess I'd made, fragments of china and glass, the plastic cases that had popped open to spill shiny blue and silver discs across the carpet.

There was a gouge out of the wall where I'd first thrown the phone.

"OK…" He finally looked at me, standing there, clutching the photo frame, panting. Blood running through my fingers.

"I'm fine," I said.

Amir eyed the debris at my feet. "Can see that."

Then he stepped in properly and squatted down, picking up one of the ancient DVD cases and slipping the disc back inside. A workout one Mum never has the time to use.

"You don't have to help."

"I know," he said, and carried on helping.

I was in for it when my parents got back.

Genevieve Tatlock had called Mum on her mobile, but Dad was the closest to home and he found me sitting at the dining-room table, superglue squidging out of the cracks in the vase Mum had inherited from Nan.

Not all rage is loud.

I watched as Dad sat in his chair at the end of the table and reached for the first-aid kit.

"Give me your hand, Yousef."

When Mum arrived, he'd redone Amir's botched attempt at dressing my wound and we collected what couldn't be

salvaged into a bin bag. After that, she asked Amir if he'd give us a minute – one that turned into half an hour, in which my parents took turns telling me off for trashing the joint, for impersonating Dad, for how I'd shouted at the woman from the Rec…

Mum suggested booking extra counselling sessions, but Dad rolled his eyes and made a pointed remark about how well they'd been working so far.

"I don't want extra sessions," I said.

"You'll have extra sessions whether you want them or not!" Mum jabbed a finger in the direction of the front room. "Please, Sef. This is not healthy."

After we agreed a sum for me to pay back the damage, they called Amir down and then, their faces as calm as if they were telling us they'd decided to buy a new fridge, they told us the things they thought we should know. The things they'd hoped never to have to tell us.

"Kam's made strides since he went to the Recreare." Mum only needed to say that for my benefit – Amir knew those strides, had been walking the path with him. "And we're proud of how hard he's worked to get where he is. So proud."

There was a catch in her voice and Dad reached across to take her hand.

"Kam is severely disabled," he said, a word I'd never heard used in our house before then. "Hard work does not change that and although we hoped for the best, it has not happened."

"What do you mean?" Amir looked from Dad to Mum.

"What your father is saying is that Kam's condition is

complicated and he continues to need a very high level of care. We'd hoped he could continue to receive this at the Recreare." *Hoped*. A word that rang out as loud as a gunshot. "Kam moved there on a short-term basis, but long-term care requires a financial assurance that we can't give them."

"Why not?"

"We don't have enough money, Amir. Your uncle's been helping and we've looked at everything we can do, but we don't have enough."

"How much do you need?" I asked, only daring to dart a look in my parents' direction, ashamed of how I'd shouted that same question down the phone only hours earlier.

"It doesn't matter how much, Sef…" Mum said.

"What if—"

"There are no 'what ifs'." Dad spoke up, lifting his glasses to rub his eyes. "It is too much. This is not just about the next six months, but the rest of your brother's life. Now is the time for us to think about putting what we do have to the best possible use. We must find something that we can afford."

Amir was frowning, confused. "How does everyone else manage?"

"Compensation claims…" Mum began, her words bitter pills forced down my throat, the poison of their meaning seeping into me.

"Then we get one of those!" Amir stared at them, desperate for hope.

Mum glanced at Dad. "Amir. We've tried. There's no money," she said. "Kam will have to move before March."

The second I left the front room, I messaged Moz, ready to grovel over what a dick I'd been about the money. But Moz is as quick through his moods as he is through his infamous hook-ups and I pitched the idea I'd been toying with for the last few days, expecting him to go for it.

Chicken only works if you think the other person won't pull away. Moz's reaction was underwhelming.

I won't pull away.

Then I will. I don't want to die.

Why do you tell me that if you want me to believe it???

Because it doesn't matter, the viewers aren't going to believe it, they're not stupid, they know neither of us wants to die – and the second they think it's framed is the second you lose them.

So you think us going "We'll play chicken if you raise forty thousand quid" isn't going to work?

40K??? Are you high? 20, like before.

IT'S NOT ENOUGH.

IT'S THE BEST WE CAN DO.

I smacked the screen of my phone against my forehead a couple of times, trying to get it together before I replied.

That's all we asked for last time. Can't we ask for more?

Not if you want to reach the target.

Whatever. So chicken's out...

Didn't say it was out, mate. This is a private chat right?

Please don't send me a picture of your dick.

Like you'd be so lucky. I meant you're not sharing this with your girlfriend?

No. But I forgot and had to add, **She's not my girlfriend.**

Whatever she is, are you game to prank her? Properly.

As I said before: there's nothing I wouldn't do to save my brother.

PART THREE: CLAIRE & SEF

FEBRUARY

SUNDAY

SEF

Ahead of me is a wall of white light and I hold out for as long as I can. Longer than Moz.

We swerve and I'm roaring with the effort of keeping my hands locked around the wheel, the car sliding sideways. It's all happening too fast and as the car snakes beneath me, my foot slams down stupidly on the brakes, arms yanking the wheel the other way, throwing us into a full spin. Claire screams at a deafening *bang* and the judder of something smashing against us. The impact jars my arms, my shoulders, my neck and my teeth clack together, slicing into my tongue.

I'm shaving along the edge of death, laughter sparking out of me, lighting up the dark.

The car slows and stops, and my foot falls off the clutch so the engine bangs, jolting us forward one last time.

There's pain in my chest and shoulders and sides, cramp in my wrists, blood on my tongue, my body on fire with being alive.

Wanting to feel the same fire burning in her, I lean over to kiss Claire…

"WHAT THE HELL?"

She lashes a sharp, violent slap across my face, then

launches her whole body at me, straining against the seat belt as she pummels and punches any part of me she can reach, shouting and screaming at me.

"I *hate* you – why did you do that – you could have killed us…" She's sobbing, too angry to take in enough air to breathe and she starts choking.

I reach out, but she shoves me off.

"Don't touch me!" She unclicks her belt and pulls at the door handle. "Unlock it."

I do and she's out of the car, staggering away from me towards Moz. Scrabbling out of the car, I run after her.

Up ahead Moz is already out of his car and whooping at the night sky. "That was AMAZING!"

He holds a fist up for Claire to bump and she slaps him, too.

"Ow!" Moz presses his hand to his face looking utterly shocked. "What was that for?"

The noises Claire stutters are hot rocks spitting from a volcano before the lava flow wipes out the island. I reach for her arm, hoping to quell the rage, but she spins round, anger concentrated on me.

"I said don't touch me. Ever."

And then she's off, marching away across the track.

For the first time in his life, Moz looks like he isn't so sure of what's happening.

"You need to sort this out, Sef," he says, walking back to his car. "I'm going to give you two a bit of space – this better not have been a massive fucking waste of my time."

I hear the rev of an engine, one throatier and more powerful than poor Mrs Bennet. Moz has gone, then.

"Claire! Where are you going?" Feet scuffing on the loose gravel behind me.

"Home." I flinch away from the hand Sef's reached out to hold me back and keep marching forwards. Everything hurts, the burn on my neck and an ache in my chest where the seat belt bit into me, the skin on the palm of my hand from slapping Sef and then Moz. My heart hurts so much I can barely withstand the pain of it.

"Don't be daft. I'll drive you—"

"I will never get in that car again."

"Won't you?" Behind the words there's a flicker of a smile, a hint that he's thinking of the things we've done in the car that have nothing to do with his driving and he's sidling closer like he thinks that's all it takes to change my mind.

I put my palm flat to his chest, stopping him from getting any closer. His eyes are so dark it's hard to tell the swell of his pupils from the brown of his irises, the excitement, the edginess rolling off him in waves.

This is who he is, isn't it? My boyfriend, my best friend, my co-performer … whatever else he's pretended to be, this is the truth.

"It's over," I say.

"What are you saying?"

"I'm done," I say. "I can't be with someone I can't trust."

329

"Be with?"

"I'm breaking up with you, Sef."

"As in…?"

"As in everything."

There's a second of silence between us – an impossible ocean of hurt and love and broken trust that neither of us knows how to cross.

"Claire…" He's moved closer and he's reaching up to touch my face, to run his thumb across the overlong hair by my ears. It's the move he made the night we first kissed and I don't mean to lean into the feel of him, but I'm going to miss him touching me like this and…

SEF

This is it. She'll change her mind. She can't. I need her and she needs me and it's going to be fine, we can get through this – we just…

Claire pulls away, sucking her lower lip a little, biting back words she doesn't want to—

No.

"Claire?" My voice doesn't sound right. It's trembling.

"I'm sorry, Sef, but—"

"I love you." The words come without my permission – an explosion in my heart and fear of what they mean floods through me. I *need* her.

It's come too late. Claire's mouth is parted in shock and I want her to tell me she loves me too. Anything to let me know that what I've said *means* something—

"No one who loves me would risk my life for a bet," she says, gently.

There are too many emotions fighting within me to know what I'm going to say or how I'm going to react, as if I've lost control of myself as well as everything else.

"You say it like what we're doing – who we're doing this for – doesn't matter!" I'm surprised at the way she's recoiling from me until I realize I'm shouting. "This wasn't just some bet – we're trying to save Kam!"

Claire's gone still and white.

"*You can't save him!* Kam will *never* be the way he was before – you can only help him live *this* life…"

But my hands are up at my face as if I can block out the pain of what she's saying, because I have to be doing more than helping him, this has to be worth more…

"We are helping," I say, "He needs money—"

"He needs his brother not to have killed himself in the process!"

And with those words, everything falls away, my hands slide down to my sides and Claire slips beyond my reach. She doesn't know what she's saying. Kam does not need a brother like me. He deserves so much better, so much more. Whatever she thinks I am to him, it is nothing compared to what I should have been.

CLAIRE

"Is this it?" he says quietly, as if my words have flipped a switch and now he's shutting down. "You're really

putting an end to this?"

"I can't be a part of it. Kam's life isn't worth more than mine. No one's is." I want to touch his face and kiss his forehead and tell him that Kam's life isn't worth more than his either, but he's pulling away, nodding.

"Sure, whatever. We're done. I get it." And he's backing away, turning and striding back to the car, slamming the door and revving the engine, wheels spinning angrily as he drives off in a spray of gravel, leaving me there in the abandoned industrial estate with no clue how to get home.

SEF

I drive away regretting everything that has happened, everything I have said and everything I have done – not just tonight, but every lie I've ever told, every truth I was too frightened to admit to her.

Not that it matters. None of it does.

I drive recklessly, taking corners too fast, pulling out round cars that are staying within the speed limit. I don't care about anyone or anything.

Anything except Kam.

I park badly. So badly that I scrape the bumper of the car behind. I drive off and park even further away from my house and hope no one noticed what happened. The camera's been rolling this whole time and the battery's dying, but Claire's left her bag in the back with the cables inside – along with a cardigan and her purse. All stuff I'm going to have to give her back.

Upstairs I set everything up to transfer off the camera and get my phone out to check for messages. There's one from Claire and my heart leaps into my throat before I actually read the words.

You can use the footage from tonight. Wouldn't want to have nearly died for nothing.

The laugh it wrings from me isn't pleasant.

I compose a hundred and one different replies and send none of them. Instead I message Moz to ask him if he'll edit the footage and he calls me back from the car.

"Made up with your lover yet?"

"Finished with her, actually."

I expect him to go on about it, gloating that he'd guessed all along, but after a short pause, he says, "Are you OK?"

This tiny kindness from Moz nearly unravels me. But I wasn't calling him for comfort.

"I'll survive," I say bitterly. That's what I've been doing, isn't it?

Moz re-evaluates my tone and asks why I'm calling.

"Look," I say. "I know we agreed that Claire would work on this, but…"

"Send me the files, I'll do the editing."

"How long?" I ask.

"I'll get the teaser up as soon as I can, but there's no saying how long it'll take to reach the target for us to release the full thing."

I already have a tab open on the donations page – we're only two thousand short of the target for this dare – so close

yet still so far from what Kam needs. I'm more optimistic than Moz. I have to be.

"Moz." I hear the authority in my voice. "My family have been told to look at new homes for my brother. I'm going to have to do something else or we've no chance of making a difference."

"Brother?"

There's a pause in which I realize I've not exactly been straight with Moz, either. "Yeah. Kam's my older brother."

"Mate…" There's a sigh on the other end. "I'm sorry, but even if we post for another dare, it'll take longer to raise the money. Diminishing returns—"

"So we post a teaser until the money's raised."

"A teaser of what?"

I close my eyes and think of the bravest thing I've ever done. The stupidest.

"Let me think on it," I say. "I'll have an answer for you by the time you've got the editing sorted."

CLAIRE

Seren makes me a hot drink, stirring sugar into my tea with one of Hallie's toddler-sized spoons. The plastic handle is green with anatomically questionable dinosaurs all over it. I keep staring at it after she drops it into the sink ready to be rinsed.

"Claire?" Seren hands me the mug. "I'll do whatever it is you need me to do. Talk, listen, make you some food…" My stomach contracts at the thought. "I can commandeer

the front room and turn the sofa into a den, hunt a unicorn down and steal a vial of its tears … anything. OK?"

And I put my tea down to look at her and hold my arms out for a hug, my best friend stepping into my arms without question and wrapping herself around me. Like with her and James, when I felt at my most desperate, Seren was the person I turned to (and her dad, who is very suspicious as to why they just drove out to an industrial estate in the middle of the night to collect me).

Up in her room, I ask if she can lend me a jumper as it dawns on me that I left my bag in the back of the car I swore I'd never set foot in again.

The only thing I walked away with is my phone.

I look down at it now, wishing it would tell me something other than the time. Like where Sef is and what he's doing, how he's feeling.

Seren reaches over and gently removes it from my grasp.

"What happened?" she asks.

My tears ebb and flow with the telling of it, the betrayal of the boys teaming up to prank me like that, the rage as I relive the fear of believing I was going to die, feeling stupid now that I haven't, because when you think about it, Moz would never risk his own life even if Sef would…

"You don't think that's true, though, do you? About Sef, I mean," Seren says, handing me yet another tissue to add to the soggy little pile I've collected in my lap.

Without being there in the car, without seeing the way Sef was laughing, the manic gleam in his eye before he hit the accelerator, it's hard to believe it could be true.

But I was there, and I know.

"I think he'd risk everything for Kam," I say.

SEF

I'm going to make a video of my own. There's nothing set up to post on our channel tonight, but the time for daft little stunts is over, anyway – the last few weeks have stripped away the pretence that this is about anything other than money.

Instead, I'll make one to drive interest to the donation fund and bait our viewers for the chicken video – a video that doesn't require maintenance to get people watching it. No more bantering with people in the comments. I'm as done with all that as Claire is.

Combing my hair flat and giving it my best Dare Boy style, I set up Claire's camera and start to film myself as if I'm about to go and meet Moz and Claire.

Pulling my mask on, I sit down on my bed and look right into the camera.

"Hey hey, lovers, it's me, Dare Boy, getting ready to record the most epic dare your pretty little eyes have ever seen…"
It's so easy to slip into the character I've been playing for the last six months that it's almost second nature to mess around doing V-style dance moves in front of my eyes.

There's a knock on my door and before I can get myself together, Mum pushes it open.

"Mum!" I yank my mask off, catching Amir's eye as he peers over Mum's shoulder on his way back from the

bathroom, the collar wonky on his checked pyjamas.

"I heard you talking…" Mum frowns like she thinks I've got someone in here, although where I'd hide them, I'm not sure.

"Yeah, to the camera –" I nod at the camera on my shelves and the lie comes to me so easily it feels like the truth – "I'm practising a monologue for Drama."

It's obvious she's wondering where the camera came from, but instead she glances over to where my digital alarm clock spells out the time in enormous red digits.

"You've got the whole of half-term for this, Sef. Is there any need to do it at five minutes to midnight on a Sunday? I can hear you murmuring from along the landing and I've work in the morning."

I hadn't realized I was being that loud – too used to the privacy of Uncle D's caravan.

"Could I just have five more minutes?" I have to get this done now or what's the point? "I'm just about to nail one of the lines. OK?"

She purses her lips and holds up her hands, five fingers splayed, backing out of the door – although Amir presses forward, the nosy beggar.

"What monologue?" he asks.

"Not one you'd know," I say, bouncing my heel, impatient for him to go.

"Why the mask?" he nods to where the material is balled in my hand.

"Why all the questions? Since when have you given a shit about what I do for Drama?"

"'For Drama'," he repeats, air-quoting at me before he gives me a dismissive, "Whatever."

I wait until I hear his door shut, then bring the camera close so I don't have to talk so loud and start over.

MONDAY

CLAIRE

My parents find me crying in the kitchen. I put a hot chocolate tab in the coffee machine, but didn't click it in properly and there's grainy chocolate goo everywhere.

I'm extremely upset about this.

Inconsolable.

Over a capsule of hot chocolate.

Mum rests a hand on my shoulder and guides me gently over to the breakfast bar in my chocolate-covered pyjamas while Dad cleans up the side.

"I'm so sorry…" I say, stuck on repeat. "It was an accident."

"I know, darling." Mum squeezes my shoulder. "No one would deliberately sabotage their own attempt to make hot chocolate."

And she kisses the side of my head like I'm a little kid.

I feel like one.

There's a clunk on the marble as Dad pushes a fresh mug of chocolate under my nose and I catch sight of the cufflinks in his shirtsleeves.

"Big meeting today?" I sniffle, trying to change the subject.

"Big enough for the lucky links, not so big that I've got to leave before I find out what's wrong with my one and only daughter."

"Nothing's wrong," I say. "Just a bit emotional. Girl stuff."

Except Mum knows I had my period last week because she had to give me a tampon out of her handbag to take to school.

"Claire…" Mum rubs a hand across my back and I lean into her. We've never been a family of affectionate gestures and all the cuddles I've had recently came from Sef. The thought surprises a little sob out of me and Mum presses me even closer, rubbing a hand across my shorn hair. It's longer now and I've been thinking about getting it cut properly into some sort of style – one I think I might like to keep.

"Is there anything you'd like to talk to us about?"

I think of the channel, how much time I've spent lying to them about what I've been doing at the mysterious "Film Club" – skipping school, the food fight… Of all the things I've done, though, me getting into Sef's car last night would frighten them the most. If I tell them one thing, I'll have to tell them all of it.

Seren once said that honesty isn't everything and right now, I think it would be too much for all of us. So I take it one step at a time.

"I've been seeing someone."

SEF

I sleep in so late that it's gone lunchtime by the time

I surface. First thing I do is turn my phone on, checking the video's gone live overnight and seeing the comments people have left speculating what I'm doing and when the video will go up. There's a message come in from Moz – he must have stayed up into the night editing and he's seen the new video on our channel.

Nice one. Add in a link to my channel, though, yeah? This fucking footage is MAMMOTH. Reckon the earliest the teaser will go up is Wed.

My heart withers at the wait, but Claire used to go on about how fast Moz was and if he says Wednesday's the soonest he can do it, then I'll have to accept it. Not like I'd be any faster.

There's a message from her, too, sent this morning. One word.

Hi.

Hi. I reply without thinking.

I saw the video this morning. That you recorded on my camera presumably.

Yeah. Sorry. Had to download the footage and I thought…

But she's been typing at the same time as me.

Wasn't trying to be narky, btw. You can keep the camera for as long as you need it.

Thank you.

It's only once I've sent it that I realize I've added a kissing emoji. In an attempt to put that behind us as fast as possible, I type another message.

I can bring the rest of your stuff over if you want?

Um … maybe not. Kind of told my parents about you.

Ah. I could drop it off while they're at work?

But even I know that's not a good idea. That if Claire opened her front door, I'd want to step inside and do more than hand over her bag.

I can get it at school next week.

Even your purse?

My parents aren't really letting me out, tbh. Just promise me you won't lose it. K?

"Fuck!" I slam my palm into the wall next to my bed with enough force for my skin to go numb before the pain flares up.

Sure.

CLAIRE

All I want to do is message him back and tell him I miss him.

Which is pathetic given that it's less than twenty-four hours since I last saw him walking away after *I broke up with him*.

"Get it together," I tell myself.

Two minutes later and I'm rewatching his video on my laptop.

As I said: pathetic.

SEF

Planning is so much harder when you have to do it yourself.

"Get off!" I shove Cheddar from where she's trying to

sit on my notepad and she tumbles off the table with a squawk.

Amir glances up from watching something shit on telly and clicks his fingers for Cheddar to come to him. But he's looking at me.

I ignore him and reread a list of bullet points that make no sense.

"Bollocks." I tear the sheet out and rip it up.

"You OK?" Amir is leaning on the arch. He looks calm, and old. When did I become the angry one?

"Fuck off, Amir."

But it doesn't work the way it used to. He doesn't get all affronted. He doesn't sulk. He stays where he is.

"Want to talk about it?"

"No." A defensive reflex without thought.

"School stuff?"

I put my pen down, take my glasses off and rub where they've been pressing behind my ears. This pair has never been comfortable. I'm so tired, so sick, so … powerless.

"No. Not school stuff."

"Kam stuff?" I look up at that – all the confirmation he needs. "I'm the same. Keep going in circles, thinking there's something I can do, but then…" He shrugs. "Maybe this is OK, you know? The Rec's not the only place out there—"

"It's the best."

"Is it?" I expect him to ask me how I would know, but the question is as much for him as it is for me. "Or did we just think it was because that's where he had to be? Were we all just making ourselves feel better by saying it?"

Kam's accident has changed us all – Amir the most. My little brother, all grown-up.

TUESDAY

CLAIRE

I've got to stay in and revise for the mocks I've been pretending will never happen. Yesterday Dad called the house – "Do I need to pick up milk on my way home?" Today it's Mum – "Can you check the calendar? I can't remember when my hair appointment is." I'm sure they think they're being subtle, but Dad was the one who did the shopping at the weekend and Mum lives her entire life off her phone.

That's what happens when your parents find out you've had a secret boyfriend for the last three months. Imagine how hard they'd find trusting me if they knew about all the sneaking around I've done for the channel…

Across my screen I've got about ten tabs open on different revision sites covering everything from French idioms to electric circuits, and yet I can't help opening one more…

The video Sef made is the only upload since Sunday and I check out the most recent comments. At some point someone started speculating on the fact that neither Truth Girl nor Dare Boy had been seen since this video was posted and as is the way with the internet, there are a few people getting carried away with the drama.

OMG. Do you think those guys are all right?

Videos only post Sundays + Wednesdays. CTFO.

No comments though???

This only went up early Monday morning. They're probably having a break.

What if something happened? I'm worried.

me2

db/tg if u are reading these comments can u maybe let us know ur ok?

WTF r u gonna do if their not?

Has anyone heard from MozzyMozza?

I feel bad about this, like maybe people really are worried, but at the same time I really don't want to get drawn back into it. Besides, knowing Moz and Sef, this is probably all part of the plan.

SEF

The caravan is a shit tip and I open all the windows as wide as they'll go in the hope of getting rid of the last of the banana fumes. Tomorrow I'll have to bring the vacuum cleaner down here, but for today, I set about dismantling the set, unpinning the backdrop, charting our dares by the map of weird stains spread across the sheet. There are bin bags in Uncle D's cupboard and I fill one with leftover foodstuffs – marshmallows and cream crackers and an assortment of the foulest possible herbs and spices that I fed to a blindfolded Claire until she correctly identified each one.

She's not going to forget fenugreek in a hurry.

Slowly, surely, miserably, I move my way around

cleaning up the mess we've made of everything. Of the caravan, our friendship, the channel. Somewhere between stripping the bed and emptying the bedroom bin, I start crying, tears edging silently down my cheeks, my breath wet as I carry on with what I'm doing, taking out fresh sheets and googling how to do hospital corners the way Uncle D does it, swearing at my phone because I don't type in the right thing.

When I'm done, I think about lying on here with Claire. Not the sex stuff, although, yeah, the sex stuff, but also wrestling around trying to tickle her feet, her kicking and squeaking and laughing. Falling asleep and waking up with her squashed up against my chest, my nose buried in the back of her neck. The warm, clean, welcoming smell of her skin.

Taking all the comfort another human had to offer.

All the hope.

I fold this sheet up the same way I did the backdrop and put everything by the door, ready to take the rubbish to the refuse site and the washing back to my car.

"I tried," I whisper to the room, when what I mean is that I failed.

WEDNESDAY

CLAIRE

I get a notification to say that MozzyMozzaMeepMorp has posted a new video and promptly set a record for the

fastest email-to-link click in the history of the internet, my fingernail tapping impatiently on my laptop casing as my cursor hovers over where the skip ad button will appear and:

Black screen.

A flicker of light hinting that the shot was taken in a car, the sound of an engine revving added in over the top.

Black screen with a text overlay on a single drum beat.

FROM THE TEAM THAT BROUGHT YOU THE FOOD FIGHT …

A split-second shot from the camera set up next to the wheel of Mrs Bennet and I recognize myself onscreen, laughing with Sef – a sound drowned out by the engine effect.

Black screen and drum beat.

… COMES A DARE SO DANGEROUS …

Same angle, longer shot, the engine changing gear as you see me tensing back in my seat, Sef's arms braced on the wheel.

Black screen and drum beat.

… YOU WON'T WANT TO DO THIS AT HOME.

And as the pitch of the engine rises, there's a series of shots barely long enough to register: from someone's camera looking through the windscreen to the distant flare of headlights; Moz whooping and punching the air; Sef shouting at me; me, arm raised as if to protect myself from imminent impact, the engine fading masterfully into the sound of someone screaming.

The screen flares bright once more, the once-distant headlights almost filling the frame.

Silence and then:

DONATE
TO
SEE
THE
VIDEO

A single shot of Moz, his face made up like he's cut his lip, blood on the side of his head as he points to the link below.

"It's worth it." And he winks at the camera before it goes black.

I've been holding my breath, braced in my chair like I'm right back in the car, my heart hammering in horror. I take a moment to relax, get some oxygen back into my body and then, the same way hundreds, maybe thousands of other people must be doing, I click to watch it again.

THURSDAY

SEF

It's been slow for a Thursday. Although it could just be me who's slow. I've been on the gateline checking tickets for the nine (ish) o'clock showing of *Akira*, for which a group of comic-book girls have shown up, talking loudly about the sorts of things I only know about because of Amir. The sort of knowledge I'd have once used to my advantage.

"Settle this argument, OK?" one of them asks. She's wearing a vintage *Final Fantasy* T-shirt and has her hair

pinned up into two little buns the way Claire used to wear hers on the channel before we shaved it all off.

"What argument's that?" I rip her ticket and hold my hand out for the last one – although the girl won't meet my eye, and I ask her, "You're fifteen, right?"

"Yeah, I'm, like, seventeen." The girl rewards my question with the mother of all stink eye from under the rim of her beanie.

"Sorry, of course you are. Um…" I say, quickly changing the subject. "What was the argument you wanted me to settle?"

Beanie girl gets in there first. "Sarah wants to ask you some bullshit question about the best anime film you've shown this week because she wants to flirt with you—" *Final Fantasy* girl identifies herself as Sarah by giving her friend a slap on the arm. "But we're already late for the film, so can you just tell her your email or something?"

Despite her mortification, Sarah gives me a very direct and inviting look and I feel myself sliding towards old habits.

"I'll still be on shift when you come out. Gives me one-hundred-and-thirty-nine minutes to form an opinion on anime…" And I step aside to wave them through, enjoying the way Sarah seems to be impressed that I know the running time, as if that means I'm a fan. Which it doesn't. I know the running times of all the last films on my evening shifts.

Once they've gone, I drift over to where Mia glitters disapproval as she wipes down the counter with unnecessary vigour.

"Back to your old tricks, I see…"

"Mia…" She ignores me, concentrating on a blob of chocolate that's melted on the warm glass.

"One smile from a pretty girl and you can't help yourself."

"It's not like that," I try.

Mia glares up for a moment and I feel a lot like that chocolate. "The way it wasn't like that with Claire?"

"It isn't any more." I go round the counter and sit on the floor, my back pressed up against the fridge as I tip my head back and stare at the lights.

Mia's stopped her aggressive wiping and is looking over at me, her scowl softening slightly.

"Things not going well with Claire?"

"She broke up with me." I can sense Mia's waiting for more information, too aware of how I behave to side with me automatically. "I … she…" I press the heels of my hands up to my eyebrows to try and squash away the headache that's come on from a lack of sleep and a lot of stress. "I did something she can't forgive."

"Sef…"

"Not that," I snap, annoyed at her for thinking the same as Claire once had. "Flirting's not cheating, for fuck's sake, OK?"

I've never lashed out at Mia like that and she reels a little at the fury of it. When she steps back from the counter, I assume that she's gone to wipe tables somewhere I won't yell at her and my head falls forward against my knees.

One less friend to worry about, I guess…

"Sef?" I feel her sit down on the floor next to me, the top

of her arm resting against mine. "Are you all right?"

"You don't need to worry about me," I say, not looking up.

"Yeah, sure. But if you ever need to talk, I'm here, OK? I know you've friends all over the place, but you have one here too."

But I'm shaking my head into my knees, wishing she would take that back. Mia doesn't need a friend like me. No one does.

FRIDAY

SEF

I vacuum Uncle D's caravan.

SATURDAY

CLAIRE

"Just ring him." For all she's sympathetic, Seren has limited patience for problems she can't fix.

Rich turns round from where he's sitting in front of us on the floor. Gemma is out with her friends, Rich is with his. "Stop interrupting the film."

"Claire's interrupting it with her melancholic phone-checking."

"I'm not checking it for messages from Sef," I say, as Rich gives up and pauses the film. I don't even know what we're watching. "Donations reached twenty thousand pounds this afternoon and I'm refreshing Moz's channel in case the full chicken video goes live."

For all I'm trying to disengage with my online alter ego, there's a part of me that's cross at having to wait for the video to be broadcast across the internet like I'm just another viewer. It's hard to let go of the ownership that comes with creating a monster.

"Moz tweeted about –" Rich peers at the progress bar that's come up on the screen – "twenty-three minutes ago that the chicken video would go live in half an hour."

"I didn't know you were a Moz fan?" I wriggle my toes on Rich's back in surprised affection, but he pushes my foot away.

"I'm not, but I'm a Claire Casey fan and I knew she'd be stressing out over this. Which is why I suggested she came over to my house to watch a film."

Behind him, on the sofa, Seren and I exchange a smile and I hand her my phone with the timer set for seven minutes.

"You can unpause the film, Denver Richards. Claire's paying attention now."

Seven intolerably long minutes later, the timer on my phone goes and without me having to ask, Rich pauses the film and we all squash on the sofa as we gather round my phone.

SEF

If you could award Oscars to YouTubers, Moz would be a contender. The full-length video is nothing short of stellar and at the end, there's a tiny post-credit take of Moz styled up in his "viewer" guise, glasses drawn on his face as he pretends to talk to someone off-camera.

"Did you see that? Those guys are insane." He turns back and reaches towards the end as if to press something on the screen. *"Donating now…"*

I hadn't known he was going to do that until he transferred it to me and for all the bravado, all the snark and the sarcasm and the squabbling, in that few seconds, I wanted to kiss him. For all his faults, I guess Moz is as much of a friend to me as he can be.

CLAIRE

I couldn't watch it too many times at Rich's or my friends would have stopped me. They were horrified enough watching it the first time, Seren with her hands to her face, whispering, "Oh my God, oh my God, oh my *God*…" through her fingers and Rich with his hand on my arm, squeezing tighter and tighter as we watched the seconds leading up to the moment Sef swerved.

But at home, with my lights off and the glow of my phone hidden under my duvet, I watch it again, taking in the difference in tone between this video and the food fight. For all Moz's whooping and Sef's laughter, it's not fun. Not

just because of me, clearly out of my mind with fear in the passenger seat, but because of the manic edge visible in the way the boys are behaving, like maybe they too were scared…

Onscreen the video cuts to a shot taken from the back of Mrs Bennet, the silhouette of me pummelling the driver picked out against the light cast from Moz's headlights.

He's not used much of what happened afterwards, keeping the focus solely on him because none of what me and Sef said or did would be usable, but the viewers don't know that and there's a lot of concern in the comments asking whether Truth Girl is OK.

I rewatch it one more time, asking myself quietly whether Dare Boy is OK.

SEF

When Claire's name flashes up on my phone, it's a sweet release of the tortured anticipation that's been building since the video went up, because I know that she'll have seen it. That for all she walked away, she's still watching.

The chicken video looks about as terrifying as I remember it. Three screaming face emojis.

As you said, wouldn't want you to nearly have died for nothing…

That sounds so callous.

Sorry. I know that wasn't funny. I don't know what's wrong with me. Are you OK?

Nope.

She's typing something else.

You?

Not really.

Not about us, Sef. The money side of things...?

You said you didn't want to be involved with that.

I said I didn't want to watch you try and kill yourself. Doesn't mean I don't care about you. (Kind of the opposite, you doofus.)

Despite everything, I smile at my phone.

Did you just call me a doofus???

Yes. Right there, in writing. Get it printed on a T-shirt.

Even as I smile at the screen, I can feel my throat tightening, sadness swelling inside.

I know we're not together, but I want you to know we can still talk.

What if I don't want to talk?

Then I'll listen to your silence.

I miss her so much that it's a physical pang and little snippets of words only make it worse.

I love you. I type. And then I delete it.

Nothing I say can make her believe that any more.

SUNDAY

CLAIRE

Although we started the week frosty after my revelation,

Mum's unbent enough to tolerate me eating Parma ham and cereal straight from the packet despite leaving half my dinner each night and on the way to the Recreare, she asks me how I'm feeling.

"Sad," I say, truthfully.

"And you've not spoken to him since you broke up?"

"A couple of messages, Mum. Nothing more."

"But you'll see Seth in school?"

"Sef," I correct her. "It's short for Yousef."

"Oh." That single syllable packs in a large amount of re-evaluation.

"He's Kam's brother." I nod towards where we're driving. "The middle one."

"Oh." More frantic recalibrating.

"That's why we got talking in the first place."

"Will you tell Kam that you've broken up with his brother?"

"I've never talked to him about it." I shrug, not wanting to have to explain to Mum that the nature of Kam's condition means all our conversations are focused on the things we do together, not apart. Time passes for him differently than it does for me.

He's not himself today. Or maybe he's feeding off my mood – it's hard to tell – but the closeness I felt last week has faded with the days that have passed and Kam is so withdrawn that he barely even looks at me.

"Kam?" I try and draw his attention away from where he's staring out of the window so I can ask if he'd like me to push him closer, but all he does is strain to turn further away.

I let him, because this is the only way he has of telling me to leave him be.

Instead, I open up the book and keep reading, assuming that his silence means this is OK. Afterwards, I lay a hand lightly on his arm to attract his attention as I say goodbye, but all Kam does is tug his arm away.

"Can I have a word, Claire?" Nurse Goethe is waiting in the doorway and I follow her away from Kam's room down to some chairs by the nurse's station. Indicating that we should sit, she takes out a sheet of paper from the plastic wallet she has clutched to her chest. "I've been keeping a record of your visits and see that you've been reading to Kam since the thirtieth of September, but you need to keep visiting until the end of March to fulfil the requirements of this award, is that right?"

"Yes," I say. My blood has started to prickle, realization crystallizing inside me.

"You've built a fantastic rapport with Kam in the time you've known him and I know you'd hoped to continue reading with him –" everything in me is about to break – "but I'm afraid arrangements are being made to move Kam elsewhere for his Level 2 care."

"No." The word trembles out in a whisper. "Please…"

Nurse Goethe sees my distress and places a hand on my shoulder. "I'm sorry, Claire, but his family…"

And I'm too busy shouting at her inside my head to hear her excuses, as if this is a decision made on anything other than money. Money that Kam's parents have stretched themselves to find, that his uncle's travelled halfway across

the world to make, that Sef and I have risked everything to raise…

"… we need to look at you reading to someone else after next week."

SEF

No one's home. Mum, Dad, Amir, they've all gone up to see Kam this afternoon. They asked if I wanted to go with them.

"Come and see him before he has to move," Mum begged. "You won't have many more chances, Sef…"

"I know," I said. And yet here I stayed.

Dad wouldn't even look at me after I left the dinner table.

In Kam's room, I set up the camera, sellotaping a sheet of greaseproof paper on the window in an attempt to diffuse the overbright light beaming onto my face when I sit on the bed.

There's been backlash to the way we handled the chicken video. Some of our fans feel like we played them, abusing the relationship I've been at pains to build up over the last six months.

"I owe you an apology," I tell the camera. "For those of you who thought something serious had happened after last week's video and who saw the teaser on Mozzy-MozzaMeepMorp.

"I'm here to let all of you know that no one got injured when we did the dare." I close my eyes for a beat, then,

"But there are other ways to hurt the people you care about and me and Truth Girl, we…" I swallow back the memory of her fear, the way I'd been so caught up with the excitement of it all that I'd been stupid enough to think that there was a way to charm her out of it. "I really upset her with that prank and I don't think she's ever going to forgive me. Are you?" I wish I was saying this to her face and not to the lens of her camera. I think about her watching this, on her phone or her laptop.

"She shouldn't, either. Six months ago, Truth Girl thought of a way to help me, to help my brother – our friend – and none of this would have been possible without her. I owe her everything. She's been my partner in crime, my best friend and my only hope."

I rub a hand across my mouth, hiding the way I'm struggling with all this.

"You might think the worst thing to do is to break a person's heart, but last Sunday I broke my best friend's trust. First I let my brother down and now my best friend." I sniff back the tears. "Everything I love, I ruin. I'm such a fuck-up." I laugh at myself, bitter and hateful. "He was right. It should have been me. But it wasn't. And now he's … it's … fuck." It's too hard and I have to stop because I can't breathe. Seconds, maybe minutes of filming where I'm just crying on my bed until I'm sick from sorrow, pissed off at how pitiful I am. I need to get this video made, need to get it edited and uploaded.

I start again, forcing myself to say what needs to be said.

"I've got one more chance to make this right, OK? There

isn't anything more I can do to keep him after this week. We need the money and we need it now. Check out Moz's channel on Wednesday for another teaser of what I'm going to do. The full thing will go live once wc hit the target."

I watch myself point to the bottom of the screen where the link will be.

"One last dare and I'm done. Stay tuned."

MONDAY

CLAIRE

I've been in a foul mood all morning. Something's wrong with the Wi-Fi and my data ran out at the weekend. I want to know whether Sef has posted a new video on the channel. With all the anger directed at us from our viewers, I don't see how he can't…

Not for the first time, I wish I hadn't cut myself off from him over half-term. I want to be able to tell him about what Nurse Goethe said on Sunday. It still feels like we're in this together, even though we're apart.

"Give me your phone." I hold my hand out the second I sit next to Rich on the bus.

"What? Hey!"

I know his passcode – it's the same one he has for his bank card and the alarm at his house. I tap through to our channel, tutting as the bus wobbles, making me clumsy, but there it is, a new upload.

I take a moment to look at Sef onscreen, refreshing my memory, wondering how it's possible for even a teeny-tiny thumbnail to give me that familiar gut twist.

"Are you going to watch it or drool over it?" But Rich doesn't even wait for an answer before he presses play.

As I watch, leaning in close to hear the video over the rattle of the bus and the hum of the passengers, I start to get a slow, crawling sense that something is very, very wrong…

The sixth-formers register at lessons and my best chance of finding Sef at this time in the morning is to go to the common room over in the annex. It is literally my idea of hell, squashing past people idling in the corridor, all of them staring at me as I pass, conspicuous in my uniform.

I hear someone ask their friend if they know me.

I hope they don't.

I lurk nervously in the doorway, scanning the room for Sef, hoping he'll see me before I see him.

"Hi, are you looking for someone?" The voice behind me is female and I turn round to come face to face with Laila.

Most people look prettier in their selfies than in real life, but not Laila and the sight of her draws all my deepest insecurities to the surface. Why would Sef ever have wanted me when he can have girls like her?

"Hi, um… I was looking for Sef Malik?" My voice rises too high at the end and I have to clear my throat.

Laila's smile falters a little. "Sef doesn't usually show until his first lesson in second period. You'd be better

coming back at lunchtime if you want to speak to him." Her lips tighten a little. "Or I could pass on a message?"

"No…" I duck my head forward in my years-old habit despite no longer having any hair to hide behind. "I'll come back then."

My insecurities sweep me out of the room so fast I'm able to make it to my first lesson before the bell goes.

Despite Laila's suggestion, I can't find Sef at lunch, either. I checked the car park on the way across, so I know he's on the premises. The common room's not so full this time and, after asking a couple of people who shake their heads and shrug me off, I'm on the verge of giving up until I walk out of the door and straight into Sef's friends.

For a moment none of us say anything and I'm certain from the look that crosses Finn's face that he knows exactly who I am. Matthew Lund is harder to read.

"Sorry," I manage, like a damp squib.

"No worries." Finn moves to the side as if to let me pass and I'm so tempted to leave it there, to walk away from having to talk to people I don't know, but: Sef.

"I – er – you're friends with Sef Malik, right?"

Finn tips his head to the side like this might be the case, but it's Matthew Lund who mutters, "If you can call it that."

Not sure what he means, I carry on cautiously, "I was meant to meet him here to collect, some, er, equipment I lent him."

"Claire, is it?" Finn holds up the bag I'd not noticed him holding. "Sef heard you were looking for him earlier. Said to give you this."

It's my bag. My purse and my cardigan and ... my camera's in there too. What dare is he going to do that he doesn't need my camera?

I feel a fresh wave of panic wash over me. "I – er – thanks. Look, can you tell him to call me?" I don't care what that implies. "I need to speak to him."

Matthew Lund raises his eyebrows and gives me a knowing smile that makes me want to scrub his brain clean, but Finn – the nice one – nods and says he'll let him know. There's nothing more I can say or do and with a crashing sense of disappointment, I turn away and head back to the main school.

SEF

The toilet door bangs open and I push up off the wall when Finn says, "She's gone."

"Thanks, mate," I say. "I couldn't face it just now."

"Whatever." He holds the door open for me. On the other side of it, Matty greets me with a frosty stare.

"Secret relationship over?"

I shrug, uncomfortable at how much of my life has suddenly become public knowledge.

"Good to know you're as much of a flake around your girlfriends as your real friends..." Matty turns away, shoulders hunched, and I want to yank him back and tell him it's not like that. That they don't want me really, that I'm broken and pathetic and not worth the worry.

"Don't ever ask me to cover for you again, Sef." Finn's

looking at me like he doesn't even know me any more. "That girl's worried about you."

"She doesn't have to be," I lie.

Maybe I don't know me any more.

CLAIRE

Sef. Call me. Please. I saw the video. I'm worried about you. What's this dare you're planning to do?

But I've already messaged him variations on that theme every chance I've had and he's not replied to any of them.

I try calling too, but there's no reason he'd speak to me when he won't even reply by text. There's got to be something I can do to get through to him, but I can't think what. Six months I've known Sef. I've licked toothpaste off his chest, had his toe up my nose and eaten his earwax. I've held him at his most vulnerable, kissed the tears from his skin and whispered comfort into his ears. I've bloody well *had sex* with him…

And yet I don't even know his address.

How can I have shared so much of myself with someone only to come away knowing so little?

Even though he doesn't work Mondays, I try ringing the cinema and asking for him, then, as predicted, when I'm told he's not there, I ask for Mia. She's *always* there… But not tonight.

I'm so frustrated that I actually feel like I'm going to explode.

I try Moz again – although he's so unreliable that when he actually picks up, I'm half convinced it's his voicemail.

"Hey hey, loser."

"Moz?"

"Obviously."

There's music in the background, so loud that I feel like I have to shout. "It's Claire! What are you up to?"

"My mate's birthday – in some bar in Soho. Come join us!" I look at the time, confused as to how it got to be this late.

"No – that's not—"

But there's shouting and cheering at the other end and I doubt he can hear me.

I message him instead. **Tell me what you're planning with Sef. It's important.**

Moz replies with a ghost emoji.

MOZ THIS IS SERIOUS. I'M REALLY WORRIED ABOUT HIM. TELL ME WHAT THE PLAN IS!

But I don't like his serious reply any more than I liked his silly one.

He's doing the dare tomorrow. We've set it up so that whatever's recorded on his phone goes straight to me and I'll edit the footage.

What's he doing? When?

Afternoon sometime – no idea what. He's been shifty about this one.

Aren't you worried???

Should I be? Come on, it's Sef. He's not going to do anything *that* dangerous.

But Moz and I have different definitions of dangerous.

The next day, I look for the one person I can think of who might help: Amir. I find out his form from the school office, but when I go there at lunch, the Year 8s that are there don't know where he is. When I try again at afternoon break, his form room is empty.

"Claire?" It's Rich's sister, Flo. She walks past to get something from her locker in the corner. I hadn't realized the two were in the same form. "You after something?"

"You don't know Amir Malik, do you?"

"You mean Mally?" Her face lights up.

What? "I – er, I guess?"

"We've got a library lesson next." I follow her along the corridor to the library. "Is he in trouble or something?" Flo doesn't look like she believes it.

"No, I just need to chat to him about his brother."

"You know Kam?"

"The other brother."

"Oh." And she nods, giving me a curious look. "That brother."

In the library, Flo leads me over to where Amir's sitting with a group of other Year 8s. He's laughing – and something in his manner reminds me of Kam in those pictures with his friends.

"Mally?" Flo nods towards me once she's got his attention. "Claire's been looking for you."

Curiosity flits over his face. He's nothing like the sullen student I remember from the start of the year, shoulders hunched and a scowl on his face – a memory immortalized by the few things Sef has said about him, implying Amir is a mildly intelligent ferret that can walk on its hind legs.

But brothers aren't always the best judge of a person and now he's standing taller, hair long enough to tuck back behind his ears, Amir looks like he's growing into someone kind of cool.

"Hi," he says.

"I need to talk to you about Sef."

And any trace of laughter leaves his face. "You know Sef?" And then, a sharpening of focus. "Are you *Claire*?"

SEF

Last lesson of the day for me is Drama during period four. I sleepwalk through it – doodling on my notepad, not even pretending to pay attention.

My classmates aren't people I'd call friends. I've messed about with these guys, grumbled about lessons and said some of the most despicable things to their faces as part of an exercise, flirted with them at lunch even, but nothing more and I'm grateful to be able to spend time with people who'll leave me be.

I'm not in the right space to talk to anyone.

When the lesson is over, I leave, driving off to park up by the river, where I sit with Mrs Bennet's nose pointing at

the viaduct, checking the views and the comments on all the videos we've made since we met Moz, heading over to Twitter to banter with him. I've been doing this on and off since Sunday so we don't accidentally trigger some kind of hysteria.

Apparently Claire isn't the only person worried about me after watching the video I posted on Sunday.

Imagine how bad it would have been if I hadn't edited out half of the things I'd tried to say.

I pull my mask down and snap a selfie to tweet to Moz.

And the countdown to the dare begins... Half an hour to go, ladies and gentlemen and everyone in between.

Moz retweets it and it gets hundreds of likes within minutes – the sort of attention I thirsted for when I was staying up all night trying to drive interest in what we were doing.

It doesn't matter how many people watch, it never seems to be enough.

There's a message come through from Amir.

Can you pick me up from school? Feel sick.

Sorry. Call Dad.

Seriously? Are you in a lesson or something?

Or something. Call Dad.

I pull my mask off and pop it into my pocket, my nerves jangling with anticipation when my phone buzzes again, but it's not Amir.

I miss you.

I can't help it: I miss you too. Sorry I didn't catch you yesterday.

That's OK. How about you catch me today?

I want to so much.

When?

Now?

CLAIRE

I can't, I'm sorry. I love you.

His reply flushes my blood cold.

"It didn't work," I tell Amir. We're standing outside the library still, not sure where else we can go, or what we should do. "Do we call the police?"

"What do we tell them?"

Neither of us has an answer for that. It's not like Sef is missing – he's just being difficult.

"Can I see the video again?" he asks and I give him my phone. Cupping it in both hands, holding it landscape, he frowns into the screen, tutting when he tries to skip to the end and gets caught buffering. It was awkward, explaining about the channel, and Amir said very little, until I told him how desperate Sef was to raise money for Kam and I was worried what he was prepared to do.

"All for Kam?"

"Yes."

For a moment it seemed as if he was crumbling from the inside out.

I watch the video over again and try to decode what Sef's saying, where he could be and I grab Amir's arm in a flash of hope.

"I think he's gone to film Kam up at the Rec!" It's such a relief that I actually feel weak.

Only Amir doesn't look even faintly convinced – he's shaking his head, frowning, his mouth pulled back in a twist of confusion. "Seriously? How can you even suggest that?"

I don't understand.

"My brother's not been to see Kam in all the time he's been there and you think he'll do it today just to make a video?"

"What? Yes, he has."

Amir and I stare at each other, a wall of incomprehension standing between us. Only...

"He has!" I say more forcefully, and then, "Hasn't he?"

The car park is on the wrong side of the bridge for where I want to be and I give Mrs Bennet an affectionate little pat before I leave her.

You get a scratch on her and I'll kill you.

Kam would *not* be happy about that massive dent in her nearside wing where that chunk of tarmac flew up during the chicken dare. Nor about the scrape on her back bumper from my terrible parking.

Yet another thing I've managed to fail him on.

I walk slowly over the bridge, squashing myself up against the stone wall to let a group of East Bank kids past, then hop over the stile that leads down to the path where

a young couple's romantic summer's walk was ruined by Kam's body plummeting into the water. If they hadn't been there, then no one would have been around to dive in and pull Kam out – his friends were stranded on the viaduct, the only way down to jump.

Like it's so much cooler to get trashed and jump into the river?

The land rises up from the banks of the river in a curve so steep I have to grab on to the weeds with my hands to help pull myself up. It was summer when they came up here, Hamish and Danny strong with alcohol, my brother just plain strong the way he always has been. Had been.

I think of him hanging off my legs to drag me down from the fence when I tried to impress my friends by taking that dog on. The way he would sometimes try and pick Mum up when she was cooking in the kitchen, her shouting at him to put her down.

At the top I stop, out of breath from the climb, my hands prickling and sore. There's new wire along the line of the train track – an even newer notice. A sign that they put up after the kid that tombstoned off the viaduct back in June made the front page of the paper.

You can't tell from the photo they used that it's me.

The sun blares yellow in the clear, cold air and I walk along the track towards the middle of the bridge, alert for the sound of trains – not sure what I'll do if one comes. It's not like it's that wide up here. Over the middle arch, I decide to film so that the town will be in the background,

the Rec sitting high up on the hillside. Putting my bag on the ground, I lean out over the wall and look down at the water below.

The drop looks a lot further than I remember. My phone rings. Moz.

"Hey hey." There's no laughter in his voice. "Where are you?"

"At the secret location as per the schedule."

"Claire just sent me this weird message asking me to call this off. She's worried you're doing something stupid."

"Sounds on brand for Claire."

"Tell me you aren't doing something stupid."

I don't reply.

"Because I give a shit, you know?" He's so serious. "About you."

"That's very sweet of you, Moz."

"How much do you need?" He says it so fast I barely catch the words.

"What?"

"Money. I have a lot of it."

But I'm here now. "Let's just make the video, OK? You've already spunked money on this, so we may as well see it through, right?"

"Sef—"

"Are we good to go? Yes or no?"

"Sure."

And he hangs up.

Mr Douglas emerges from the library. He's the most casually dressed of the school staff and today he's wearing a T-shirt with a My Little Pony reading a book and the slogan LIBRARIES ARE MAGIC.

"Amir, your lesson started five minutes ago." He switches his attention to me. "Yours too, I'm sure, Claire."

Amir gives me a desperate glance. "I'm worried about my brother, Mr Douglas."

"Of course..." Like Flo, Mr Douglas immediately assumes the wrong one.

"I mean Sef. He's missing!" Amir says, but Mr Douglas has no patience for that.

"That's enough now, I saw him this morning. Miss Casey has somewhere she's supposed to be too."

And he stands there, glaring Amir into the library and me around the corner. As soon as I'm out of sight, I check the message that's buzzed through from Moz.

Called him. Says he's still doing it. Sorry.

I'm running out of time, but I've an idea of where Sef might have gone...

I've never tried running from my school into town and I'm grateful for the gradient as I heave and pant and sweat my way towards the bridge.

My mind can't stop turning over what Amir said about Sef, so many things sliding into place. Why he never talks about Kam, why he must have found being with me so

much easier than being with anyone else, because I never pushed him on anything. I wonder if I should feel angry with him for this, and I wonder why it is that I don't.

I remember how worried I was when I first went to visit Kam. The sleepless night before, thinking there was a weakness in me that was about to be unearthed. I'd been so frightened of finding that out about myself and yet I shucked off that fear without a second thought.

That's the thing about fear. One minute it's the only thing you can think about, your whole world consumed by imagining nothing but the worst, and the next – *poof* – it's gone. Forgotten.

Did Sef face his fear and fall apart? Or has he been running from it all this time, watching it multiply in the shadow that follows him?

I feel so achingly sad for him.

The bridge comes into view and with it the car park on the far side and for one glorious moment hope soars up from within, until…

"No."

I see Mrs Bennet parked on the far side of the bridge and I know that I was right. I'm already heaving in air, lungs aflame with the effort, but I dodge across the road, ignoring the angry drivers crawling in the queue over the bridge. Across the stile and onto the footpath, I force myself to keep moving, my muscles straining as I hurry onwards.

If I'd told Sef I'd stay, if I'd seen this through to the end, he would never have come here – we would have worked something out.

I'm crying from the effort and the fear of being too late…

But I can't be. There is no choice and I will dredge the strength from the tips of my toenails if that's what it takes to reach Sef before he starts recording.

S E F

Since this is a one-take kind of deal, I want to make sure the app's working and I hold the phone up, resting my elbow on the top of the wall in an attempt to stop myself from shaking.

"Hey, Moz. Text me if you get this…" And I leave it running because I daren't be stopping and starting it in case something goes wrong.

A few seconds later his message rolls down from the top of the screen.

Got it. Where the fuck are you? Looks freezing.

I've no time to be chatting about the weather. It's time for the truth. I take out my mask and the picture I have of Kam, the one from the shattered frame in the front room and I clamber onto the wall so that I'm sitting with my feet dangling out over the river, watching the distant dirty water rippling and swirling beneath my trainers.

It makes a good shot.

"That's the River Lay," I say, turning the phone, tapping the screen so the lens flips round to show me looking down. "And I'm sitting up here on the viaduct, twenty metres from the surface of the water. Do you dare me to jump?"

I tap the screen again so it's filming the water once more.

"Twenty metres is a long way, isn't it? My brother should know. It's the same drop that left him in a coma for seventeen days and damaged his brain so that he can't do any of the stuff he did before."

Tap back to selfie mode and hold up his picture.

"This is who I'm doing all this for. My brother, Kam. My hero." My voice wobbles dangerously. "Only… I don't get how it happened, yeah? Because this jump is totally survivable. Because I jumped it over a month before he did."

I take a moment, try to steady my hand.

"I jumped off here for a dare because that's what I've always been good at and then … the day my brother got his results, I teased him about it. Told him he didn't have it in him. That he wasn't brave enough."

Don't cry.

"And you know what? He did. Only he borked it. And do you know what else? I'm the reason there's no money to pay for his care."

A sob escapes.

"There wasn't a sign when I jumped off here for a laugh, but there's one there now." I jerk my thumb to where I've come from. "Because of me. Says no one's responsible for what happens beyond it. And that's why there's no money to pay for his care – which means it's up to me to make this right. To make up for the biggest fuck-up of my life. Kam needs the money and the one thing I've always been good at is doing a dare." I pull off my mask and look right at the camera. "This is who I am. And that's the truth."

I struggle up, not worrying about the crap footage of

my phone in my hand as I pull myself to stand on top of the wall.

CLAIRE

There's a figure on the bridge and for a heart-stopping second I worry what it is I'm about to see as Sef stands there, tall and spindly against the sky, looking down at the river below.

I'm so certain he's about to jump that I see it before it happens.

Only it doesn't.

Slowly, carefully, Sef stoops down and sits on the wall, still precarious, still terrifyingly close to the drop down to the river, but sitting. Not standing. Not jumping.

Not sure if this is the right thing, not sure of anything any more, I call out his name and raise my hand in a wave.

A moment later and Sef holds his up in reply.

Fear that something will happen when my back's turned makes it almost impossible to concentrate on climbing up the bank, my hands stinging from grasping at clumps of grass, knuckles grazed from the hard ground. I hurry so fast through the hole in the fence that my jumper and tights catch on the ragged ends of the wire.

There has never been a more beautiful sight than that of Sef still sitting on that wall.

Panting and hot, in pain from the climb, a stitch burning a hole in my side, I walk to where he sits and lean forward to peer over the edge.

The sight of it is enough to make me dizzy and I feel a lurch of horror at the thought of Sef standing up here.

"I've done it before," he says quietly, his attention not on me, but the water. "Jumped off here."

"There's no need to do it again." I don't tell him that I've long suspected this to be the case, but step a little closer, so my arm is resting against the side of his thigh, and think about stuff like how cold the water would be, how there's no one else here to help him if he hurt himself…

"But I was fine." He sounds so bitter about it.

"You were lucky."

"It's my fault he came up here, you know." For the first time since I got here, Sef glances at me, so quickly that he's looked away before I can react. "I as good as dared him to do it."

"Sef…" I slide my hand closer to his and trail my little finger against where his hand rests on the brickwork.

"And if it hadn't been for me –" he hangs his head, a teardrop falling to land on his jeans – "there wouldn't be that sign …"

He stops and I slide my hand over his, our fingers locking together.

"They put it up after I jumped. I didn't know, not until my uncle told me about paying for the Rec. No liability, no money."

All of it slides into place – why it's the money that matters to him more than anything else. The desperation born of believing he's to blame.

"I'm sorry, Sef," she says, and she slides her arms around me, hugging my middle.

"That's not the worst thing I've done…" I tell her. I don't want to be alone any more. I don't want to lie. I've finally found a dare I'm more scared of than the truth and the discovery has unlocked me.

"You haven't done anything. This isn't your fault."

"But it's my fault I've not been to see him." She stills. Listens. "I love him so much I thought I'd do anything for him, but … I can't even go and look at him. Too scared to face up to what he's become and…"

As I lean forward into my hands, Claire's arms tighten around me as if she thinks I might fall and a nervous "Sef!" escapes.

"… I'd rather risk my own life than find out what Kam's doing with his. That's not right."

"No," she says, still clamped around me. "It isn't. So perhaps we could maybe stop risking your life and you climb back over to the safe side, where all we have to worry about is getting squashed by a train?"

She presses her face into my back, planting a kiss on my T-shirt.

"It's all right to be frightened," she says. "Living is pretty scary."

Fears like mine can't be fixed overnight and it's taken a lot of counselling for me to get here. Counselling that was there for me from the start, if I'd been able to accept it.

If I'd believed I'd deserved it.

"Sign here and I'll get you a visitor's badge." The woman behind the desk is businesslike and it's helpful, somehow, not feeling like she might be judging me for not coming sooner – because how could she possibly know?

They all offered. Mum, Amir, Uncle D. Even Dad. But having them here would make me feel like I owed them something, their expectations shaping how I behaved.

This is something I owe myself and my brother. No one else.

I slide my hand into the one that's waiting, her fingers slotting together with mine.

That doesn't mean I wanted to do this alone.

"You got this," Claire says quietly, walking with me to the staircase, one step at a time closer to seeing Kam.

I've talked to people a lot about the accident. My counsellor and my family, but it was Danny who helped me the most and all it took was the truth.

"What did you want to know?" he asked as the pair of us sat in Mrs Bennet, parked up miles away from town.

Below us, through the rain-spattered windscreen, the fields stretched down to the town nestled in the crook

of the dull brown river, the bridge lined with cars. The viaduct.

"Why was he up there?"

"Same reason I was. Same as Hamish." Danny shrugged. "We wanted somewhere to hang out, somewhere better than the pub, you know? A place we'd feel like the only people in the world." When I looked across, I caught him in a smile, in a memory of everything he'd had before the worst had happened. "For a while there, we were."

"What happened?"

"A bat."

"A what?"

"A bat. Flying mammal. As in blind as a…" He wasn't smiling any more. "A bat happened."

I watched, waited.

"Kam was sitting on the wall, back to the river, like, and me and Hamish had just cracked open another round and then…" A sudden, sharp flare of his hand right up towards his face had me jumping back in my seat. Danny noticed, stared at me for a second. "Yeah. You've got the idea."

He turned away to stare out the window on his side, his voice muffled as he raised a hand to his mouth, nibbling at the ragged flesh around his thumb. "One minute we were laughing, the next Kam had flinched away as something swooped towards his head and…"

It was a long time before he finished his sentence.

"… a stupid fucking shitting bastard bat."

Nothing at all to do with what I'd said to Kam earlier that day.

Doesn't change the consequences, though. Someone still has to pay for his care.

Neither of us had known that the app on Sef's phone was still running after he'd sat down. Every word of our conversation had been live-streamed to Moz, Sef's chin in the corner of the frame, the rest filled with sky.

And Moz put the whole thing up on his channel.

If Moz thought he'd seen me angry after the car stunt, I was apoplectic with him for this one. Had I not been too worried about Sef to leave him, I'd have travelled the hour and a half it took to get to Moz's house and live-streamed me tearing a strip off him for exposing so much of Sef to all the tens of thousands of unsympathetic eyes and hearts, opening up the boy I was desperate to protect to a new wave of vitriol.

Claire. I get it. I really do. But please trust me. Just one last time. I'll take it down tomorrow, but just wait, OK?

He hadn't given me any choice – and, for once, I'm glad of it.

When we started this, I'd been so sure of humanity that I genuinely believed strangers on the internet wanted an excuse to donate to a good cause. A certainty that drained out of me with every day that passed, every credit we didn't get, every gross comment about me or Sef. The grossest ones that sought to question Kam without even knowing who he was.

I'd long lost faith that more people wanted to do good than bad and yet Moz – the most morally grey human I know – is the person who gave it back.

One week after he posted the video, the people of the internet, land of the truly free, raised enough money to make a difference to Kam's life. For the next six months, at least – but the care he'll have in that time might mean he'll stand a better chance of a more independent life beyond that. They're still donating now, no longer to Kam, but to a charity that helps more people like him.

I'm not sure if how we went about it was right, but one way or another, Sef and I, we did a good thing.

SEF

At the top of the stairs, there's a pair of double doors. Across the top of the doors, there's a sign that says I am about to enter the Bueller Wing.

One step at a time.

Claire presses the buzzer and a nurse comes to open the door. He smiles at Claire before he smiles at me and asks, "Here for Kam?"

And I nod. Once. My grip tightens in Claire's and she glances up to check on me.

"I'm OK," I tell her – tell myself.

We follow the nurse along the corridor and he stops by one of the doors, leaning in to check something and he nods.

"He's just here."

With every step, my world narrows until I'm barely even aware of my body, of my surroundings. All I know is that I'm about to see my brother for the first time since September. Approaching the door, I become aware of what lies beyond, the enormous *Moon* poster on the wall, the row of pictures along the top of the chest of drawers exactly as they were in the picture that Amir showed me at Christmas.

From the doorway I take in the walls lined with the posters and pictures that used to hang in our home, the globe on his windowsill. The present wrapped in newspaper that must have been sitting there since Christmas, waiting for both of us to be ready to open it.

And then I take in the person who lives here.

For a long, long moment my brother and I search each other's faces, trying to work out who exactly we are to one another before he looks away, mouth moving, preparing to speak.

"Come in," he says.

And I step inside.

Enjoyed this book? Tweet us your thoughts.

#TruthorDareBook @NonPratt
@WalkerBooksUK @WalkerBooksYA

FLIP THE BOOK OVER

TO READ THE NEXT PART...